Lies that Bind

"Enthralled from the start, I found myself pulled deeper and deeper with each chapter, consumed by beautiful prose, diabolically depraved characters, and a storyline that unspools magnificently. *Lies that Bind* coaxes its readers in with the arrival of a mysterious stranger who threatens to shatter what's left of the life Lorelei and Adele have built together—but we all have our mysteries, don't we?"
—Alexis Dubon, author of I*t's Going to Be Fine* and co-editor of *No Trouble at All*

"Viciously sexy. A tale about pain in and out of the bedroom—especially the self-sacrificial secrets we keep, thinking that we spare our lovers suffering. A devious delight of dramatic irony, *Lies that Bind* gives readers a front-row seat for every delicious twist of the knife, the cruelty of which the leading lovers cannot —yet—fully comprehend.
—Briana Una McGuckin, author of *On Good Authority*

"Slick, devious. *Lies That Bind* invites you to a game of magic, lust, and manipulation, where the pages run with sweet blood and feverish delights. A tale of briar heartstrings, waiting for you to submit."
—Hailey Piper, Bram Stoker Award-winning author of *Queen of Teeth*

Enjoy the lies,

Little Dove.

Lies that Bind

by Rae Knowles and April Yates

Rae Knowles

Brigids Gate Press

Lies That Bind

Edited by Elle Turpitt

Formatted by Stephanie Ellis

Cover illustration and design by Daniella Batsheva

First Edition: February 2024

ISBN (paperback): 978-1-957537-92-4
ISBN (ebook): 978-1-957537-91-7
Library of Congress Control Number: 2023952304

BRIGIDS GATE PRESS
Overland Park, Kansas

www.brigidsgatepress.com

Printed in the United States of America

To the women who want to scream and the women who want to make them.

Content warnings are provided at the end of the book

Disclaimer

This is a work of fiction written by adults and intended for an adult audience. It is not intended to demonstrate appropriate relationship dynamics or healthy ways of engaging in BDSM. If you are sensitive to any of the following content warnings, consider skipping this one: intimate partner violence, emotional abuse, self-harm, drugging, references to incest and sexual assault, explicit sexual content including: light breath play, knife play, bondage, degradation, dubious consent and non-consent.

If you are experiencing intimate partner violence, help is available.

US National Domestic Violence Hotline 1-800-799-SAFE

UK Domestic Violence Helpline 01772 201601

Chapter 1: Skeptics and Believers

Lorelei

The air is heavy with the smoke of cigars the gentlemen refuse to put out.

They're friends of Mrs. Crawshaw, our oldest and most trusted client. They've never been to a sitting before, they think it's all a bit of a lark, something to be sniffed at. It can't possibly be real.

Adele enters the room, a vision in white linen.

She sits at the head of the table, and even in the gloom I see the younger of the gentlemen take her in with keen eyes. Why wouldn't he?

Golden blonde hair, complexion like cream, the blush of her cheeks in the warm room, the color of ripe strawberries, and her eyes …

In the darkness, they are the indigo of a peacock's feather, but in the sunlight, they take on the pale, almost violet hue of cornflowers.

They seem impossibly big in the gloom.

The young man opens his mouth to speak to her, but whatever he is about to say dies on his lips as Mrs. Crawshaw shoots him a withering glare.

She knows well the etiquette; she has sat at this table many times over the years. I was seven years old when I first saw her. She doesn't remember me from back then. My role was, shall we say, backstage, helping the previous owner set up before retreating to the shadows.

"You will direct any questions to me whilst Madam Adaline readies herself." I say this to the entire room, but I direct it to the two smoking gentlemen.

Adele makes the room wait. She sits, eyes closed, taking deep breaths. Once a suitable amount of time has passed, I ask if she's ready.

"I'm ready." Adele's American accent adds to her popularity with the gentlemen about town but also gives weight to our endeavor. Even in Matlock, people have heard of those famous American spiritualists such as Alice Bailey and the great Madame Blavatsky. Our patrons ask in hushed tones whether they had a hand in training *Madame Adaline*, which Adele answers with a coy shrug, allowing them to believe as they wish. I admire her ability to sell an air of mystery, despite the effect of this same distance on our private lives.

A young woman sits to the side of Mrs. Crawshaw silently sobbing; she lost a child, the poor girl was found face down in the garden pond. It takes only a moment of carelessness for tragedy to occur.

I don't like having women with grief as fresh as hers at the table. I normally tell them it is too soon for the soul to have manifested on the astral plane. But we need the money she's willing to pay, and she's plenty of it to spare. I take her hand and we close the circle.

Adele stiffens, every muscle pulled taut as piano wire.

She starts to babble, the words spilling out one on top of another, all clamoring for attention. It is up to me to bring order. "Spirits, calm yourselves. We only wish to speak to one at a time."

Silence.

I cast about, trying to remember the name Mrs. Crawshaw wants to contact this week. "We wish to speak with Emily, is Emily there?" Three thuds reverberate around the room. Mrs. Crawshaw gasps; this never ceases to amaze her.

The table shakes before rising a foot from the ground, then slams back down.

From Adele's hands a gauzy sticky substance oozes, glowing faintly green.

The cigar hangs limp from the young gentleman's lip, his face the same hue of ashen gray as its smokey tip. The candle flames extinguish, plunging us into complete darkness.

Adele speaks. "Ida, my duck, is that you?"

To my utter surprise I recognize the voice as one that has sat around this table a dozen times or so. A friend of Mrs. Crawshaw's who passed a little over a year ago, she had been waiting until the time was right.

"Oh Emily, it's so wonderful to hear your voice."

"Yours as well. As you know, I can't stay long, but I want you to know that I'm all reyt."

I can't see Mrs. Crawshaw's face but her voice is thick with tears when she answers. "I'm so glad you're well on the other side."

"Oh, I am, don't you be whittling about me."

Then silence.

I clear my throat. "Does anyone else wish to speak?" Silence. "I think this might be all for today."

"My baby?" The bereaved mother sobs.

"They're being looked after," Emily says through Adele's mouth. "You'll be reunited one day."

Adele slumps forward, spent from the session.

I break the circle and turn up the gas sconces on the wall. "Ladies, gentlemen, I'm afraid that is all for tonight. Madame Adeline's vitality needs time to replenish."

I usher them out of the room; the younger of the men stops at the door, staring at Adele, no longer trying to hide the hunger in his eyes.

"Can I help you with anything else, sir?" I spit the last word out, no longer caring if he comes back.

"No." His lip curls in a sneer. "I suppose there isn't anything *you* can do for me." Most people are blind to who, what I am. Others sense it straight away, this otherness.

"I dare say you're right."

He follows his companions out.

Once alone, I walk back to the table where Adele still sits, her face buried in her arms. I run my fingers along the nape of her neck.

She shivers slightly before looking up at me, a smile on those beautiful lips of hers.

"Was that okay?"

I cup her cheek and capture her in a kiss. "Sweetheart, you were wonderful."

Skeptics sat down at the table, believers rose from it.

***

The tricks of the trade are simple and painfully obvious. Once you know them, that is.

The thuds are from the wooden heel of my left boot. Lead pellets fill the hollow of it, lending it extra weight.

The table is lighter than it appears. I'm able to lift it up with the aid of a flat piece of metal attached to a leather cuff round my wrist. Slipped into a slot in the table's edge, I can manipulate it all whilst my hands are clearly on show, palms resting flat against the surface.

The 'ectoplasm' is gauze, covered with potato starch mixed with zinc sulfide and silver, which causes the ghostly blue glow.

The rest is all down to Adele, to her gift for mimicry, and an astounding memory.

Her skillful tongue uncannily replicated the cadence and rhythm of Mrs. Crawshaw's dear departed friend's speech.

"I wish you hadn't said that about the baby," I say as I tidy the room, straightening the candle sticks. "You know how I feel about bringing kids into it. It sets up expectations we can't meet." I look at the gooey mess on the table; it'll take some scrubbing to come clean. I doubt the varnish will survive. "She'll come back wanting to know more."

"What was I supposed to do? The woman's out of her mind with grief. And we need every paying customer we can get." She looks downwards and adds, in a mutter, "It's not like the money's pouring in from anywhere else."

The words are true, but that doesn't lessen the sting.

Adele is used to a finer life than this one. I promised better, and so far, I have failed her.

"Perhaps you might enlighten me on how you made ends meet before the shop."

"I …" I fucked about in exchange for gifts and money, Adele. "I had ways and means."

"Ah yes, of course." She sets down the mop, a bit too hard, letting it sway before tipping over. "*Ways and means,* as you've mentioned many times. If only I knew more about these mysterious *ways and means*, we might lessen the weight of our debts."

"We manage to keep the bailiffs from banging on the door."

"Mother would be so proud," she grumbles.

"You could always go back to America, Adele. Maybe you could take me with you and show me this fine life that you used to lead?"

She winces. "You know I can't do that."

"Then why bring them up at every turn?" I sigh, it's always *Mother this* and *Father that* with Adele. It's as though she enjoys rubbing in the fact that I don't come from privilege.

"I'm sorry. It's been a long day; I suppose I am just exhausted." She laces her hand around my waist.

"I'm sorry I can't give you more." I pull her closer to me. "But you do realize that life's most pleasurable activities are free, don't you?" Placing a kiss upon her neck, I whisper, "I could carry you upstairs, my queen."

Adele giggles and I go to one knee, offering my arms. She sets herself into them, raising her hand high with a loose wrist. "Yes, please do. I am dead tired on my feet and can't possibly face the stairs." Flicking in the direction of our upstairs bedroom, she says, "Quickly now!" in a posh accent.

"I'm going to have to have to be honest with you. I'm not entirely sure I could carry you. You must remember I'm just that tad older. I can, however, lead you lovingly by the hand up the stairs. Would that do, my lady?"

"Well then." She slips from my arms, looking at me down the bridge of her slender nose. "You are fired as my head of staff. But"—she extends her hand and I take it—"I shall keep you on as my partner."

"Most gracious of you."

"We Hughes' are known for our graciousness." Adele starts in the direction of the stairs, but I take jogging steps to pass her, dipping into a bow before I lead. "And our beauty," she adds with a wide smile.

"Come on then, let me get a better look at all that beauty and show you what money can't buy."

Chapter 2: Tawdry Things

Adele

Quartz bends the light pushing through our curtained windows, warps it in such a fine and lovely way. I catch the full spectrum of color in my palm, let it paint my flesh with blues and greens and red while the memory of Lorelei calling me *Your Majesty* bounces delightfully through my head. The crystals lie on a plush velvet cloth the color of eggplant. Well, velveteen, velvet's cheap cousin. In my mind Mother reminds me as much. She points out, too, that our stones lack quality. *Tawdry things, those. Have you seen the fine crystal set your aunt left us? Now* that *is crystal worth having.* Her admonishments followed me across the sea. Even in the cramped quiet of our shop, I cannot escape her, her disappointment. Her reminders of our—my—failure.

The clanging of our bell sends a jolt of wakefulness through my arm, and the crystal in my hand clatters back to its fellows. On our threshold stands the gentleman from last night, his pale hair in a natural curl at his temple, accentuating his smug grin.

"Madame Adeline, how fortunate I've caught you." As he strides toward me, he peppers dirt in his wake.

"Mr—" I extend my hand to shake, but instead he grasps it, wraps it around his hip and smothers me in an embrace.

"Wainwright," he says, allowing me to break away. "Is that gardenia I smell?"

"No," I say, taking another step back. "It's lavender. What can I do for you, sir?"

"Well, actually, I came to discuss what I might do for you. Dinner, to start. What do you say?"

"I, um—" Blessedly, I'm spared having to complete the sentence when a woman joins us in the shop.

"Am I interrupting something?" she asks with a pointed tone. Long dark hair frames her chiseled jaw and pointed nose. Both beautiful and strange, her clothing is a patchwork of fabrics, each bearing a different pattern or design. But the clamor of color and embroidery does nothing to distract from her penetrating gaze and the way her tongue darts across her upper lip.

"No, not at all." I cringe at my own tone, which has risen an octave over its usual meekness. "Please, come in. Can I help you with something?"

Mr. Wainwright's smugness has turned to impatience as he holds a finger aloft to silence this new visitor. "So," he says to me, closing the gap between us. "Tomorrow night?"

I step to move around him, diverting my attention to the woman instead, but he grabs my arm roughly, nails dragging against my skin as I twist it from his grip. Instinctively, I cover my scratched arm with the other, pulling it close to my body.

"Sir," the woman says. "If you don't mind, I'm short on time." She waves him toward the door. I cast my eyes down, both grateful for, and impressed by, her brusqueness.

Reluctantly, he abides her, muttering disapproval on his way out. When the door shuts behind him, she continues.

"I'm in search of quite a special piece," she says, sauntering further inside as if she both belongs in our shop and is too good for it.

"Perhaps you might be more specific."

Lorelei's voice startles me, I hadn't realized she'd returned to the counter from the backroom. Her gaze wanders over the window, where Mr. Wainwright has stolen one last look at me before crossing the street.

"A particular spirit photograph." The woman gestures above her head. "A man in a top hat and the sheen of ectoplasm." She fingers the air about her breasts. "Just here."

"I'll check in back." Lorelei turns, dark red waves brushing her shoulder and, in my periphery, I think I see the woman wink. Our curtain rustles as Lorelei's curvaceous frame disappears behind it. No sooner has she left us than the woman has taken graceful strides toward me and placed her hand upon my shoulder. My skin gooses and I halt my breath.

"You've not introduced yourself." Her words tickle my ear, her breath hot on my neck.

"Ade–Madam Adaline." The words twist through my constricted throat.

"Viola," she says, brushing a strand of hair from my shoulder.

As I turn to face her, my head is heavy as lead, and I catch a smirk upon her lips. Our curtain rustles. Every nerve in my body is set aflame. True fear snakes up and down my spine. I am caught. It's a sensation I haven't felt since Father caught me playing in his office so many years past.

"Couldn't find that particular photo, however—"

I brace for Lorelei to discover my closeness with this stranger, for her biting words and lingering days of stony silence, but when I glance toward her, I find Viola at our counter, leaning upon it and eyes wandering as if bored.

It's five paces to the counter with two rows of shelves in-between. How could she clear the distance and not a s—

"No matter," Viola says. "It was good of you to humor me and check."

Lorelei fans a grouping of photos across the counter and Viola turns toward the door. "However," Lorelei raises her tone, "we have a great many other spirit photos which might strike your interest."

Without turning back to face her, Viola says, "Good day."

Lorelei's eyes turn to green lightning at the woman's rudeness. My cheeks go hot. Her jaw cracks open and I think she might rage when another spews venom instead.

"Witchcraft! Lovers of Satan!" It comes from the street, from the throat of none other than Beatrice Eyre, our self-appointed nemesis, who seems to spend less and less time at her market stall and more harassing us in the street. "You'll steer clear if ya know what's good for ya! Naught but evil in there." Through our shop window a man with a dark mustache slants his derby hat to avoid her eyes and skirts past her.

Viola looks on, one hand on our knob, with an amused lightness about her expression.

Beatrice fixes her gaze upon the strange woman through the glass. "You there!"

Viola points to her own chest in mock surprise.

"Extricate yourself from that wickedness while you still have the Lord's blessing upon you!"

Viola shrugs and looks back at us, tossing a melodramatic hand over her lips.

"Come now, quickly!" Beatrice waves her arm as if ushering Viola off a sinking ship. A strange tugging sensation within my chest pairs with an intrusive thought: *Don't let her go,* but Viola slips through the door to our bell's jangling tune.

Lorelei strips her cleaning apron and swats her hands against one another on her approach to the door. Her lips have already begun forming the words to frighten off our pesky shop neighbor when Chester joins the fray. Barely over three feet tall, I often think the length of him is filled with naught but profanity, that he's spent his ten years of life mastering the arts of mischief and insult.

"A reyt twat, ye are." He launches a wad of spittle which lands just inches from Beatrice's worn leather shoe. "Bugger off then, and take yer rank stench with ye!"

Entranced by the fray, I find myself at Lorelei's side, peering through the door with no memory of moving there. Viola has erupted into a fit of laughter, flushing Beatrice's cheeks to a darker shade of purple.

"Yer all hellions, all scum," she spews at the sky and stomps off with knees too high in each step.

"Fishmonger, my arse," Chester says loud enough for Beatrice still to hear. "The smell comes from between 'er fat thighs, ye know."

Viola covers her mouth but the smile is visible within her eyes. She pats Chester's head twice. "You're a good boy," she says before disappearing into the dusty street.

Chester bats at his nest of hair, righting the ash brown strands to their proper disorder. "Who's that then? Not from 'round here, is she?"

Being a tourist town means very few people are actually from *'round here*, but his meaning is clear: this woman does not belong.

"No." Lorelei's feet remain planted, her eyes hovering over the spot where Viola stood last. I cross my arms around my midsection, as if I might hold my secret lust from her sight. But a creeping dread tells me she knows. "Come on then." My lover circles her arm around Chester, auburn hair aflame in the daylight, and ushers him inside. He strips his satchel and begins rifling through.

I make an effort at busying myself, brushing the sheen of dust from some old volumes as Lorelei enquires about Chester's morning. He places bits of this and that about the floor: a tarnished pocket-watch, a silver locket with cracked glass, coins coated in vibrant teal muck from submersion in water—plucked from the fountain one town over, no doubt.

"Give them here," Lorelei says, retrieving a bit of soda and an uncut lemon from behind the counter. With the reverence of beholding some holy thing, Chester places the items one by one into a small bowl and Lorelei gets to work removing the tarnish. "Got a half a Bakewell tart in back if you'd like."

Chester nods eagerly, and his young age can finally be seen in the scampering steps he takes to the back room to sate his hunger. I tighten my core. If Lorelei suspects my lust, it is now she will speak to it.

"Unusual for you to take such a forward role in assisting our customers." Her attention remains fixed on the locket which she buffs hard with a bit of cloth.

"I—we could use the money." My tone has an edge I do not intend.

Lorelei *hmphs*. "Quite the observation, indeed."

I need to save us before we descend into squabbling. "I thought perhaps a patron so clearly well-traveled might be one worth a bit of extra attention."

Lorelei's hands stop working. She meets my eyes. "You would know, being so well-traveled yourself."

The rest goes unspoken. Though I was not deliberate in granting my words dual purpose, I can't help but consider how it might feel to give Viola the *extra attention* Lorelei seems to imply. I am quite sure she would make use of me in ways my lover seems to think me useless, or old hat, perhaps. As she returns to scrubbing, I grab the broom and make long, useless strokes across the floor, pushing bits of dust and errant hairs this way and that as I replay our argument in my mind. So many times now, we've gone round and round, each rehearsing our parts so thoroughly I think one could stand in for the other if necessary. And yet we find no way to avoid it.

The broom's spindles grate a soothing sound against the hardwood.

Why can't I touch you? I start.

I let you touch me.

Yes, you do, but not in that *way.*

It's different. You know that. I still take care of you, pleasure you—don't I?

Pleasure. Does a porcelain doll feel pleasure at the combing of her hair? You think me equally fragile. Equally useless. It's the part I never say; thinking to speak it would be a bridge too far, might crack the dry, weather-beaten leather that binds us.

Chester emerges from our back room, jam staining the corners of his lips. "What you reckon that rammel'll fetch us?"

"A few shillings, at least."

Realizing the starkly clean square foot of floor before me, I return the broom to its resting place upon the wall, leaving little hills of dirt to scoop up later. "I can take you to the pawnbroker if you'd like. Some fresh air would do me good."

"Would be prudent to wait a few days at least." Lorelei's eyes narrow. "Should any ladies or gentlemen notice their pockets recently made lighter and come looking for their trinkets."

"Stop yer wittlin'," Chester fires back. "Does thou really think me that thick? Any ladies or gents with light pockets got on the train an hour back. Lest their trinkets manage to float down the Derwent in chase, they'll not see them again."

I feel Lorelei's contemptuous stare upon my back as I step onto the street. A breeze pushes my hair back, and despite the grit blowing with it.

I exhale the stale air from the shop—all resentment and unfulfilled promises—and inhale the possibility …

"Bit early in the day to be squiffy, init?" Chester calls. "Yer headed the wrong way."

I turn on my heel, realizing at once that I've not followed the street to the pawnbroker's shop, but down the same path Viola crossed. I can only hope Lorelei has not seen and Chester will write off my missteps as absentmindedness, or drunkenness, though he has never seen me indulge in even a drop.

"How's your mom?"

My shoulders relax as Chester descends into his usual tirade. He's called her a trollop no less than four times before we reach the pawnbroker, and I think I must've sufficiently distracted him from my ill-intentioned wandering up the road.

Mr. Williams is a kindly man, thank God for us. He pushes his spectacles up the bridge of his nose as he inspects Chester's wares. I must admit, they look a great deal more sellable since Lorelei's polishing. His musings about their approximate age and condition are drowned out by mathematical calculations in my head.

The rent, plus the ten pence we owe the butcher, minus payment from the friend of Mrs. Crawshaw—

"Twelve shillings for the lot."

"But sir, the quality—" Chester starts, emulating Lorelei's posh manner of speech.

"It's the best I can do."

"But sir!"

Mr. Williams frowns, raising a quieting hand. "Twelve shillings."

I take him at his word. "Thank you, Mr. Williams." Though you'd never think it, with his immaculately pressed trousers, crisp white shirt and his gray beard properly trimmed, Williams came from humble beginnings himself, and helps us in the ways he can.

Chester extends a grubby hand for coins and Williams abides. No sooner have Chester's fingers encircled the bounty than he is jogging out of the shop and down the street. I smile at Williams, and am about to bid him good day when a hand settles on my shoulder.

I stiffen, having thought the shop empty but for Williams and myself. The pawnbroker's eyes settle on whatever person stands behind me. As if dismissed, he nods and enters his back office. My pulse races, a sharp, sweet scent filling the room, and I turn to see her.

Viola.

Chapter 3: Sharper Than You'd Think

Lorelei

Adele arches her hips to meet my hand. How I'd love to pin her where she lays, withdraw and feel her squirm beneath me, but watching her like this, eyes closed, her bottom lip between her teeth, the sheen of sweat on her furrowed brow, I wouldn't dream of treating her as such.

Nothing excites me more than her pleasure. And after seeing how she stared at that woman today, how that bastard Wainwright grabbed at her, I need to show her I'm the only one who can treat her with the care she so deserves. I continue to work Adele, alternating the speed of my thrusts, ignoring the burn of the muscles in my wrist. I should have confronted that bastard instead of holding my tongue and letting *that woman* come to her rescue. I picture grabbing them each by the throat, their faces replaced by Adele's as she releases a labored breath. Shaking away the violent images, I remind my hand to be gentle.

The ticking of the clock seems all too loud, a distraction, a herald of the passing minutes, the prospect of bringing Adele to a satisfactory conclusion slipping farther away with each click. Is she close? She seems close. Eyes clamped shut, nose screwed up. Concentrating.

I increase the pressure, noted by the tensing of her abdomen. If she fantasizes, I cannot blame her. It's not as if I don't drift elsewhere too, spicing reality with imagined flavor too depraved for sweet Adele. Her initial slickness is all but spent. Tick. That damn clock. Her hand clenches around my wrist.

I stop.

"Sorry, I—"

"It's alright." I climb up beside her and let myself collapse, stare at the water-stained ceiling.

"I could …"

Her fingers trace idle circles on my stomach before they move lower. I part my legs for her so that she may trace smaller, tighter, faster circles upon me, closing my eyes as she takes my left nipple into her mouth, her tongue keeping the same time as her fingers. My mind drifts. I dig my fingers into the sheet to keep from grabbing her by the hair, but I imagine I do, that she mewls at the twinge of pain, that her cornflower eyes plead with me. I'm just about to come when her hand moves lower still. My eyes snap open as I capture her wrist in my hand, stalling her movements.

"What … You don't have to do that." I don't mean for the words to come out so harsh but I cannot change them now.

"I—"

"You know I don't—like that."

"I'd've thought you might have learned to trust me." Adele turns her gaze away from me. "After all these years."

How can I tell her it's not that?

"You know I trust you, implicitly." Except when I don't. Except when you lock eyes with other women, beautiful women.

"Then why won't you let me touch you?"

"I do let you touch me. I was very happy with you touching me. I was about to become even happier still."

"You know what I mean. Why won't you let me …"

She won't say it, it's too coarse of a thing for her to say. I'll say it for her.

"Fuck me."

She nods. "Yes, why won't you let me?"

I'm in no mood for this conversation. I get out of bed.

"I've asked you time and time again. Have I not earned an explanation?"

Slipping on a shirt, I manage to bite back any words I might speak in anger, but it will not save me from hers.

"So, I'm plenty useful to you as a showpiece for the shop, and you found my purse quite useful in adorning it with the latest charlatan gadgets, yet my use in our bedroom has firm and mysterious limits."

I glance at the ticking carriage clock on the dresser; it's gone one in the morning. I pull on a pair of trousers I keep for wearing around the house and shove my bare feet into my boots.

"Where are you going?" she asks petulantly. If there's one thing Adele hates, it's being ignored. She'd prefer for us to argue because at least then she's still the focus of my attention.

"I'm going for a walk." I pull on a jumper and go to the door. "You are welcome to finish yourself thinking of whoever you were just now." I regret it instantly.

"Hah!" It's a contortion of a laugh, shot through with muffled pain. Adele's ire has pushed her voice to a fever pitch. It bounces off the walls, chasing after me as I descend the stairs. "Perhaps I will dream up another, one who might welcome my touch rather than run from it."

If I didn't know better, I'd think she meant it. "Don't bother waiting up for me."

***

After the heat of the bedroom, the night air is blessedly cool. Summer is coming to an end and with it the tourists and their purses. People still visit during the autumn and winter months but not in the numbers they do during the height of summer, and we've barely made it through.

I'm a failure. For all my blustering and aspirations to rise above my station, I've seen none of it to fruition. Perhaps my former patron was right: I needed more guidance, more connections before striking out on my own. But the price …

Those solitary, painful days of healing resurface in my mind as I walk down the promenade, at last reaching the bridge that connects the prom to Lovers Walk over the river. This is my favorite place in the world when it's quiet like this. Free from the tourists who pass to and fro across it each day, I can watch the few remaining lights skate across the water. I lean back against the cool iron, close my eyes and think. Was there any reason other than my own sentimentality to stay here? Those in town who run the hydros and thermal baths have a steady stream of customers throughout the year seeking their healing properties. Hell, our best-selling item is the bottled water we claim helps with hair loss. Maybe …

Footsteps interrupt my thoughts; has Adele come to fetch me home?

I turn to find the woman who came in the shop today, the one who had captivated Adele so. The one I saw look at Adele with a wicked gleam and a lick of her lips.

"Rather late for a walk, isn't it, Lorelei?"

How is it she knows my name?

"No law against it," I say as I survey this rival for Adele's affection. She matches me in height; one of the things Adele had always liked about me was that I was taller than her. It made her feel safe. And the woman's clothing is certainly finer than mine as well, which speaks to her having money. Money, and the security which it brings, is something I can't compete with.

No, Adele might be momentarily distracted by this woman but it will be no more than a few idle daydreams. I know this type of woman. I used to be this woman. She'd cast Adele aside as soon as she grew bored, and if there's one thing Adele knows I can provide her with it's constancy.

"Left Madame Adaline home alone, have you?" she says, her eyes flicking in the direction of our home. "Maybe I ought to pay her a visit. I hate to think of her alone in a cold bed."

"Stay the bloody 'ell away from 'er!" I ball my fists, nails digging into my palms.

"Mind yourself," she says. "That carefully cultivated accent you learnt by fucking all those society women is slipping."

Have we met before? There're so many nights from those days that are hazy around the edges.

"And to think I thought you'd have better control of your tongue than that." She leans in to whisper, "Maybe it's Adaline who has the talented tongue. I bet she wouldn't need much coaxing from me to find out. I—"

I've never struck another woman before. Sure, I'd been in scuffles in my younger days, but I'd never really, truly hit anyone. If I had I'd have realized you shouldn't strike someone in the mouth; human teeth are sharper than you'd think.

"Fucking bastard," I hiss between my own clenched teeth, clutching my hand to my chest.

She laughs even as she brings a finger to her mouth and wipes away a spot of blood, looking at it with a mixture of amusement and perplexity. This is a woman not used to being hurt.

"You silly, silly girl."

This rankles me further; she can't be that much older than I.

She offers me her blood-stained hand. "Show me," she says, her tone warm and gentle now.

"No."

She sighs in a resigned manner as she takes my wrist, turning my hand this way and that. "Flex your fingers."

I do.

"A few scrapes and you will have some swelling, but nothing is broken here. You'll still be able to take *care* of her. But I wonder, Lorelei, does she take care of you?" She places a kiss on my inner wrist before relinquishing her grip on me. And though I try to tell myself it's the cool night air that makes me shiver, I know it is *her.*

"Run along home now, Lorelei." She turns away and walks in the direction of Lovers Walk. I watch as she disappears into the darkness before I turn away in the direction of home.

***

There is a visitor on the front step when I arrive.

Chester sits fidgeting with a piece of knotted string. This isn't the first time he's shown up in the middle of the night and sadly won't be the last.

"Ey up, lad," I say, sitting beside him. "What yer doing round 'ere this time of the morning?" He knows I don't really want an answer, even in the near darkness I can see the wetness on his cheeks, the bruise forming on his left eye.

"Fancied a walk, didn't I?"

I nod my head. "Nice night for it." We sit in comfortable silence for a moment. Neither of us have to pretend to be anything when it's just us alone. "Yer know," I say slowly. "If you were feeling tired after your walk, thou could 'ave knocked on the door. Adele would have let you in."

"I did, no answer. Didn't want to knock any louder in case I woke yer neighbors up."

"Not like you to be so considerate." I gently elbow him.

"Yer know me, proper little gentleman I am." His gaze lands on my hand, the knuckle scraped and already swollen. "Did you deck 'er?"

"Chester! You know I'd never hurt Adele. I've told yer times many there's never any real excuse to hit someone, especially a woman."

"Jesus, Lore, I know that! I meant t'other woman, the strange one."

I look down at my ruined hand. "Well, she deserved it. And how did you—"

"She followed us t'pawn shop."

"Did she, now?" I cast my eyes to the other side of the river, knowing that somewhere in the darkness, she lurks. "She'll be gone soon enough, I reckon." I stand up and dig in my pocket for the key. "Let's get inside."

***

Once Chester is safely curled up in the chair in our sitting-room, I go to our bedroom. I dawdle at the door, running over the words I wish to say to Adele.

I'm sorry, I shouldn't have left you …

The reason I don't like to be touched like that is …

I brush my fingers across the handle before snatching them away.

I can do this. I take a deep breath; I can be honest with her. Expose wounds, long hidden, to the air and the light in the hope they may finally start to heal.

I can fix things between us.

After long moments I enter the room, only to find Adele is no longer in our bed.

Chapter 4: Open Your Mouth

Adele

Out the door and through the darkened streets I run, but not to pursue Lorelei, to flee her. The scent of me clings to our sheets, hangs musky in the air, a ghost of my guarded companion. And I'll not be haunted by her. Not tonight. The clanging of our bell fades into the distance as I dampen the blow of Lorelei's rejection with the heavy cloak of night. Words unsaid between us become invisible hands pushing me from the home we share. I know Lorelei will go to the Jubilee bridge, so I head in the opposite direction.

You may have beat me to leaving in a huff, but you've not the fortification of spirit to outlast me in a siege, darling.

Halfway down the lane, I realize I'm clothed only in my nightdress, and wrap my arms around the thin fabric separating my nakedness from the world at large. The street below turns from dirt to cobblestone underfoot as I rehearse arguments, me ever the victor, Lorelei apologizing or left speechless. In the imagined silence of my partner, another voice creeps in. Viola's whisper curls inside my ear, *Meet me at Lovers Walk*. Though I'd no intention of abiding her unseemly request when the words parted her lips at the pawn shop, I find my feet ushering me toward Matlock Bath and into uncertainty. Past the promenade I go, slowing my pace only when a stitch in my side demands it. The shuttered shops grant some assurance of privacy, but the clouded sky thickens the darkness to such an extent I can hardly see some twenty paces ahead. A twitch of fear spurns me on and, eager to find company, even if it be with an alluring stranger, I cast nicety aside and continue down the well-trodden path at Lovers Walk.

Ancient oaks groan under the pressure of a passing wind. The distant squawk of an unseen crow reminds me of my vulnerability, the possibility of nefarious eyes upon me, crouched behind a boulder or tucked in a thicket of brush. Moonlight glistens off the rolling lake, and a strange thought wraps it itself around my throat. I envision a sea monster, old as a pagan god and just as ruthless, breaking the surface and dragging me down to the icy depths. I am about to turn back, to face my loveless lover with head hung in defeat, when a crisp voice croons from behind.

"You came."

The simple words send a shiver through my marrow. I'm suddenly aware of the puffiness about my eyes, and press my finger beneath each before I turn to face her. She seems taller than before. Cloaked in a jacket of deep purple with a smart, wide-brimmed black hat, she approaches with gentle steps.

"And you've been crying," she adds, wiping a tear from my cheek. She puts her thumb to her lips to taste me. "How sad."

My feet spring roots. My tongue goes numb in my mouth. I find I can't move, nor answer her. Whether she's bewitched me or I've just submitted to my powerlessness before her, I know not. But I remain in my spot as she extends her palm to my cheek.

"Little dove." She clicks her tongue, and I'm unable to stop the rush of blood between my thighs. I want that tongue tickling across my skin. Inside me. Exploring the places only Lorelei has known.

Lorelei. The thought comes with a jolt of pain. *What am I doing?*

"Tell me your troubles." She takes my hand in hers and, as if by some new magic, I find myself following her like a leashed dog as she sits on a large, smooth stone. A gesture from her hand is all it takes for me to sit beside her. Her skirts brush against my nightdress, and I'm grateful for the opaque fabric, that she can't see the goosed skin beneath.

"Well?"

I sneak glances to a swollen place on her upper lip, notice her eyes fixed on mine. A tiny crevasse sealed with fresh blood. "It was improper for me to come. You must forgive me." I mean to rise, to excuse myself with what grace I have left, but I move not.

Her palm presses against my back.

"It's … domestic troubles. Nothing so unusual."

I smooth back my hair, a petty attempt to mitigate my foolishness. Though I'd never be so invasive as to ask directly, perhaps she, too, grapples with domestic unease, evidence sketched upon her bloodied mouth.

"Your lover, then?"

The bounds of propriety constrict my ribcage. One careless word and all of Matlock will alight with rumor of my unnatural predilections, just as it happened in New York. "My housemate."

"Your housemate, yes," she says, tugging at an errant thread in my nightdress. "And lover, Lorelei."

My pulse pounds in my ears. She cannot know. How have I betrayed myself? "I assure you, it's nothing as—"

"You needn't worry, little dove. There are secrets far more malevolent and depraved dwelling inside the vault of my spirit." Her lips curl into a smile both sinister and sincere.

I believe her.

"I am quite the same." Her curled finger raises my chin so I cannot escape her gaze. "So beautiful, you are. Such full lips. Your eyes wide and blue enough to sink into."

I tremble. An intoxicating mixture of fear and desire quickens my breath. I wet my lips, and she releases me.

"Lorelei and I …" My eyes wander over the lake's mirror shine. "It is not as it was. As I thought it might be." A winged silhouette swoops from a cluster of branches and breaks the surface with its clawed foot.

"Things rarely are as we hope they might be." Her tone is so steady, so sure, I feel as though I am audience to a divine being. "And yet, we continue to hope."

In this close proximity, I notice the gentle wave of her hair, not flat brown but a hue like mahogany, though perhaps it is some trick of the eye, a reflection of her purple dress. As if in some dream state, I reach for the closest lock. It's silken in my hand, and I wait for her to recoil, to chide me, to hurl threats of exposure, but instead she says, "I see the desire of your heart."

The slickness between my legs bleeds down my thighs, and I press them together in a desperate attempt to relieve the throbbing ache of need.

"Open your mouth."

My heart drops as she stands. The command of her voice stirs a secret desire, one too malevolent to speak. I gaze up at her, my jaw naturally cracking open.

"Wider."

Silence bares down upon Lovers Walk, as if every living creature has stepped aside to allow the strange woman to take center stage. There is a moment. I know if I go further, I will have transgressed, crossed a boundary from which there is no noble return. I'd thought, once, if I could share a bed with a woman, that would be enough. But something is missing still, a void Viola's domineering presence threatens to fill. In a still mental space, not quite myself but pleasurably calm, I do as she bade me, stretching my jaw as wide as it will open.

"Good girl." She extends a finger, placing it inside. My center gathers into a knot as she presses down upon it. Every clenching muscle inside me relaxes. I wish only for another command, to do her bidding with obedience unparalleled.

"On your knees, little dove."

She withdraws her finger, and I slide from my stone seat and land roughly. Branches scratch my knee caps, but the pain only flares my desire. I look up to her once more, hungry for her.

"Tell me your true name."

"Adele," I whisper.

"Adele, you will please me, if you can."

I reach for her layered skirts, the satin cool in my hands.

"Wait."

I stop breathing, fear snaking up my spine.

"What do you say?"

The words flow easily from my lips, escaping my chest like steam from a kettle. "Thank you, ma'am."

A grim smile tells me I've done well in answering such, and a nod beckons me to continue. Needing not but that, I thrust her skirts up to her thighs and gasp at the loveliness of the hosiery beneath. Finely woven fishnet stockings run three quarters up her leg and are affixed to her waist with a black garter belt. She wears no undergarments, her most intimate places greeting me. A ripple of shock at the lack of pretense is followed by fiery lust. Viola wants me, invites me closer. I don't welcome her into my mouth straightaway, but instead drop and spread kisses over her ankles. Her taste is both sweet and spiced like cinnamon, and I become frenzied as I work my mouth and tongue up the inside of each thigh. She coos and moans above me, and when I rise high enough to begin to taste her, she thrusts my head into her opening, my tongue landing just where her lips part.

"Yes, Adele." Her voice is throaty, low, and her slickness slides down my throat. I have so craved it, so coveted this feeling—animalistic desire. I thirst for more, caressing every fold of her skin and slipping my tongue inside her between rolling circles over her most sensitive spot. I burst with pride as her breath becomes heavy and even. My fingernails dig into her hips and she, in turn, pushes my head even more firmly upon her, until her moans crest into a strangled yelp that echoes off the lake.

"Well done," she says as I untangle myself from her skirts. Her pleasure coats my lips and chin, and I move to wipe it away when she grabs my wrist and spins me around, bending me over the stone on which we sat. "And now I'll show you how you should be fucked."

She is not coy, not gentle like my usual lover. Nightdress tossed over my back, she enters me with two fingers, a girth that makes me cry out.

Her other hand wraps around my mouth, stifling my moans of pleasure and pain as she works me, thrusting my torso into the unforgiving stone. Once again, she wriggles her fingers into my mouth, this time hooking them into my cheek and forcing me to face her. Her look is one of amusement as the pressure builds and my breath hitches.

"Is this what you wanted?" she asks. "Is this what you crave?"

Just as I think I'll climax, she withdraws her fingers, leaving a devastating emptiness in their wake. I think I'll scream in frustration when I feel her slick hand caress the spot I tend to when I'm alone, and my emptiness is filled by her thumb.

She stops moving.

"Go on," she says, brow arching. "Work for it."

Gripping the stone for purchase, I rock back and forth against her. The sound of my wetness only drives my desire further, deeper, and it takes only moments of bucking against her for it to crest into wave after wave of pleasure. My hard nipples press against the thin fabric, and when she withdraws from me, I collapse onto the hard stone, panting.

As I catch my breath, she sits beside me, stroking my hair away from my face. Her dripping fingers hover over my arm, and I think she might take my hand. But instead, she pinches a bit of skin at my wrist and sinks her nails into my flesh, drawing up a thin layer.

I shriek, the searing pain clouding my vision, and watch as she opens a bloody strip in my arm. Horror and panic strike me at once, and I recoil, stumbling backward, clutching my arm to my chest.

"Don't look as shocked as that, little dove. You and I both know what *little* damage I've done."

I look down to my arm, though I already know what I'll find. My demonic ability exposed, a secret even from Lorelei, which now this stranger might witness.

"Show me." Her voice is a hiss, and I shake my head no, but she advances with the speed of a feral cat and yanks my arm toward her.

Before both our eyes, my skin stitches itself back together, not even a scratch where it had been removed.

"I knew it." Her eyes narrow to slits. "I knew that I had found you."

Chapter 5: She was Running from Something

Lorelei

I've seen no one all morning.

Chester scarpered on home as soon as it was light enough and not a single customer has graced the shop.

I should have gone out looking for Adele when I saw that she still hadn't come home, but I know Adele well enough to know if she doesn't want to be found, she won't be. I remember the first time I met her.

Every relationship I've had, hell, most every interaction I have with people has its roots in illusion. Adele was no different.

I'd been sent on an errand to Liverpool, evidently the only place to purchase a particular style of lace, or so the girl I'd been trying to court at the time insisted, when I first saw her. She stood out from the crowd not just because of her beauty, but because of her obvious good breeding.

She stood a little straighter than the surrounding people. Her clothes were another point of difference, for, although not ostentatious, they were perfectly tailored and cut from the finest materials.

She was guarding a trunk, its leather not yet scuffed or cracking with age, and from the way her eyes darted about and the way she chewed her bottom lip, it seemed she was wondering what she should do next.

I ran a hand through my hair. Contrary to convention I'd always preferred to wear it loose, and approached her.

"You look as though you could do with some help," I said, ensuring I pronounced those pesky *h's*.

"I'm fine, thank you." *She's American!*

"It's really not safe for you to be here by yourself. Have you lodgings booked to which I can escort you?"

She looked at her feet. This trip was not planned. She was running away from something.

"I promise I won't hurt you."

Her gaze lifted upwards and she looked at me, really looked at me.

I noticed the way her eyes flicked downwards, taking me all in, the way she bit her lower lip as she did so. And, in that instant, I knew she was like me and why she was so far from home.

If Adele has decided to run away from me, and who could blame her, I know she has the fortitude to make it as far as she wants. For all I know she may be on a train heading down south at this very moment.

I walk over to the crystals that lay on the aubergine cushion that Adele always insists on calling eggplant, recalling how convinced I was, at first, that she must be teasing me with such a ridiculous name.

You're making it up. It sounds made up.

And where do you suppose words come from, prey tell? Are they mined from the earth?

No, I had the notion that they were plucked from plants. Much like eggs are, apparently.

Though I know Adele wiped them clean only the day before, a thin layer of dust covers them. Our love was once like them, shimmering and full of color, but at some point, we stopped trying to wipe the dust off.

The bell rings. I steel myself to deal with a potential customer but when I turn around Adele stands there still in her nightgown, hair disheveled her eyes shot red, either by a bout of crying or by lack of sleep, I cannot tell.

My first instinct is to ask her where she's been, but I don't trust myself to ask the question kindly. I wait for her to speak first.

"Good morning."

"It's practically the afternoon."

"Oh." She puts her head down as she crosses the room, and that's when I notice the red-and-rust-coloured spots littering the back of her nightgown. I do a quick calculation of dates in my head and come up short. And I'm certain that I hadn't been so rough with her as to cause her to bleed.

"Adele?" She turns and looks, not at me but some point behind me. "You know you can talk to me, don't you?"

"Yes, I know." Her tone is flat, lifeless. "I'm going to get changed, I've got errands I need to run."

"They can wait," I say, then, before I can stop myself, "Stay with me?"

"They need doing. Not every want can wait." All at once the anger I'd felt at her disappearance, that I'd tried so hard to bury, came rushing to the surface.

"Very well, after all who am I to stand in the way of such pressing matters."

She's changed and out the door again in ten minutes. I watch her walk down the street as dark clouds start to gather far on the horizon.

Chapter 6: Another Twist of the Blade

Adele

The hue of Lorelei's eyes are all I see when I finally arrive home. The color of jade, not the vivid green of an uncut stone, but a green that has been softened by time, like a well-loved ornament handled repeatedly over years. Could one who loves me such as Lorelei does, strives to protect me as she does, ever speak to me with the abhorrent disdain which sets my body aflame? Never could I ask it of her. I would sound mad, fit for a whorehouse. And simply the act of asking would sour it. On the longshot that Lorelei was willing to stoop to such lows as to play this fantasy, I would ever see it as an act of charity, a willingness to play into my debauchery for my pleasure alone.

Her words warp, the sound distorted as if bounced around the walls of a stone tunnel. The initial rush of transgression having worn off, changing from my soiled nightdress does nothing to dampen the cloying embrace of icy guilt.

Lorelei's concern for me is a knife, for I know it is undeserved. But had she taken more care to notice my needs, I would not have been lured in by temptation. Still, I am filled with shame for betraying her. I can scarcely stand to be in her company at all, which I'm sure she reads as punishment for our row. Another twist of the blade. The old fear once again sets its teeth in me: I was born *wrong.*

So I take my leave, mumble something about needing fresh sage, and loose myself upon the busy street, hoping to drown my angst in the faces and voices of a crowd.

A crowd is what I find, and for a time I find the bustle a salve to my moral failings. It's market day and the traders are out in force. I peruse softening fruits, fresh cut flowers, and fish on ice from rickety wooden stalls, the peeling paint on their signs making their names barely legible. A brother and sister, no more than twelve, dance a jig as their father plays a pipe and tabor. There's such merriment in their steps, their knees so high, smiles so wide, I clap along in time with the rhythm, forgetting my troubles for the moment. The boy extends a hand, dirt nestled in his nail beds, and I reach for it to join him in dancing when the bellow of an old crone makes the father stop playing.

"A witch!"

The accusation stops both the boy and girl dancing, yanks their joyous expressions into curious frowns.

"You'll keep your children a great distance from 'er if ye know what's good for ye!" Beatrice careens down the promenade, her frock varying shades of brown and her nose wrinkled in disgust. "Tangled up in the dark arts, this one." She twists her lips as such I think she might spit upon me, and I move to back away when she snatches a bit of twig from my hair. "Aye, ye see?" She points an accusatory finger to the children and back to me. "Up late night with the devil 'imself, were ye? Debasing all that is holy, signin' yer name is his dark book, no doubt!"

The father ushers his children away, and while I know she speaks falsity, as perhaps those around us do, could they sense that her words are not altogether devoid of truth? I raise my palm to cover my flushing cheeks. Passersby give me a wide berth, and my eyes dart for a path of quiet escape, finding a familiar woman leaning on the corner of an alleyway. How is it that she seems to be wherever I am?

Viola grants me a coy smile, and in my haste to exit, I think her a preferable alternative to my current, public humiliation, and move swiftly in her direction.

"Go hide!" Beatrice calls after me. "Nestle in the jitty there with the rats and other forsaken things."

When I gather the courage to look up, Viola has gone, but to change direction would only draw more of Beatrice's ire, so I continue along my path, feeling Beatrice's judgment boring holes in my fragile countenance until I round the corner. Viola nearly knocks me off my feet.

"Causing quite a stir today, are we?"

The swelling of her lip has settled a bit, but a dark scab cuts through it, and the surrounding area shows the greenish tint of a bruise.

"Ma'am." My voice cracks and quivers. "I wish only to find my way to the herbalist. I should like it if you stepped aside, so I might find my destination with no further … tumult."

"And yet you still find yourself compelled to address me so reverently."

Compelled. As I am now compelled to meet her intoxicating gaze. I swallow hard. While I might not undo my regretful actions, I can certainly refrain from spiraling down even further. "I made a mistake. Last night. A woeful error which causes me great suffering. I hope I can rely on your discretion." The prospect of living more rightfully lends me strength. "Lorelei is …" I do a quick check of my surroundings to ensure none can overhear. "The love of my life. To lose her would be unthinkable. I'd be destitute, heartbroken."

Her stony face appears unmoved.

"Inconsolable."

She *hmms*. "Discretion is what you wish?"

"Yes, ma'a–Viola."

Shifting her weight from foot to foot, she glances skyward as if considering. "On the point of your"—a sneer crosses her lip causing the wound to reopen slightly—"*preferences*, I believe I vowed my discretion just before you showed me your molars."

The flash of memory crackles in my gut.

"Isn't that so?"

I can only nod.

"And on the other point, your"—she runs her fingertips along my arm—"oddity. A secret like that has worth enough to be measured in coin."

The insinuation lights an ember of panic. "We've not much money to off—"

"That much is clear." Her eyes wander my threadbare dress. "So what are you prepared to offer in place of it?"

A trickle of rain wets my head, and I look upward to see gray clouds amassing in clumps.

"Come." Viola swoops an arm around my shoulders, whisking me further into the alley, beneath the protection of a tin overhang. "I see your imagination is somewhat inhibited by"—she gestures about my face—"*feelings* of late. So I shall make a suggestion. I have business in America. New York, to be quite specific."

I calculate what little money we might have tucked away in a drawer. "Perhaps we might scrape enough together to buy your passage."

"If money was my aim, I would've chosen a more fitting patron. No, what I seek is locals. Locals with enough guile that they might sneak me aboard a vessel bound for New York."

"Sneak?"

"I find myself without travel documents, you see."

Not short on intellect, I know her to be deceptive, and reasons for her prohibition from travel tick through my mind. *A criminal? A smuggler?* Then my eyes fall once again upon her busted lip. *Or perhaps she is running from that.* A pang of sympathy swells within. "I should like to help you." Rainwater pours from the cracked gutter as the storm gathers strength.

"But?"

"But what would I tell Lorelei?"

Viola reaches a hand beneath the makeshift waterfall, which fills her palm in a blink, then lets the water cascade down to her elbow, soaking her elegant silk. "Money is quite tight of late, is it not?" She holds her palm before me, and I watch the water seep from the cracks between her fingers until her hand sits empty. "Your speech sounds quite familiar to me. East coast of the Americas, am I wrong?"

"No."

"So perhaps you receive a letter about the passing of some distant uncle, and an urgent trip is needed to collect your inheritance. Would Lorelei not be *compelled*?"

The word sends a shiver, and I realize how the wind's picked up. I think of Lorelei, tending to our empty shop, thinking me cross with her still. "She is too sharp. Should Lorelei catch me in a lie, it would be the end of us."

Thunder cracks in the distance, rumble echoing off the stone walls. "I can't risk it. I'm sorry." I push past her, determined to get home. Back to the warmth of our cozy loft, to the warmth of my familiar love.

"I'll think on it," I call over my shoulder. "There must be some other way." Halfway down the strip of road, I turn, expecting to see Viola in pursuit. Water droplets roll from my brows into my eyes, and I wipe them away, but still find nothing. The alley sits empty, but for the driving rain.

By the time I reach our threshold, I'm soaked through and through. My skirts hang heavy, and my footsteps leave puddles in their wake.

"Gone for a swim?" Lorelei leans upon our counter, and I'm startled to see her in the shop rather than our quarters, the storm having driven any potential customers from the street.

I motion to the river of water streaming down our windows. "Caught me before I could make it to the herbalist." I strip my bag, balancing it on the coat rack, and watch water trickle from its seams.

"Smudging will have to wait for another time, then."

"Another time."

"Just as well, sage is more suited to chicken anyhow." She circles around the barrier. "Let's get you out of those clothes before you catch your death." With a nudge on my hips, she turns me to face the counter and loosens my bodice.

"Shouldn't we go into the room?" I eye the street, its image melted through the thick, pouring water.

"A storm like this will have even the voyeurs inside." A jerk at the strings lets the bodice fall around my waist, and she gets to work unfastening my petticoat. When it drops, I crouch to gather up the sopping mess.

"Lorelei." My voice falters. "I am sorry about last night. I didn't mean to—"

"What would you say about this morning?"

Her scorn, though expected, spurns me into our bathroom. In only my shift, now translucent from the downpour, I'm far too exposed to plead within her sight. "I shouldn't have stayed out so long." I wring my clothing into the tub and slide my shift to the floor. When no response comes, I glance up to see Lorelei standing in the door.

"What happened?"

Between Beatrice's tirade and Viola's strange request, I hadn't time to compose an account of my night and morning. I inhale deeply, prepared to offer the painful truth, when Lorelei steps inside and bends down to inspect the dirt and dried blood scuffing my knees.

"What animal did this to you?" Her voice is hot with rage.

I fold my arms across my breasts. "Would you fetch my robe, please?"

"It's that man, isn't it? From the last seance."

It would be so easy to agree. I nod.

She stomps from the bathroom, tossing my robe behind her. "I saw the way he looked at you, the hunger in his eyes."

Shimmying on my robe, I pursue her. "Lorelei, please."

But she's already grabbing her coat.

"It's torrential." I see the fresh wounds on her knuckles. "And what have you been up to? Striking at our walls again?"

As her fist clenches around our umbrella, I see deeper punctures. Not a wall, then. "Have you been in a fight?"

She makes for the door. "And it won't be the last. Get some iodine on you before infection sets in. I'll take care of—of *him*."

Our bell signals her departure. I learned long ago that Lorelei is not one to be swayed of her opinion, especially when she's in a state of anger. There's a nip of pain and a feeling of relief when I think on how I nearly told her of my betrayal. Perhaps it's best she doesn't know. Confessing may assuage my guilt, but it would simply transfer my pain to her, and that is not my wish. I find the mop in the corner closet and begin to soak up the largest puddle, the one beside the coat rack, and my hand draws my attention. The skin is pruned, white, swollen, and wrinkled, but this is not what draws my interest. Rather, it's the faint separation—I squint my eyes. Surely, they deceive me? I look closer. A gasp.

Not a trick of the eyes. The pruned skin in fact has lifted from the surrounding tissue. The mop hits the floor with a clang. With a trembling finger, I prod, and the gentle nudge exposes a tangled mess of sinew beneath my flesh. Long, thin bones are visible between the pinkish ropes of tendon. My stomach turns over, and I scurry to the bathroom to retch over the toilet. When I've emptied myself of everything but the bile lingering in my throat, I splash some water on my face, wincing at the sensation of cold on exposed nerves, and wrap a towel around the offending portion of my hand.

My heart races. I think back to the first time it happened, this grotesque, secret thing. Nine years old, I'd taken to amusing myself in my father's study. Despite his stern warnings, I continued to play there when he was out on business, giving the fireplace pokers ample space and not, as he would say, *frolicking about like a wild hare. How dangerous could a study be,* I thought. Father worked long hours there, and no harm came to him. It was naught more than a desk, a leather chair, a fireplace, and wall to wall shelves overflowing with books of all sorts.

That's what drew me in. The promises they held of adult knowledge, things thought too mature for children, all contained in their pages. A day prior I'd discovered the extent of *maturity* contained within, stumbling upon a slender text with worn pages. Unfamiliar with the title, I'd flipped through, my young eyes lingering over detailed line drawings of a feminine form. Saliently I remember the elegant curve of her thighs, the swell of her breasts. Veins shot through with terror, I'd snapped the book shut in wild fear—of being caught, yes, but also of the strange reaction of my body to the imagery.

On the day everything changed, I scaled the sliding ladder, intent on borrowing a vermillion volume with gold lettering. *The Art of War.* I'd had a spat with my brother, George, that morning, and thought perhaps I'd find some tips on how to make his day particularly miserable. I'd thumb through for inspiration and return it to its spot before father returned home the following day, none the wiser.

Getting to the book had been no problem. I reached the top rung, plucked the book from its spot. But it was heavier than I'd anticipated, and the weight threw me off balance. On my descent, I tumbled down to the hardwood floor, my leg catching on the fireplace poker. It tore clean through the flesh, hot blood spurting with every heartbeat.

"Adele?" George called from down the hall, his attention drawn by the clatter.

Terrified I'd be discovered by him, I restrained my impulse to scream and responded to him in the voice of Angelica, our maid. "Just me, dear. Cleaning up."

I'd only recently discovered my uncanny ability to mimic the voices of others, and it satisfied George's curiosity then just as it's served me on many occasions since.

I pushed the book away from myself, not wanting to stain it with my gore, and still thinking I might get away with the whole ordeal if I could just remain calm and think things through.

I sat up, inspecting my injury. My flesh hung in a ribbon, and I had the childlike, fanciful thought that I just might be able to put it back. As I maneuvered the skin, wincing and growing nauseous, I accidentally tugged, ripping an even longer ribbon of flesh from my leg. Blood now slickened the floor, and I opened my mouth to cry out, but then I saw it. Like magic, my leg knitted itself back together, jagged skin reaching across the bloody gash like the hundred legs of a centipede, joining together. I ran my fingers over the area again and again, expecting to feel searing pain, for my hand to be drenched in blood when I pulled it away, but found only pale, smooth skin.

I'd heard my mother's friends whisper about witchcraft in low tones during their parties. Caught a glimmer of a news article about trials in Salem years back. And for the first time in my young life, I knew shame, knew secrecy. I vowed then never to spill my secret, lest the witch-hunters come for me too. One bit of oddity is enough. My preference for women combined with this strangeness would see me to the gallows for sure. So I minded myself, body and desire, kept a close guard fractured first by Lorelei's love, now webbed with cracks like an eggshell.

When I think my hand has sufficiently dried, I lift the towel and can finally breathe fully when I see my skin has righted itself. The relief is only temporary, however, as I realize my condition has worsened. Never before has my flesh flayed itself. Always an injury has preceded the uncanny event. But this time, mere water has resulted in my unraveling.

Sunlight breaks through the cloud cover, sending beams through our window, seemingly to mock me. How can I guard this secret? Should I luxuriate in a too long swim in the sea, only to emerge a hairless monstrosity of braided muscle and bone? My head swims, the day brightening further to spite me.

I burrow beneath the blankets, the stale scent of sex another ingredient in my now thick blend of cloying shame. Drawing the linen over my head, I wish for a moment to never emerge. To live out my days unseen and unjudged, here in the mess I've made.

Chapter 7: What a Temper We Have

Lorelei

I do not know the name of the man, but it'll be easy enough to find out. I make my way to Mrs. Crawshaw's, the wind whipping the rain sideways, making the umbrella near useless. I close it; I can move faster this way anyhow. Mrs. Crawshaw lives in Matlock town proper, a mile away from the Bath, which translates to a twenty-minute stroll. But at the pace I'm going, I think I can shave a good five minutes off the journey.

I must resemble a drowned rat by the time I reach her door. The best I can do to prepare myself is to run a hand through my sopping hair before I knock.

She is quick to answer. "Mrs. Crawshaw, I trust you are well on this, I shan't say lovely, afternoon."

She opens her mouth to reply, but I haven't time for that today.

"I was hoping you might help me. I found a cufflink this morning whilst cleaning which I believe must belong to your young gentleman friend. As I am not fully acquainted with him, I was unable to take it to him directly, so found myself forced to call upon you. I do hope I haven't disturbed you." Again I do not wait for an answer. "If you would be so kind as to give me his name and address, I can pop over and drop it off."

She hesitates a moment before answering, no doubt expecting to be cut off again, but two minutes later I have both a name and a location and am on my way to confront the wretched bastard.

Guilt gnaws at my stomach the entirety of my miserable walk. I don't need Adele to tell me what happened. It's patently obvious between the blood spots on her nightgown and the ruined skin of her knees. I was the reason she went out into the night and, after she'd stumbled back home in a state of shock, instead of being patient with her, waiting for her to open up, I turned to ice.

Standing in front of his home it strikes me that I'm powerless. I may have told Adele that I would take care of him, but how?

A woman answers the door. I explain where I'm from and that I believe I've property in my possession that needs returning. She disappears back into the house.

It's a good five minutes before he appears in the doorway. The smile on his smarmy face quickly fades when he sees me. "Oh." The previous day's sneer returns to his face. "I was hoping it would be the other one."

I don't make the same mistake as last night; my punch lands squarely in his throat. He doubles over immediately.

"You—crazy—cunt," he wheezes. I take a step forward, but he is quicker than I anticipated. He slams the door in my face, the click of the lock swiftly following.

I hammer at the door.

"Come on, you thought you were fucking 'ard enough yesterday."

One strike is not sufficient punishment for what he did to Adele. I look about for something, anything to use. A drystone wall runs the length of the street. Perfect. I liberate a good-sized stone and hurl it through the window. The sound of shattering glass is inordinately pleasing to my ear, as are the shouts from inside the house.

My satisfaction is short-lived though, as a hand grasps my shoulder.

"I think you better come with me, lass."

Fuck.

***

I'm held in the cells of Matlock police station for an hour before, to my utmost surprise, I'm told I'm free to go.

"That can't be right." No fine? No being brought before a magistrate?

"If you want to stay and argue …"

"No, no, I'm going."

The day has brightened considerably during my brief incarceration, so at least the walk home will be a better one. No longer white hot, my rage has cooled to orange embers, manageable yet ready to reignite.

"Lorelei, Lorelei, Lorelei, what a temper we have." Leaning against the station's walls is that woman, the brim of her hat tilted downwards so I can't see her face, but I can hear the smile in her words. "Not even twenty-four hours have passed and there you are again, using those hands of yours to cause pain when we both know they were made to give pleasure."

I won't be drawn into whatever game she wishes to play, I put my head down and start to walk.

"Aren't you going to thank me?"

The heat within me flares as I spin around. "For what, exactly, am I to be thankful?"

She lifts her head up and fixes me with those eyes the color of honey left to darken and crystalise in the back of a cupboard. The mark of my previous night's rage upon her lip, my tongue darts, Viola's eye's following, to its mirrored spot on my own.

"You'd still be sitting in a cell if it wasn't for me. Assault. Property damage. And all against a perfectly innocent man."

"There's nothing innocent about him. He's abhorrent, my only regret is that I couldn't do more damage to him." I turn away from her and continue walking. It's not long before I hear her footsteps alongside my own.

"There was a fox once, who took up residence in my garden."

The strangeness of this *non sequitur* makes me pause in my stride.

"A lush coat he had, rich red speckled with the deepest gray." Her eyes drift right as if she's remembering. "A less astute woman might have been tempted to lure him inside, offer him food and shelter, try to domesticate him."

I grow bored with her reminiscing and move to leave when she adds, "But I knew better. He was feral, vicious beneath his beautiful exterior." Her eyes train on me. "Do you follow? Let me take you somewhere private, we need to speak, you and I."

"Whatever poison you have to spew you can do it here."

"If you want me to act as town crier and tell all and sundry how Adele fell to her knees like a whore and took his—" I put my hand to her mouth to quiet her, digging my fingers and thumb into the soft skin of her cheeks.

"Don't you dare call her that." I tighten my grip. "You understand?" She nods and lets out a moan that both excites and disgusts me. I drop my hand. "Good."

"I've a room at The Cromwell, we can talk in private there." She says the words as though I've already agreed to them.

I nod in defeat and follow her.

***

Viola—she finally deemed me worthy enough to know her name—has a room at the finest hotel in the town, confirming my assessment that she is a woman of wealth. The room is of a modern style and is situated on the top floor of the hotel. A bed bigger than I've ever seen before dominates the entire room across which Viola has left various items of hosiery and undergarments, a habit which would drive me insane in my own home. A walnut writing desk, highly oiled and polished with paper and envelopes in greens and purples littered across its surface, stands by the window which offers a view of the town below and the peaks beyond. Viola sits down upon it as she indicates to me to sit on the bed.

I've been in this situation many times before, a dark-haired beauty of means leading me to her room and bidding me to sit upon her bed. They've always been my type and, with the exception of her fair hair, the trend continued with Adele.

"I know you must believe me as you wouldn't be here if you didn't."

I nod.

"All that attention Adele attracts has been slowly eating away at you. You think you aren't good enough for her. When the truth is, it's she who isn't good enough for you."

"No—"

"Quiet. One of the saving graces of your relationship is that it's a secret from the world at large." She pauses here to examine her nails and right a ring whose stone has strayed off center. "She was seen, you know, by that woman the lad likes to spar with."

"Beatrice," I mutter.

"It's quite rude to mumble, Lorelei, but yes, her. Of course she claims that it was a demon with which Adele had her late-night tryst with, although both you and I know there's no such thing as demons." A sly smile here. "Don't we?"

"I've found they tend to take human form."

"Quite true." Viola's eyes take on a faraway look. "Quite true. What was I saying? Yes, the upside of people not knowing is that you have been spared the humiliation of her betrayal." She gets up off the desk and starts to strip in so casual a manner it's as though she's forgotten I'm in the room at all.

"Adele is a petulant girl. You need a woman, Lorelei. Not some bitch who will spread her legs—"

In the privacy of the room I don't bother with a hand on her mouth, I go for her throat.

She laughs. "Yes, this is what I wanted to see from you. That fire! Is it me you want to hurt or is it Adele?"

The question throws me, I'd never want to hurt Adele, not in the way I want to hurt Viola, though I long for her to submit fully to me. To entwine my fingers in her hair, for her to let me control her. No, the rage

I feel at this moment is not the same as what I want to do with and to Adele, but the urge to hurt her emotionally is fierce. I want to come home with the scent of this woman all over me, to kiss Adele and have her taste Viola. I let my hand drop from Viola's throat.

"Get on the bed." My voice little more than a growl.

She lays down amongst the silken garments, as I quickly divest myself of clothing, and spreads her legs, showing me how ready she is for me. I bite her inner thigh, she tastes like cinnamon, before setting to work with my tongue. Though Viola's moans please me and cause the ache between my own legs to grow, her pleasure is nothing but a side effect in my mission to cause Adele pain. I stop when I sense Viola is close to climaxing. I want to see her face when she comes, see her lips forming my name. I enter her with one finger before swiftly adding another, then another, something which I would never dream of doing to Adele. I thrust hard, fast, and Viola lets me continue my brutal punishment of her for a minute before capturing my wrist.

"I've something which I think you would like very much, Lorelei," she says with me still inside her, my fingers crushed so tight I fear they might break. As I flex them, she throws back her head, drawing in air through clenched teeth.

"I like this very much," I say, realizing to my horror that what I mean is *I like hurting you very much.*

"Oh, you'll like this better." She removes me from her, before getting out of the bed and going to a trunk in the corner. She opens it and takes out what looks to me at first like a tangle of leather straps with a …

I swallow hard as it dawns on me what Viola holds in her hand.

"Have you used one of these before?" she asks.

"Yes."

"I thought you might have. They're very much a perversion of the upper classes, and we both know how much you liked to play with them." She sits once again on the desk. "Come here, then."

I go to her.

She hands me the dildo, made of soft leather wrapped around a harder core. "Put it on."

I fumble with the straps a moment; whomever wore it last was a little bigger around the hips than I. Once satisfied it is tight against me, Viola dips her fingers between her own legs and spreads the slickness she finds there along its length. As she does, it presses against my sweetest spot. She leans forward. "Does this please you?" she whispers. "I'd hate to disappoint you." I let out a whimper. In response, Viola moves her hand faster and faster. Just when I think I could come from this alone, she leans back on the desk and spreads her legs for me once more.

This is all the invitation I need. I bend down and grab both her ankles, lifting them to my shoulders before thrusting the entire length of it into her. Then, not giving her time to get used to the extra girth, I move.

I put a hand on the desk for purchase, brushing aside the brightly coloured stationary so it falls to the floor.

She shatters on my tenth stroke, but I don't stop. I keep going until she is a ruined, mewling mess beneath me. When she cries out that she can't take anymore, then and only then do I allow myself to lose control and tumble over the edge.

And that's when I stop.

Chapter 8: The Mothers Always Return

Adele

I awake to a rapping at our door. Jolting upright, I peel away the hairs glued to my cheek with dried tears and check the room for signs of Lorelei. The only evidence of life I find is a dormouse scuttling into a hole in the floorboard. Another knock, harder this time, and I scurry to pull on the nearest shift.

"Just a minute!"

I fasten my bodice, admittedly somewhat crooked, and affix my skirts to my hips well enough that they won't go tumbling to the floor in the presence of whatever visitor demands my attention. As I emerge from the bedroom, I notice the storm has cleared, and the orange glow of a setting sun pushes through the damp window panes. Mrs. Crawshaw's friend stands upon our mat, picking at the skin around her thumbnail. I take a steadying breath. The mothers always return.

"How can I help you, Mrs—?" I speak loudly so as to be heard over the clanging bell. She pushes past me.

"Richards, and I am sorry to intrude without notice." She paces a tight circle around me, and I whirl to keep up. "It's Jessalyn, you see. Her birthday is in just a week's time and I—" Her voice cracks. More guilt lays upon my gut like lead.

"You wish to contact her?" I keep my voice soft. Though I know it's just a trick, a series of devilish tricks, if it brings her some comfort, and affords us another month of shelter …

She grasps me by my sleeves, eyes brimming with tears. "If you would be so kind as to do it tonight. Short notice, I know." There's a sharp scent of sweat, a mottled hue beneath her eyes as if she hasn't slept.

"Tonight." The shop is as I left it, mop still lying beside the coat rack. Lorelei has not been back. She could be hurt, could've been killed for all I—

"She's been heavy in my heart, you see, and I fear—I can pay you." She draws a fat purse from the inner pocket of her coat, and already I hear the jingling of coins. Parting the sides, she shows me a bounty which would pay not one, but three month's rent.

"Tonight," I say again, swallowing the lump in my throat. "Let me fix you some tea. Please, sit down."

I know full well I can't perform the seance without Lorelei. But to turn away such a generous offer would be madness. I can only hope to delay her until Lorelei returns, though who knows when then might be.

Mrs. Richards settles in the corner chair, but not before having the good sense to strike it thrice, dislodging a plume of dust. I fill the kettle with sink water, ignite the burner, and place it on the stove of our kitchen. I'm remiss to even call it such, having known true kitchens. More accurately, it's a cramped corner with a sink and stove. "My business partner is out," I say, gathering two teacups from the cupboard. "I do hope she'll be back soon."

Mrs. Richards takes on a suspicious look. "I thought she would've been back by now. It's not more than a twenty minutes' walk to south Dale. You'll forgive me, of course, for eavesdropping. I was taking tea with Mrs. Crawshaw when she dropped by."

A flush of embarrassment warms my neck. I settle on a polite smile so as not to reveal to Mrs. Richards that she seemingly knows more about my partner's comings and goings than I.

"Let us hope whatever detains her is nothing of concern." She does the Sign of the Cross, and I send a silent prayer—to a God I am unsure I believe in—that she is right.

"All the more reason for me to wait and ensure she arrives home safely."

In the pantry I find a few cubes of sugar, a novelty we save for paying customers, and place them on her saucer. "While we wait, perhaps I could offer you a reading." I strain my face into a smile and place the cups and saucer on the small table before her.

"Palm reading?" Her brow furrows slightly, and anxiety raises the hair on my arm.

"Tarot, actually. The cards can tell you about your past, your present, your future, if you so desire to know."

She presses firmly on a sugar cube, breaking its form beneath the weight of her finger. "I've not heard of tarot. I suppose it couldn't hurt." She reaches back into her coat, drawing forth another purse, and places a few shillings upon the table.

"The practice is quite old." I hope this will lend me some credence. "Originating in fifteenth century Europe, by the aristocracy, no less." Any trace of hesitation leaves her face, replaced by a subtle reverence to be amongst such company. "I'll get my deck."

I walk slowly to the bedroom, thinking casual steps might offer Lorelei the utmost opportunity to return, and open and close drawers which I know full well don't contain the cards. "It's in here somewhere!" I call.

I make an auditory spectacle of moving objects from this place to that, intentionally clumsy, and draw pensive, exasperated breaths to further prove my point.

Showmanship is not to be underrated.

I continue my farce of a search until the kettle begins to whistle. Grasping the deck off its place on the dresser, I wave them so Mrs. Richards can see before removing the kettle from the heat. I set the kettle upon a small serving tray with all the accoutrements. Thick plumes of steam paint linear clouds as I carry it to the table. It takes all my focus to keep my hands from shaking as I set the dried herbs in their strainer and pour the boiling water over top.

Returning from the kitchen, I note Mrs. Richards's teacup remains untouched. A relief, as the finer, white tea leaves were all used up, leaving only stale, lemon balm to offer. I fan the tarot deck face down before her.

"I want you to think of a question," I say, moving the cards around in circular motions on the table. "One which is heavy upon your heart." In a fluid motion, I gather the deck and shuffle, the breeze pushing back Mrs. Richards's resulting frazzled fringe. "You needn't speak the question aloud."

Her eyes glow with curiosity, initial skepticism turned fully to intrigue.

"But repeat it within your mind." I place the deck before her, a perfect rectangle. Gold leaf embellishments on the black deck glimmer even in the dying light.

Her hand hovers above them. Chubby fingers strangled by rings—which must've fit in her youth—drum the air in the space just above the top card.

"Good. Infuse them with your energy." It's a bit of an ad lib, but seems to be working as she chews her cheek with intention.

"Now, sort the cards as you are moved. Don't overthink, just move as you are bidden."

Like a child grasping a slippery frog, she lifts the deck with care, moving the cards atop one another, cutting the deck once, twice, then a final time, before placing it back upon the table.

"Perfect."

I glance at the clock. Its great arm swings sluggish, and I take a few deep breaths, hoping to hear Lorelei's steps on the street outside at any moment. But they don't come.

"The cards will reveal your past, present, and future, in that order." I take another look outside. Only the baker's wife and her children.

I draw the top card, flipping it face up on the table.

The Four of Wands.

"This is a good card. You made your home a lovely place. Wanting for little, you found your days full of deep, abiding love. You gave generously, needed little, and took even less. The circle here"—I point to the illustrated swirl—"tells me you felt quite full. Gratitude was abundant."

I flip another.

The Five of Cups.

"This will come as no surprise. The Five of Cups tells me a deep loss has severed you into two." I force her to meet my eyes. "You straddle two worlds, feeling unwelcome in either. You long for the wholeness you had, and day after day, find yourself empty. This card asks you to address your grief, to reframe it."

She hangs upon my every word. Though I wonder whether I speak more to myself than to Mrs. Richards, she doesn't see this.

"The future card will tell us what comes." I let my hand linger over it. "Are you sure you'd like to know?"

She breaks contact, searching the floor as she considers. Seconds tick by, counted out too slow by the lazy grandfather clock. Alas, her head wobbles in eager agreement.

I flip another card.

Death glares up at us from eyeless holes, his scythe embellished with gold leaf. Mrs. Richards winces. "I've had quite enough of that I think." She straightens her coat as if she means to go.

"Please, Mrs. Richards, wait. Death is not about death as we think it, rather about transformation."

She settles once more.

"It indicates more of a rebirth, of sorts. A remaking of what once was into something new." I clasp her hands in mine. "And does it not bring you some comfort, to think of turning your grief into something fruitful?"

The click of familiar boots on the street outside catches my attention. At last! Lorelei has returned. She slides over our threshold, her chin held particularly high. I take in her face, searching at once for signs of cuts or bruising, but find none. Instead, I detect a strange combination of expressions, ones unfamiliar to me.

"How wonderful you're here." I stand, gesture toward Mrs. Richards. "As you can see, our patron has returned. She wishes to contact her daughter, Jessalyn. *Tonight.*" I give the word enough inflection to convey my panic to Lorelei, while slipping under Mrs. Richard's radar.

Lorelei removes her coat and hangs it upon our rack. I inspect her once more. Still no sign of a fray. "Tonight is—"

"Perfect, I've already told her. We've no other bookings." I eye the backroom.

"Wonderful. If you'd just excuse me a moment to get myself sorted." Lorelei crosses the room, and I parse the unusual composition of her mood. There's a smugness to the arch in her back, and her smile resembles more of a sneer. Turned away from me, I see one of her buttons undone, and another in its neighbor's loop.

"If you'll give us both a moment," I say to Mrs. Richards, who produces yet *another* bag, this one containing her knitting, and gets to work on it with long, thin, mirror shine needles.

I join Lorelei in the backroom. "What happened? What were you doing in south Dale?" My voice is a low growl.

Teeth bared, she says, "Fetch the candles, Adele." So rarely does she use my name, I wonder whether she's learned of my indiscretion. *But how?* I brush off the thought. She must still be cross with me for staying out all night. I move about the shop collecting candles, steadying myself with the knowledge that had she suspected infidelity, she would not have run from our home with a mind to avenge my honor.

Lorelei and I work to set the stage, cunning enough as a pair to shield our tricks from Mrs. Richard's sight. From the corner of my eye, I catch her finally taking a sip of her now tepid tea. She grimaces, sending an ache of embarrassment through my core. *How low have I sunk?*

We begin the seance as usual. Clunks from Lorelei's boot, table rising from the floor. In my best guess at Jessalyn's voice I confirm the hopeful message I conveyed earlier through my tarot reading, and Mrs. Richards weeps with relief once more.

"Happy early birthday, Jessalyn." Her voice cracks. "Perhaps I can come back on the actual day."

My need of money does not outweigh my breaking heart, so in Jessalyn's tone I tell her, "There's no need, Mother. I am with you always. On a clear morning, I come in the morning breeze. Storms bring me on bolts of lightning, and when you watch the river, it's my image you see before your eyes settle on your own reflection. Seek me no more, for I am already found, and shall never leave."

Lorelei's boot nudges me beneath the table, but I care not. It's a kindness I do now.

Mrs. Richards goes on weeping, offering assurances of her love, with need of only the occasional word from "Jessalyn". Lorelei begins the closing ritual, and I think all has gone perfectly to plan, when I feel a wet sensation on my ankle. Both ankles.

I glance beneath the table cloth and have to choke back the scream rising in my gut. From knee to ankle, my flesh melts from my body, oozing into my shoes in burgundy and apricot puddles. I move not from my seat when Lorelei dismisses Mrs. Richards, bidding her to come back and see us any time she'd like. I detect a look that tells me Mrs. Richards thinks me rude for not rising to escort her to the door, but I am glued to my spot, still feeling my skin and blood pooling around my feet, soaking my socks.

I think Lorelei will ask me about the impropriety, and I struggle to grasp for an excuse, but to my surprise, she simply excuses herself.

"I'm going to wash up."

Grateful as I am to be hidden from her, when she closes the door, I check the time. Not even nine o'clock. Near daily, Lorelei bathes in the morning. She takes the occasional bath at night, but well past this time. Generally a midnight ritual, in which she fills the entire bathroom with steam, soaking in water so hot I faintly know how it doesn't scald her.

I slide my chair back, cringing at the screeching it makes against the hardwood floor but relaxing once more when the bathroom door remains firmly shut, and look to my legs. Exposed bone stretches the length of them, wrapped in thick musculature like garland around a Christmas tree. Intact arteries pulse with my heartbeat, and I cover my mouth to stifle the sound of my retching.

The rushing sound of water from the bathroom stops. I freeze in place. Wait for the sloshing sound of Lorelei rising to dry off. But it doesn't come. Once again, I turn my eyes to my calves and, to my great relief, they begin to mend before my very eyes. I strip my boots and socks, rinse them under the sink. I am clipping them to the drying line when Lorelei finally emerges from the bathroom.

I remove my bodice, only now fully aware of how disheveled I must've looked during Mrs. Richards's visit, and Lorelei casts her towel to the floor. Conscious to hide my battered knees behind the bedside, I take the opportunity to examine her in full for signs of a fight. Her fiery hair is maroon when damp, and hangs around the gentle slope of her jaw in loose waves. Her neck and face unmarred, my gaze moves downward, and I'm unable to stop my eyes from lingering over her ample bosom, pink nipples perked in the cool air. A droplet of water slides from her collarbone, pauses at her breast, then continues down her curvaceous form. I lose sight of it at her hip, but a mark there draws my attention.

Consumed with locating her favorite sleepwear, she doesn't notice as I squint my eyes and lean in to get a better look. There's a linear abrasion several shades darker than the pale, surrounding skin. It juts several inches over the curve of her pelvis. A cut? No. More like a burn, not unlike the friction burns I got playing that wretched game with my brother as a child, when he'd wring his hands against my wrist.

"Is your garter too tight?" I ask. "I could alter it for you."

Her lips purse with confusion, so I gesture to the mark.

"No," she says, finally. "My garters are quite alright, thank you. Though it's good to see you concern yourself with *my*—" She clears her throat. "I must've caught my hip on a knob."

As we settle into bed, the space between us feels larger than ever in our cramped quarters. A mile of unspoken words form a gorge between us, but I can't concern myself with the quality of our communication. Not right now. The image of my flesh pooling in puddles like so much rainwater around my ankles roils my stomach. I think back to the night with Viola, the strange thing she said when she saw my curse. *I knew I'd found you.* 'Twas as if she expected it. So consumed I've been with my infidelity, I'd scarcely given it much thought. She knows my affliction. Perhaps she has seen it before.

I pull the blanket over my shoulder, face away from Lorelei as she does me. I resolve myself to find Viola tomorrow. To ask her what she knows. With any bit of luck—and I'll be damned if I'm not overdue for some—she knows of some cure. In the thin reprieve of this longshot hope, I drift into sleep and dream of the burn around Lorelei's hips.

Chapter 9: Seven of Swords

Lorelei

"Have you ever been hungry, Adele?" It's still dark, no sign of dawn yet breaking. "And I don't mean in a *oh I can't wait until teatime way.* I mean really, truly hungry. It feels like burning but at the same time drowning. You burn from the pain of your empty stomach, it's become an organ of betrayal, you feel it shrink and threaten to consume itself. The drowning … the drowning part comes from when you give up hope. When you wish you could just drift off to sleep and never wake up. Have you ever felt that? Have you ever felt that when you've been with me?"

Silence. She's sulking or slumbering still.

"Maybe if you had you might understand me better," I mutter before shifting onto my side. My lower back aches something fierce, and I find no relief in this bed with its thin mattress. The soreness, along with the friction burns upon my hip, is a reminder of both my triumph and my shame. I've derived pleasure from pain before, but never in anger, and the velocity with which I took to it scares me somewhat, but that's eclipsed by the decadent rush I felt at having had my own tryst. I wonder if Adele has the knowledge, or indeed the imagination, to hazard a guess as to what the marks on my body could mean. Adele has never indicated, not that I have been completely transparent myself, that she had lovers before me; and if she had I imagine they'd be as young and innocent as she. I'd spent the years before her chasing a certain type of woman, women who moved in the circles I wished I could have. Women who I imagined must have perfect control over their lives. They didn't have to slowly poison themselves with phosphorus working in factories nor sell themselves down backstreets and in dingy bedsits.

I soon learnt that, invariably, their lives were dominated by men regardless of their background. Fathers, brothers, husbands. They'd submit to them all in public for fear of losing money and privilege whilst submitting to me in their bedrooms. Some were quite innocent in their tastes, my fingers and tongue more than sufficient for them. Others liked props, such as the one Viola had in her possession. I'd thought it a tad deviant, and rather exciting to take them like that. But whilst I could be rough, I was never full of rage, not like I'd been with Viola.

I shift onto my other side so I'm facing Adele. Her hair isn't loose as it normally is. Instead, she has kept it in her daytime braid, as if stuck in another time to avoid me. It's always been my favorite part of waking up, having her beside me, her hair spread out on the pillow and in my face. I breathe her in as I move a little closer, her lavender shampoo a strange combination of soothing and … It would be so easy to wrap my hand around her braid, to make her look at me as I moved my hand between her legs and have her take all of me within her. To claim her as mine. To feel the sting of my palm against her …

Adele shifts, a gentle sigh escaping her lips.

No! Why would I want to hurt the woman I love? What the fuck is wrong with me?

This new part of myself scares me, yes, but not as much as the prospect of losing control of myself with Adele. This combination of fury and lust disgusts me; like oil and water, they don't mix.

***

Another summer storm is raging when I awake. The ache in my back has dulled somewhat so only a slight wince escapes my lips when I get out of the bed. Adele is not in the bedroom, but I can hear her moving about downstairs. I quickly dress and go down to join her. Water lashes at the windows; I can't see more than a yard in front of them. It will be a quiet morning, a chance perhaps for reconciliation? Adele is stood watching the pouring rain, one hand idly worries at the stitches of the cushion upon which the crystals lie.

I go to her, move her braid, and kiss the back of her neck. She doesn't stiffen or recoil from me but she doesn't lean back into me as she once would. On previous mornings like this, I would suggest going back to bed to make love to her as the wind rattled at the windows and the distant sound of thunder roared. I daren't make such a suggestion today though.

"Get your tarot deck."

She looks at me with a curious glint in her eye. Too often have I spoken of the cards as nothing more than pretty pictures and glib words.

"Really?"

"Really," I repeat, softly. "Show me what my—our—future holds."

She smiles for the first time in days, weeks? Shame grasps at me once more. When exactly did I stop making her smile on a daily basis? No wonder she sought out another's attention. The past year as our purse strings, already tight, were cinched ever tighter and the specter of poverty lingered over us, I'd accused her many times of disguising flirtation with politeness. I pushed her to the very thing I'd been so afraid of.

She reaches for my wounded hand and brings it up to her lips. The kiss she places there is feather light yet carries the entire weight of our relationship. The action must have only been a few seconds long, but my racing heart stretches it into an eternity, and when she drops my hand to go and fetch the deck, she takes it with her.

I go to the counter and wait for her. You'd have thought I'd have made it my business to learn the interpretations of the cards, but when that girl on the Chatsworth estate tried to teach me, I'd been far too fixated on the plunge between her freckled breasts.

I've gleaned the meaning of a few these past three years with Adele, watching her read, but even now I lack the patience to learn all seventy-eight of them.

Adele comes back and leans over the counter. The gown she is wearing today is not one she normally wears out in public, for it is dangerously low cut, so when she is leaning forward as she is now, I am afforded a view of her perfect breasts. It pleases me to think she has chosen this item of clothing for me, though I know I shall have to try very hard to feign interest in the reading.

"I want you to think of a question."

Would you let me take you to bed?

Would you give me your body to do as I wilt?

Would you let me hurt you in ways that would bring you ecstasy?

"Have you thought of one?"

"Yes."

She hands me the deck to shuffle, and the way she bites her lower lip as her eyes flick down to my hands sends a jolt through me. We may end the morning in bed after all.

She places the first card.

"Temperance," Adele says. "A sign of moderation, balance, and harmony."

The second card is the Seven of Swords.

"Betrayal?" I ask. Even I know the meaning of this card. But is it hers or mine?

"Sometimes." The word is rushed. "It can mean liberation, parting oneself from a particular circumstance." She smiles dimly. "Perhaps our fortunes are about to change. Let's see about our future card." Her hand trembles as she places The Tower.

She stares at it with something approaching horror in her eyes, but remains silent.

"What does it mean?"

Adele sweeps the cards up and places them back in the deck.

"It's nothing." Her lopsided grin doesn't reach her eyes. "As you've always said, it's nothing but a parlor trick."

I soften my voice. "No, you believe in them and that's good enough for me. I should have told you this long before now." I move around to the back of the counter so I'm stood behind her, and envelop her into a hug. I place another kiss on the back of her neck, and I am rewarded with a small moan. I kiss her again, this time flicking my tongue out. She shivers as I kiss and lick her, pulling the back of her dress down to access her shoulders. She giggles when I nip her playfully, grazing my teeth across her skin, moans when I bite her a little harder. I spin her around, pressing her up against the wall bringing my thigh up between her legs. I press upwards, hard, as I keep a hand on her collarbone to make sure she stays flat against the wall. I keep thrusting up, grinding against her. As always, the subtle movements of her body and breathing shows she's close to completion. I turn her back around and lift up her skirts, replacing my thigh as the primary source of pressure with my hand.

"Do you like that, you—" I suppress the urge to add a harsher word to the end of my question, to see how far I can go. So instead, I bite down on her shoulder once more. She lets out a little yelp.

You do, don't you? You whore. You love it.

Spurred on, I bite again, sinking my teeth into her creamy skin, causing a strawberry red welt to bloom instantly. Adele cries out loud enough to startle me out of whatever trance I was under. She turns to look at me. I'd expected to see pain in her eyes, and whilst there is pain, it's veiled beneath a docile, faraway look. She comes against my palm, bucking into it as she rides the last wave of her orgasm. I drop my hand, my chest constricting as though I've taken too deep a gulp of ice-cold air. I've gone too far. Horrified at the mark I've left upon her perfect body, I retreat upstairs.

***

I have ensconced myself in the bathroom trying desperately to keep my breaths deep and slow.

She liked it …

She liked it when I hurt her. My body hums with the memory of it; it's what I've wanted for so long and yet I ran from it. I push myself up against the door and lift my skirts, dipping my finger into the wetness I find there. I come harder and faster than I've ever done before, biting down on my own wrist to stifle my scream.

Once I have calmed down, I take my time straightening my skirts and washing my hands before sitting on the bathtub's edge. Did she like it or was I merely seeing what I wanted? What I so desperately yearn for. I sit tapping my foot upon the tile, the repetitive movement comforting me, until I feel ready to face Adele. As my hand is on the handle, I hear her shuffling about. My heart leaps, perhaps I'd been too hasty in my thinking. I feel a shyness come about me which I am not used to. It is like Adele is a stranger to me once more. But I yearn to know her.

I listen to Adele for a moment more moving about. It sounds as though she is changing, before quick footsteps and the bell of the door.

The rain and dark clouds, like I, have hidden themselves away once more, and the street is filling up. Have I scared her away? Misread her eyes? Mistaking her pain for my pleasure? I've ruined things between us even further.

The heavy thud upon the doormat distracts me from these ever-spiraling thoughts.

A letter lies there, its envelope a textured linen, forest green in color. I don't need to pick it up to feel the quality of it.

In fine script is written our address and the name *Adele Hughes.*

Chapter 10: Fragile Hope

Adele

The Tower looms large in my mind, a menacing shadow. Shame, my ever-present companion since my transgression with Viola, whispers to me often that my fall is imminent, that I will get what I well deserve, and now the cards confirm it. Moderation, betrayal, the fall. Lorelei's teeth on my flesh materialized my inner pain, a respite sweet and long enough to allow for a temporary satisfaction. But just as the elation drains from me, panic takes its place. I chastise myself for being so reckless, the skin of my shoulder melting to my elbow.

Why? Why so sensitive now? Ever before it has taken some grave injury to cause this … reaction. When a rush of water tells me Lorelei is nearly finished in the washroom, I pull my sleeve over my masticated shoulder and flee our now treacherous home.

I find Beatrice just steps from our threshold, but if she spews her usual venom, I hear it not, for I move with such haste, the very beating of the wind drowns out all other sounds. Choosing a direction at random—at least, I tell myself it's at random—I clear four blocks.

I am of a singular mind: I must find Viola.

Certainly it is not fondness for the memory of my infidelity which draws me back to Lovers Walk, but rather a driving inclination that she might linger there. A tingling about my shoulder tells me my flesh is restitching. There's a stretching, a tightness like one might experience after spending too long hours under a beating sun. I continue my course, focused on the strange sensation, and when the heavy iron gates of Lovers Walk are in sight, I slow my pace.

Tied more loosely than usual for fear that a too-tight string would trigger my seemingly sensitive affliction, my bodice has shifted in my urgency, and I use these beats of slackened pace to straighten it and catch my breath. That is when Chester finds me.

"Adele, is that you?" His voice comes from behind, and I have the fleeting, crazed thought of running in the opposite direction before turning on my heel to face him. He scuttles up the road, face smudged by grimy fingers. "Thought you might 'elp." He shoves a finger through a hole in his tweed jacket, two sizes too large.

"I would be happy to, of course. Perhaps you could come by the shop—"

"I was headed that way just now."

My heart thrums. Lorelei is more mother to him than his own. To rouse his suspicion would surely lead to more questions from my already addled lover. Addled? Is that what she is? After this morning I can't quite—

"Adele?"

Nothing jolts one from rumination quite like the impatience of a child. "I woke with a tightness in my chest. Thought a stroll on the walk might do my health good."

"Reyt, well." His eyes drift a group of children making a commotion down the street, and I see he has lost interest. "I'll come by in a while then. In time for dinner."

"In time for dinner."

Chester scurries away, no doubt chasing after some new idea he's had, and I turn back to Lovers Walk. A fragrant aroma hangs upon the air, the bloom of an exotic flower I can't place. I'm halfway across the bridge before doubt sets in. What if I can't find her? I know nothing of her lodgings. Hell, for all I know she's found some other local unfortunate to sneak her aboard a crossing.

A gust ripples the river water below, and by the time I reach the bridge's end, despair has set its teeth in me. I was a fool to think I'd find Viola at Lovers Walk, of all places. As if our tryst could possibly have had the same earth-shattering significance to her, as it has to me. I round a corner of thick brush, not a soul in sight to witness the silent tears streaking my cheek.

Conflicting emotions battle for my attention, and I find myself unable to focus on any one thing, a cloth woven of guilt and pain and regret tied round my neck. Once round the loop to unravel it, just enough to catch my breath, and I'll head home. Should Lorelei discover my affliction and leave me, so be it. It would be just. My betrayal leaves me undeserving of her love.

A low hanging branch mangles my braid as I dip beneath it—not far enough. In my frantic attempt to untangle it, a spider's web adheres to my collar. I twist and turn, swatting and yanking and wiping my body in a flurry. Nature's assault is enough to unleash the dams. Openly, I sob. I let the sadness take root in my core, double over, and make no attempt to wipe the tears from my face or remove the remaining bits of twig from my hair. I am a failure and a freak to boot.

"I'm not opposed to watching you sob." A familiar voice from behind. "Though, I'd prefer it to be under different circumstances."

Viola, dressed in emerald with the same sheen as Lorelei's eyes, crosses the bridge spinning an umbrella adorned with black lace in dramatic fashion. Despite her evocative words, I'm relieved to have found her. Though, perhaps more accurately, she found me.

I right my posture, use both hands to clear evidence of my hysterics from my face, and push back the bulk of my ruined hairstyle, tucking it behind my ears.

"No need to beautify yourself on my account." The clack of her boot heels grows louder as she approaches, and her steps slow. "I quite like it when you look a mess." She walks a circle around me like a predator. I feel her icy stare upon the length of my body. My breaths labor, and I cannot help but yearn for her approval.

"I was looking for you," I eke out.

She places a hand upon my shoulder. "Of course you were, little dove."

"Not to …"

She tightens her grip.

"It's not a repeat of the other night I seek, if that's what you think."

Her hand runs the length of my upper arm and strays over my breast before falling away.

"I have no interest in *repeats*." She says the word as if the very shape of it leaves a sour taste on her tongue.

I should feel relieved. But I don't. Her rejection churns a deep well of resentment within. So, I press on. "You made mention of some familiarity with my … affliction." A step back. "I hoped you might guide me to the cure, should one exist. I'm quite sure you can see how an unusual malady such as this might—"

"Shhh." She presses a long finger to my lips, and the memory of that finger stirring a forbidden pleasure makes me clench my thighs together. "I won't deny that I enjoy your begging, though I'd prefer you did so on your knees."

I should decline outright. Should rage at her for even suggesting it, in the broad light of day no less! But I can't stop myself from glancing around for passersby, just in case …

"Hah!" She punctuates her laugh with a stamp of her umbrella.

As if shaken from a spell, I continue. "Well, does such a cure exist? Or have I found the limit to your worldliness?"

Viola balls her hand to a fist, then turns from me and sets about the path in the direction I was heading, her eyes lingering over a blooming Malus Rudolph. I think back to an early time in my relationship with Lorelei, when she stared at me the way Viola seems hypnotized by these blush flowers. Lorelei called this very tree a crab apple, and it took explaining my aunt's passion for botany to convince her of its proper name.

Viola stands no less than twenty feet ahead of me on the footpath, I lift my skirts and jog a few steps to keep up.

"There is someone I know, yes," she says without facing me.

"Who?" I am unable to cloak the desperation in my voice.

"A Spiritual Master, though he takes audience with so few of late." Finally, she deems me worthy of facing. "Even those as pretty as yourself."

The fragile hope which had risen in my chest deflates.

"Though ..."

And rises once more.

"I suppose if I brought you as my guest ..." A sinister smile curls her lips, and the promise of a cure is tainted by a certainty that Viola's aid will come at no small price.

"Would you do that?"

She stops and stands square with me, leans forward so we are eye to eye. "You inquire as to the limits of my generosity, seek to use my connections for your own good, and yet the limits of what you are willing to offer feel"—she takes a deep breath in and sighs—"constraining." Viola grasps my hips, fingers like a vice.

"What would you ask of me?"

Her fingernails sink into the flesh beneath my skirts. "Naught but what I've already asked. I seek a transatlantic crossing. I require nothing fancy." Viola pulls me toward her, 'til my hips press against her own. "You, of all people, know that I don't mind a bit of filth."

My breath lands upon her face, and her eyes ease shut as she breathes me in. "Done." As suddenly as she pulled me in, she releases me.

"And do remember what I said."

What you—

"There is little more tiresome than the same meal twice. Should my want of you extend to your flesh once more, it will be spiced with something far more exotic than a few fingers and a swirl of your tongue."

My jaw hangs open as I struggle to find an appropriate admonishment for how she demeans me, but my mind also reels with enticement. *More exotic?*

"Don't trouble yourself with imaginings, little dove. Should the time come, you'll not need ideas of your own. Obedience is all I require."

Stunned to silence, I watch her lengthen the space between us, and when she is almost out of sight, she calls one final command over her shoulder. "Dusk. Here. Bring your final answer, or don't burden me with the sight of you again." With a curt wave she disappears behind a thicket of trees, and I'm left in the company of my humiliation, stirred desire, and an urgent need to convince Lorelei of a trip to America.

Chapter 11: Home

Lorelei

I had placed the letter on the counter, awaiting Adele's return, casting furtive glances at it whilst I tried to busy myself within the shop. Never before would I have dwelled upon Adele's correspondences, but her behavior of late, the coming and goings, her strange mood made me suspicious. The stamp affixed to the envelope was American, as was the return address, but no postmark other than the one of the local sorting office. When Adele first moved in, she had a few letters arrive from her homeland. Postmarks adorned them, illustrating each step on its journey. I go over and run my fingers over the textured linen weave again. This one item would cost more than all the stationary we possess.

I snatch my hand away and grab the letter opener, which I had placed ready for Adele upon the counter. Just as I slide the blade in, ready to rend the paper, Chester bursts through the door.

"Lore!" He closes the distance between us in a couple of bounds. "I've had the most brilliant idea."

"Chester, were you born in a barn? Go put wood in t'hole."

He looks back over his shoulder at the still open door.

"Sorry, Lore." He rushes to close it. "I had this idea …"

His words fade as my focus shifts back to the letter, to the familiar texture and color.

"So," Chester says. "What do you think?"

I turn to face him, his brown eyes filled with expectation. "It's a fine idea." Expectation turns to elation. "Very clever."

"Can we go over to the next town and try it, Lore?"

"I don't think I can."

"I just thought …" Elation turns to disenchantment as he looks down at his scuffed shoes; the sole of the left one is barely hanging on.

I can see that his sock, once white, now a dingy gray, is sodden. "I'll tell you what."

He lifts his head back up.

"Why don't you come for your tea tonight?"

"Yes. Please. I—I haven't seen me mum since night before last." I think back to that night when I had last seen Chester, first seen Viola. How she kindled an ember within me that led first to fiery betrayal, then the white-hot heat of this morning's encounter with Adele.

"In fact, why don't you go get some of your things and you can spend the night? I'll even make up a proper bed this time."

Chester grins widely, showing the slight gap between his teeth.

"Well, off you pop, lad."

He is out the door as quick as when he had first burst in. I pick Adele's letter and the opener up, and slice into it.

It's from an uncle, something about an inheritance. Shame rips through me. What had I been expecting? A letter from a beau or admirer?

I think of what to tell Adele, having been so heavy-handed opening the thing there is no way I can return it to its envelope and it is too important to throw away …

I needn't have bothered myself with the worry, as it's taken out of my hands when Adele arrives home, just about falling through the door in her haste.

"What have you got there?"

"Adele, I'm sorry. I had no right to open it."

She snatches the paper out of my hand, slicing my thumb in the process.

"No, you didn't." She scans the letter as I watch her eyes for signs of emotion. There is none but slight puzzlement.

"I'm so sorry."

"Yes, you already said."

"About your uncle."

The blank look she gives me lasts only a fraction of a second before a smile, the fake one she reserves for difficult customers, replaces it. She lies, but about what?

"Yes, thank you." She stares at the letter a little longer before she speaks again.

What are you hiding from me?

"I have to go home."

The word *home* pierces my heart like a thorn. Here with me is your home, Adele. Not the house you left behind filled with people who could never understand you. Have I made you feel so unwelcome and treated you so cruelly as to want to run back there, away from me, away from us?

"Of course, whatever it takes. I'll find you the money."

She embraces me, holding on to me with a desperation I haven't known for a long time. The hitching of her breath tells me she is trying to keep from sobbing. I curse myself for doubting her. Adele rarely speaks of her family, and over the years I've learned not to press the subject. So, of course, such news would be upsetting, any reminder of them would be.

"Will you come with me?"

"Yes."

"Thank you."

I rub her back, and as my hand travels up to her shoulder, I remember I owe her another apology. "I'm sorry I hurt you. Earlier, when I—"

"You didn't hurt me."

"I left a mark. I shouldn't have done that."

"You didn't." She turns around and indicates for me to look. I pull her dress aside to find her skin unblemished.

"I was so sure—"

"You nipped, but were as gentle as you always have been." She turns around and places a kiss upon my cheek. "I know you would never hurt me."

"Adele—"

The moment is shattered by the ring of the bell. We both turn to find Viola there.

"You?" This ends now, but before I can say anything further Viola makes her way swiftly to Adele and, putting an arm around her, begins to talk.

"Adele, I take it you haven't told your business partner just who I am. Never mind, I'll do it. Allow me to introduce myself formally. Viola Marwood." She extends a hand to me.

I let it hang in the air. "We're closed. You may come back tomorrow if you like, but I doubt we have whatever it is you're looking for here."

"I'm Adele's cousin. I happened to be in London when I received the telegram about Graham's passing. Knowing that Adele resided here, I decided to come up so that we may undertake the journey home together."

This woman is Adele's family?

No wonder she crossed an ocean to get away from them.

"I didn't recognise her as being little Addie at first. She's turned from girl to woman, and, of course, it was no help being told that silly, fake name. I suppose she never did grow out of *girlish* things."

"You don't mind, do you, Lorelei? Making the trip with Viola?" Adele asks, her voice small.

I suppose it would be easy enough to avoid her once we're on board.

"Of course not," I say, trying to ignore the growing pain behind my temple. "I don't mind at all."

***

The rest of the afternoon was spent on logistical matters. Viola had passage already booked upon a ship, *Challenger,* set to leave from Liverpool a fortnight hence.

"I could easily book you and Adele a suite. I'll pay, of course."

"That's most generous of you, but I can pay for Adele and I." How, I wasn't quite sure, but there was one thing I could sell: a silver cuff I'd been gifted in another lifetime. A cuff that I'd kept hidden from Adele because it would elicit too many questions. Such as why it bore the inscription, *Always & Forever*, R. Perhaps that would be enough to cover the fare.

"Suit yourself."

Chester came back that night with a fresh bruise and tears that he managed to keep concealed in front of Adele but let flow in force when it was just the two of us.

"She's gone, Lore. Just up and left. I begged her to take me with her, but ..."

"It's okay, you know you'll always have a place here, with us." Except we won't be here. We'd be leaving for Liverpool to set sail for America soon. My aunt there, I'm sure, would look after him during that time, until we returned.

Chapter 12: The Tower

Adele

Challenger is a monstrous thing. Large as a city block, it emits great plumes of dark steam from four, massive canisters. And as the time to board draws closer, just an hour out now, it emits the most horrendous scream. There's a hollowness at my center, only in part from not eating more than nibble over the past several days. No, the void is largely composed of icy dread. The image of The Tower haunts my steps, and despite Lorelei's steady presence at my side and hundreds of passengers flocking about, I think I have never felt so alone.

Does she truly believe that this woman is my kin? So it would appear, and yet, though she would certainly deny it, there's a suspicion in Lorelei's eyes. Surely, she can smell the degradation on my flesh like so much filth? No doubt this is what caused her to sink her teeth into me—a desire to punish, even if she cannot yet place the exact reason for it.

It was agreed that Viola would meet us here an hour and a half before boarding, but she is nowhere to be seen. Coins rattle in Lorelei's pocket, a reminder that though we have scraped together the little we have to afford passage, the exercise is entirely pointless without Viola's accompaniment.

How full of rage Lorelei will be when the moment finally comes, when I have to tell her there is no Uncle Graham, no waiting fortune, that the last of our money was spent on an aimless venture across the ocean, a journey that ends with the end of us.

What madness is this?

I dig my fingernails into my palms and ready myself to pull Lorelei from the crowd, to confess all. If our story is to end, it might as well be here, on familiar soil for her. There is no sense in dragging her across the sea. I can travel with Viola alone, find this cure, and perhaps return. Given time, Lorelei may find it in her heart to forgive me.

"Lorelei, I have to tell you something." Even those words from my lips offer a landing place for my uneasy gut. Yes, this is right. She faces me, eyes like a doe staring down a hunter's barrel.

But, alas.

There is something else there too.

Looking back at me from the emerald reflection of Lorelei's iris is the face of my shame, lip curled into a menacing grin.

"Have you told her?" Viola wraps her arm around my shoulder as if we are not just kin but old friends.

Every nerve in my chest comes alive with fire and fury.

"It's the most excellent news." Her voice is disembodied, a joyous mockery of reality. Viola circles her body so she may look from Lorelei's face to mine and fans a ticket. "I was able to get us first class passage after all. It was a bit of a bother, but you needn't thank me. It is truly my pleasure to make the journey alongside such lovely company."

Lorelei stiffens.

Viola regards me with a frown. "So you haven't told her the little surprise we cooked up?" She *tsks.* "Come now, we'd agreed. You would get to revel in the moment while I took care of the business piece."

So precarious is the situation, I stutter to speak at all. Whether to my rescue or detriment, Viola speaks again in my stead.

"Well?" She addresses Lorelei directly, and I watch my lover's eyes take in every inch of me and Viola in turn, calculating, discerning.

"That was most generous of you," she says finally. Her tone is soft, but her eyes are narrow.

"I hope you won't disparage me for taking the helm," Viola says, squaring shoulders with Lorelei. It's as if both have forgotten my presence. "I do know how you like to *seize control.*" There's a strange inflection on the last words, but if the exchange is some veiled taunt about my affair, it's coded with a guile I cannot crack.

Lorelei's forehead relaxes. She takes my hand. "A wonderful surprise, my love. To travel first class will be a delight."

The crowd pushes toward the pier, and Lorelei allows us to flow freely with it, making our way toward the ticket taker.

"It's the finest stateroom money can buy." Viola raises her voice to be heard over the humming crowd. "A balcony, private lavatory, a dressing area, and two queen beds. I think you'll find it a pleasing accommodation for us all."

The Tower. I see its shadowy spires in my mind's eye, the crumbling stone plummeting seaward. A shared room. I roll the thought over and over in my mind. There is no happy end here. No possibility that a voyage of two women and a mistress, in a shared room over two weeks, draws to a serene conclusion. But the crowd pushes on, and I with it.

Our boarding and the monotonous recitation of safety procedures passes in a haze. I eye every deckhand, every mechanic, any sailor in uniform, waiting for Viola to be grabbed, dragged off the ship for lacking proper paperwork. Then I think, *No. They've summoned the authorities.* And I wait for officers to rally around her, slap her in handcuffs. The image offers a bittersweet dash of relief, but we reach the door of our stateroom without incident, Lorelei unusually quiet. And when Viola slides a great, bronze key into the lock, I know I've been taken for a fool. Paperwork was never Viola's motive. So what, then, was?

As we step over the threshold of our shared quarters, we are greeted by brilliant daylight streaming in from an oversized window. Outside, the ocean laps with a calm I envy. The carpet is plush, dyed with rich colors and patterned with classical designs. Two beds—larger than any I've seen since leaving my familial home—are draped in layer after layer of pillow and blanket. At its center, a grand chandelier leers down at us, its crystals casting every color of light upon the gold wallpaper. If Viola's wealth was ever in doubt, it is now certainly confirmed.

Whatever reason she has for getting us onto this ship, it's not a need of money or paperwork. She sprawls herself onto the closest mattress, her thick, dark hair fanning out around her, and rubs the fine sheets with her palms. "Isn't it glorious?"

I look to Lorelei, attempt to read her face, but it betrays nothing.

"Which bed do you prefer?" Viola asks, though I cannot be sure to whom the question was directed. Lorelei places her bag upon the empty bed.

"This is just fine," she says.

"Just fine?" Viola jolts up to a sitting position. "Have I disappointed you?"

Lorelei shifts her weight. A strange tension lays heavy on the air. I busy myself unpacking some belongings.

"It's beautiful, Viola. You've outdone yourself."

"There are a number of fine restaurants aboard the ship," Viola continues, "but if you would enjoy the quiet of the room, I would be happy to call on room service."

Lorelei mumbles something I cannot quite hear.

"Anything that pleases you," Viola says. This has sharp edges, and I shoot Viola a cutting look. *You mock me.*

She only smiles, my discomfort an amusement.

Whether onto Viola's game or simply stifled by the strangeness in the room, Lorelei rises from the bed and excuses herself with a mention of exploring the ship. I should follow, but too many unanswered questions float about in my gut. Like drunken birds, they crash into my organs, and I accept the opportunity to question Viola alone, offering Lorelei a dim smile when she glances back at me, doorknob in hand.

I hold my breath as her steps dim down the hall. No sooner has the sound diminished to nothing, than Viola corners me at my bedside.

"Does it rile you," she whispers, "to have your shame placed squarely in your face like this? To have Lorelei think we are family? To drive her half to madness with suspicions that, whilst well founded, she must dismiss on the grounds that surely such things cannot happen between blood?" She winds a strand of my hair around her finger, applying a bit of downward pressure so I have to crane my neck to meet her eyes.

I ignore the burning sensation in my scalp and force myself to straighten my back. "You deceived me, boarded the ship with no trouble at all over paperwork. What is your true reason for manipulating Lorelei and I into making this crossing?"

At this, she unravels my lock of hair from her finger, pinches a few strands and yanks them out.

I cry out. My yelp sends Viola into a girlish giggle, and she draws my plucked hairs beneath her nose, taking in the lavender scent of my shampoo. "You needn't concern yourself with why I might enjoy the company of two lovely women such as yourselves. And what does it matter? I gave you my word I would introduce you to my friend—"

"You have not."

"Well, little dove." She softens, caressing my cheek with the back of her hand. "Then I give it now." A flutter of warmth ripples in my chest.

Turning back to her luggage, Viola unfastens her hair pins, releasing her braid and combing it with her fingers. The thick, dark pleats reach the small of her back, and I experience a deviant desire to reach out and caress them.

"You won't tell her, will you?" My voice is shamefully meek, cracking with the question.

Before she answers, she places a silver hairbrush, a compact, and a bit of rouge on the ornate vanity beside her bed. She sits in the tufted chair, emitting a pleasurable sound as she rests into its deep red cushion. Looking not at me directly, but through my worried expression in the mirror, she says, "Not today."

It is as if her slender fingers have wrapped around my heart. My face must betray my panic, but rather than sympathy, it seems to elicit in Viola a feral delight. She continues, her every feature smiling as she says, "Perhaps tomorrow, little dove. I'm not quite sure." She raises her brush and begins to stroke her hair. "Or the day after that."

Tears well in the corners of my eyes, the realization that I am trapped with her, powerless to stop her.

"Though I'm so enjoying the foreplay of your hitched breaths, your hypervigilance at my every word, the wideness of your eyes from a simple change in cadence, I might stretch this game until our last day." She finds my eyes once more in the mirror's reflection.

Every organ twists, contracts, and invades the space of the others. Sweat beads along my collarbone.

"You wouldn't, would you?" It's more plea than question.

In a swift movement, she turns to face me. "You dare to pretend these reminders of my hold over you don't draw a slickness between your legs."

I swallow hard.

In a flash she crosses the room, lifts my skirts and thrusts her hand between my legs, stopping just before her fingers meet my flesh. "Shall I check? Confirm my suspicions?"

Before I can answer, she backs away. I right my dress, pressing at the fabric more times than necessary, as if firm enough swipes might erase how close I came to allowing her to debase me—again. It is just in time, for as I feel the redness drain from my cheeks, there's a rattle of Lorelei's key in our lock, a twist of the knob. I wipe budding tears from my eyes, jump to my feet, force my shoulders to fall, and plaster on a terrified smile.

"Lorel—" Mid-name, I halt, for Lorelei is not alone. Behind her a small figure lurks, sneaking furtive glances from beneath a mess of mousy, tousled hair.

Chapter 13: As Though it was Burning

Lorelei

Though I am loath to leave Adele with that woman, family or not, I cannot stand to be subjected to her mockery any longer. I can only be thankful that Adele is so sweet and so innocent that Viola's jibes and veiled words pass her by.

"If you hurt her, I'll show you real pain," I say, low enough so only Viola can hear.

"Anything that pleases you." The cut on her lip is almost healed, but her mocking smile is wide enough to split the wound. The tiniest bead of blood wells there, her tongue lightning quick to lap it up.

"I'm going to have a look around." I'd have expected Adele to follow me. I shouldn't have to ask, but she makes no move. I hold my tongue and take my leave.

I make my way through the halls and out onto the crowded deck. A man is complaining loudly about his missing pocket watch, his wife, equally loud, is telling him he must have left it in their cabin. I clasp the railing as I breathe the salt air deeply in an effort to as surge the turmoil in my stomach. A combination of not having found my sea legs and the worry of Viola telling Adele not only of my betrayal, but the violent nature of it.

"Catch the little bleeder!" The cry comes from the complaining man, unable to move because of the throng. I see a blur of brown hair and tweed jacket no taller than the railing rush past. I reach out and manage to catch Chester by one of his ears.

"Oi! Get off me tabs."

"Shush," I say to him, keeping my voice low. "Do you want to get in more trouble?"

He shakes his head.

"You know what to do."

The man has extricated himself from the crowd and is making his way to us. I make a show of keeping hold of Chester by his ear, him squirming and trying to get away. "Mum! Stop it."

"No, not until I see what this gentleman has to say."

Chester reaches up and clasps my free hand in his, pressing something into my palm.

He drops his hand just as the man reaches us.

"He belong you?"

"He does, unfortunately." I let go of his ear and slap the back of his head, stopping just as my hand brushes his mop of hair. Chester starts forward slightly. "What have you done now, John?" I raise my hand again. "I swear to high heaven lad if you don't tell me …" Chester cowers as I turn to the man. "I'm so sorry. Can you tell me exactly what it is he's done?"

"He took my pocket watch."

"Empty your pockets, John."

Chester turns his pockets out, nothing in them, save lint.

"You must be mistaken, sir. My son has nothing of yours." I grab Chester's hand and pull him towards me, passing him back the watch.

The man's eyes darken. "You've got it. The little bastard gave it to you."

I put my hands up, showing them empty before pushing my sleeves up.

"I have nothing of yours. You must have misplaced it."

He looks as though he might argue further with me, but I keep my gaze steady, never breaking eye contact.

He falters first, looking away.

"Come on, John, let's go find your father." I drag Chester alongside me. "Throw it overboard," I whisper to him.

"But Lore, the quality!"

"Throw it in the water. You cannot afford to be found with it."

Reluctantly, he walks over to the railing. Reaching his slender arm through the bars, he throws the watch into the water.

***

"Have we interrupted something?"

Adele's eyes are rimmed with red and shining, the only color left in her face.

"No, not at all." Viola crosses the room, reaching out to Chester who recoils from her and runs to Adele.

"Chester!" Adele calls.

He slams into her, knocking the wind out of her so her next words come out as little more than a gasp. "What are you doing here?"

"I …" He glances over at Viola and clings to Adele tighter. He came to protect us. My heart both leaps and sinks at this. His attachment to us could be his downfall.

Adele is too focused on Chester to see the fury in Viola's eyes, gas flames contained within amber glass. Both enticing and repellent.

"Seems like our little stowaway needs a place to sleep." Her tone is light, but the words are said through a clenched jaw. "Of course, he is welcome to stay here with us. It may get a little cramped." Her gaze drifts downward until those burning eyes are firmly fixed on the spot between my legs. "But I don't mind sharing a bed."

I cannot have Chester in the same room as this woman.

"Thank you, but no. We can utilise the room Adele and I already paid for. I'm sure Chester would not care to be stuck with us three women."

"Whatever you think is wise, Lorelei."

"Adele, will you come with me to get Chester settled in? We can explore the ship together." I lock eyes with Viola as I say this; I will not allow her to tear us apart.

"Yes," Adele says. There's something in her tone that says she too would relish the opportunity to spend some time away from this woman.

"Make sure you take a coat, Addie," Viola says. "It gets chilly up on deck."

***

Once Chester is safely ensconced in the safety of the cabin—which I can't even get myself to call modest, for it is pure squalor—with a promise that he will not leave its walls until morning, Adele and I go to dinner in the first class dining room.

I've moved within these circles before, but Adele ... Adele is a native. She has an ease about her that I will, for all my efforts, never be able to emulate. Whilst I must think carefully about which piece of cutlery to pick up next, Adele plucks them from the table in a manner so natural it seems almost mechanical. I'm glad once we have finished eating, and I am finally able to relax somewhat.

Situations like these also serve to remind me that I cannot be seen to do the little things for Adele that I yearn to do. I cannot pull out her chair for her. I cannot lean across the table and wipe away the droplet of wine that clings to the corner of her mouth. I cannot, when it is time to leave, offer her my arm. I am powerless.

On our way out, we pass a painting of a woman in white, a parasol in her hand. Adele seems particularly enamored with it. Her gaze lingers, drinking in every detail.

"Beautiful," she says so quietly I can scarcely hear her.

"Yes," I say, looking at her. "Beautiful."

***

The lights from the ship glint in the water, forming a carpet of stars. It reminds me of the first time I took her to the bridge. It had been late November, colder than it was now. I'd told her about how I'd watched the beacons for the Queen's jubilee being lit, how their reflections made the whole river look as though it was burning.

I wanted to say more that night, to tell her that's how I thought of myself: as fire and water.

That I wanted to burn her, to near consume her in my fire, before cooling and soothing her. But she was so sweet and innocent. I couldn't do that to her, so I smothered the fire and, in doing so, let the water turn to ice.

I grasp the railing in my hand, so frigid in the night air it burns. I don't mind that though. It will keep me focused on what I need to say.

"You could have told me." I keep my gaze firmly ahead, my tone soft, unable to stop myself from wondering if I had just told *her*. If I'd told her why I can't … would she still have strayed? "If you told me you liked … If you told me that I was unable to fulfill a need you have. I'd have understood. I'm not saying you would have had my approval, but I'd have listened."

Adele stiffens, color draining from her face. "Lorelei, I—"

"I've known plenty of women who like to f—who enjoy both the company of men and women." I turn to look at her; her expression is one of worry freshly turned to puzzlement. I look away.

"I know, Adele—I know that you went with that man willingly."

I turn to face her again, see the protest live and die upon her lips.

"I'm so ashamed," she whispers.

"Don't be ashamed of the desire you feel."

But be ashamed of the betrayal hangs like ice crystals in the air between us.

I defy the shame of my own betrayal and edge closer to her so our elbows touch. Her breath is coming in short sharp gasps as she tries to hold back the tears that threaten to spill. I put a hand over hers, brushing my thumb over her wrist before entwining our fingers. If I can offer her this gentleness over her indiscretion, is that not penance for my own?

We stay like this a moment as I let her come back to herself, before I draw her to me.

I place a kiss on the side of her neck, "I forgive you," I whisper. "And I'm so sorry." Her body goes taunt before relaxing back into me. "I'm so sorry for everything." *For everything.*

"I'm sorry too." She breaks away from me.

"I suppose we ought to go back," I say, really meaning that I wish we could go back to a month ago. I watch as she walks away, then she does something she's never done before: she stops and puts her hand out in invitation.

I take it.

We walk back to the room hand in hand, only breaking apart when we happen upon other passengers.

"We don't have to stay here," Adele says as we stand outside the door. Every fibre of my being tells me that I should agree. That we should go to the modest room we paid for and spend the rest of the crossing safely out of Viola's sights. But I am a hypocrite. I confronted Adele about her transgression whilst glossing over mine. Offering forgiveness and assuming that she would give me hers.

"No, you deserve to travel in luxury." I kiss her deeply and wrap my arm around her as we enter the room. Viola is reclined on her own bed; a slim leather volume lies discarded beside her, her gaze narrowed. I turn Adele around so her back is to Viola and lick the ticklish spot behind her left ear. It never fails to elicit a giggle. Viola's gaze turns darker and her mouth contorts into a sneer as Adele's laughter, as clear and light as a bell, rings around the room.

It pleases me, to affirm that Viola does not hold sway over me, that I belong to Adele and Adele alone, but I also fear what's to come.

***

"You better go get your boy."

I open my eyes to find Viola inches away from my face, her eyes holding a glee in them unmatched by what I've seen before. Adele stirs beside me in the bed but does not wake.

"I said you better go get your boy, Lorelei." She draws back from me and stands to her full height. "He may be in the infirmary," she says, examining the nails on her right hand.

I'm out of bed and at her eye level in an instant. "What did you do?"

"I didn't do anything at all. I merely suggested that valuable things could be found within."

I'd love for nothing more than to wipe the smug look off her face, but instead I walk past her to the chair where I'd left the previous day's clothes. I dress quickly and with no regard for propriety. She's seen it all already.

Once fully clothed I go to her; leaning in close, I whisper, "I'll deal with you later."

"I look forward to it."

I am barely out the door when I come across Chester.

There's a pained look on his face, a sheen of sweat upon his brow. As he walks, slightly swaying, there's a tinkering of glass.

I cross the distance between us, scooping up Chester just before he falls.

"What have you done?"

He digs a bottle out of his pocket and hands it to me. "I thought it was cough syrup," he murmurs into my neck. I look at the label: *Syrup of Ipecac*. Fuck! A powerful emetic used to induce vomiting, nasty stuff.

"How much?"

"Just a swallow."

Good, not too much. Though the effects will come soon.

"Am I going to die?"

"You are a daft bugger. But no, you're not going to die. You are, however, going to be as sick as a dog."

He retches.

"But, please God, not on me."

I manage to get Chester back to the room and to a washbowl before the contents of his stomach spew forth. The sound of Chester's vomiting finally rouses Adele, who rushes to dampen a washcloth to wipe at his face.

"Seems the boy needs to find his sea legs. Perhaps he might do that elsewhere, where I won't have to smell it."

Adele casts a sharp gaze towards Viola. "There's no need for—"

"It's fine," I say. "I'll take him back and stay with him tonight. There's no sense in us all suffering."

"Yes," Viola drawls. "We all know how you hate to see people in pain."

Chapter 14: Neither Yours to Give, Nor to Withhold

Adele

The acidic scent of bile coats the air. A deafening silence. Though the small clock on the bureau reads three o'clock, the eerie quiet mixes with the strangeness of the hour, and the very idea of time or place, reality or dreaming seems to lose its rigid edges. I sit in bed, blanket hugging my shoulders, and Viola's stare holds me prisoner in wakefulness, my body responding as if I'm locked in a chase.

"Amuse me, Addie." She curls the length of her hair around her forearm, sights locked onto me like a weapon.

"Please don't call me that." I swallow back memory, rolling the sheet linen between my thumb and forefinger. *Just down the stairs and through the hall,* I remind myself. *Not so very far, should I need them.*

"Very well then." Mattress springs creak with her movement, and I know without looking that she's risen from the bed. "Since you asked nicely. Amuse me, *Adele.*"

The word slides over me with the uncanny smoothness of snake's skin. Lorelei and Chester haven't been gone five minutes, and the relief I felt at Lorelei's forgiveness—albeit for the wrong transgression—has already been forced into retreat by Viola's war games. But I am better prepared now, on firmer ground with my true lover, strong enough to resist the foul temptation before me.

"All that is past us," I say, impressed with the timber in my voice. Though, feeling her gaze upon me, I dare not face her.

I wait for a pithy response, but as none comes, tension thickens the air.

"Whatever twisted thrill you desired, bringing us aboard this ship, you shall not have it." Finally, I brave looking into her honey-brown eyes. Deep as wells they are, full of sickly-sweet secrets.

"Thrill is neither yours to give nor to withhold."

My eyes drop to the silver rings dappling her slender fingers. Moonstone, onyx, and emerald I recognize, but the braided pattern of the thickest is unusual. Not a design I've seen. Within reaching distance, she stands unrelenting. A reasonable woman would back away. This closeness, after I have so openly rebuffed her, is unseemly at best, bordering on aggression at worst. And yet, Viola is no reasonable woman. She remains poised to strike, my pulse beating away the seconds as she lingers.

"I appreciate your discretion," I say at last, thinking that perhaps some words of finality will prompt her to retreat to her bed. "And understand your silence is something you may or may not uphold on my behalf, as you have made so clear. But I do not wish to repeat my prior errors in judgment. Nothing s—" I cannot bring myself to utter the word, "inappropriate will happen again between us."

At this, she fishes two fingers into her dress and draws forth a long, silver chain. Some amulet dangles from its end, encased in silver, and she draws the cylindrical shape across her bottom lip. "I am not looking to fuck you, little dove." She tugs at the amulet's helm, loosing a small, thin blade from the encasement. It glistens, even in the low light, refracting glimmers in bottomless irises.

Trepidation turns to fear as she slides it over my shoulder, allowing the edge to first tickle, then scratch. Something stiffens inside me, and all instinct to move from this predator falls away, even as she presses a firm finger atop the blade. Warmth gathers at my shoulder, surrounding the focal point where the metal bends my flesh. Heat crests into a biting sting in the shape of a line, and I clench my jaw and shut my eyes to keep from flinching. I may be unable to run, but I will not give her the satisfaction of seeing me squirm.

The sting slides. I see the shape of it behind my eyelids: a horizontal fissure weeping a drop of scarlet. Her other hand curls beneath my hair and cups my neck, and with a bit of pressure she guides my chin upward, my eyes flicking open to greet hers.

Not the shade I remember, but lit from within as if embers flare just beyond her pupils. I see it before I feel it, the flick of her hand, the blur of flesh as she yanks it away, then the ripple of sharp pain followed by a warm rush trickling down my arm. I don't look. Cannot break away from her stare of my own volition. The hard line of her mouth cracks into pursed lips, and as she dips her head, I think, for a moment, that she might drink of my blood like a vampire. But instead she blows air onto the fresh wound, and my fortitude can hold no more.

I wince, muffle my cry by sealing my mouth.

"Good girl," she says, pushing a bit of hair from my face. Tangling her fingers into the locks at the base of my skull, she takes a firm grip. I test my range of movement, trying to cock my head to meet her eyes once again, but she clenches her fist, fixing my stare onto the smooth skin of her neck.

Pressure on my collarbone and a flutter of movement tells me she's gone to work there. Razor thin metal seeks to meet the protruding bone, and the thin layer of skin is all too happy to part, allowing them to make acquaintance. The warmth of injury spreads throughout my body, traveling out from my chest and down into my fingertips, settling in my gut and cascading 'till it reaches the bare soles of my feet.

I am reminded of that night in the park, when my feet sprouted roots. Finding myself so much like a stone, so unable to move, to even flinch to avoid Viola's carving hand. Tears gather in my eyes. I feel fear, remorse, sadness, thrill, regret, enticement. Safety. I feel everything all at once. It breaks the bounds of my lids and slides down my face, Viola's eyes tracing the path down my cheeks and dropping to the curves of my breasts.

"That's good, little dove." She drops the blade, allowing it to dangle, smearing rusty stains across her nightdress. Taking my head into the crux of her arm, she presses my face against her chest. I can hold back no longer. I begin to sob.

"Shhh," she says, pressing me even more steadily into her. Her free hand wriggles into the space between us, finds the slice at my collarbone and digs inside.

I gasp, a strangled sound, but she silences me, tightening the muscles in her arm until I can scarcely take a breath.

"It is good to break," she says, rubbing her hand roughly over my bloodied chest.

There she holds me until my sobbing quiets to hitched breaths and the stream of tears begins to slow. Behind my back, her fingers comb my hair. They catch on the stickiness which coats them, but there's a care in her movements as she untangles, and despite the harm she's done me, the tenderness I feel from her now soothes me in a way I cannot quite articulate.

"It's a good start," she says. "You've done well."

Pride swells her chest, and while the question occurs to me, *what do you mean, good start?* it flutters by like a moth, and the relief and calm which settles deep in my bones burns it entirely like an open flame.

Viola peels back the blanket and gestures for me to crawl inside.

I do.

Weighty exhaustion makes me long for the embrace of sleep, and, as if knowing this, Viola extinguishes the lamp at my bedside. In the dark I feel her lean over me, her breath landing on my ear.

"I will ask something of you soon." A slight whistle as she inhales. "And you will abide me. Yes?"

A tiny, faraway voice pleads, *Say no. Ask what.* But I am too close to sleep now, and I say nothing, simply let my consciousness fall away from the waking world.

Her finger traces a circle at my temple. "Your heart travels with you on the ship, little dove." A kiss upon my cheek. "Be smart. Be good. Keep them safe."

She returns to her bed, soft footsteps leading her away while her scent lingers: sweet cinnamon and sharp iron.

The words echo in my dreams, *Be smart. Be good. Keep them safe.* I slumber deeply but find no rest there. Instead, in my dreaming, I find Lorelei.

She knows, she knows, she knows.

The shape of her face holds a vitriol unlike any I've seen before. Hands balled into fists, I freeze, thinking she might strike me. But it's worse than just that. She yanks me toward her by the hem of my dress, grabs my jaw with her other hand, fingernails slicing half-moons into my cheek. I see her do it, feel the wetness under my left eye, but it takes a moment to process that she's spit in my face.

"You fucking whore," she hisses. Lorelei releases me and my shoulders fall. I turn away, wiping my face on my sleeve.

"I'm sorry." My voice cracks. "I'm so, so sorry."

The impact of what I can only assume to be a shove sends me onto the bed. "Not half as sorry as you will be."

Face down, my loose hair obscuring my vision even if I were to turn, I don't see but feel that she's lifted my skirts, cool air on my exposed skin. There's a pinch at my hips, and I hear the fabric of my undergarments tear.

"Is this how she fucked you?" I know from Lorelei's tone that she says it through clenched teeth. "Is this what you like?"

I twist my body, thinking if she could just see my face, see my deep remorse, that she might understand the depth of my regret. But just as I catch sight of her, there's a crack that sends ringing through my ears, heat pulsing from the center of my face and radiating down to my jaw, up to my temple.

"Tell me!"

I try to tell her again that I'm sorry, but it comes out as a hitched sob muffled by the blanket.

"Get up."

I don't move, that same stuck feeling like a mouse in a trap.

"I said *get up* you miserable, spoilt, fucking bitch."

Arms shaking, I brace myself and get my knees beneath me when there's a pressure on my back pushing it into an arch. I feel the intensity of my exposure, open air licking the most sensitive parts of me, sending a chill that gooses my flesh. Lorelei presses my face into bed.

"That's quite enough, actually," she says, her voice steadying. "I think this is the most suitable position for you."

I know what's coming next. I make no move to avoid it, in fact, I part my knees slightly for more stable balance, ready to accept the punishment I well deserve. So, when I feel her enter me, it's not the warmth of her fingers that comes as a surprise, but the bite of cold that comes with them, the inflexible shape of some object that she drives inside me, not with gentleness and care for my pleasure, but with a callousness that speaks of rage and retribution.

She reaches a depth that makes me cry out, "Please, Lorelei. I'm sorry, it hurts!" But it only spurns her on, thrusting faster and more furiously. I round my back, try to change the angle so she's unable to reach the tender spot deep inside, but she responds with a rustle of movement, and something—her foot—meets my spine, driving my belly back onto the mattress.

Somehow I know, *just know*, it's the amulet inside me, that the only thing sparing my innermost parts from the slice of its blade is a thin encasement of metal and a whim of my scorned lover.

With the fiercest thrust yet, the sound that comes from my throat can only be described as a howl. And this seems to please her, as she finally withdraws, allowing me to collapse onto the bed.

"Consider your debt paid." Her voice has changed. "But not in full, little dove." Shame turns to terror, and I push the hair from my face as I turn, pulling my legs together when I find not Lorelei staring back at me, but Viola, tongue sliding over her lips, a smile as a wide as the Cheshire Cat.

I search the room, not our cabin but a dark, ancient place, illuminated by hundreds upon hundreds of tiny candle flames. The ceiling soars high above my head, not man made, but stone, jagged, a cave. Beneath me I find no blanket to cover my nakedness—for my dress has gone—but a cruel, hard altar, menacing symbols carved in a circle around me. Viola is clothed in ebony silks, a lace veil now draped over her visage. She holds a book, pages yellowed with time, and just as I move to cross my arms and hide my breasts, she throws it at me.

I block the connection with my face, but it lands at my side, between two symbols, now seemingly filled with blood. I read the gold lettering on the book's face, *The Art of War*. And then I wake, sunlight pouring through the windows, drenched from head to toe from my own fear.

"He's much better."

I don't immediately place the sounds, far away and overshadowed by my racing pulse. I sit up, wiping the sweat from my brow, tucking damp hair behind my ears.

"Lasted for the better part of the night though, didn't it?"

"Yes, Mum." Chester clears his throat. His eyes are glassy, voice hoarse. My memory returns.

"Have you gotten into the ipecac as well?" Viola's chirps at me, her voice cheery as a morning bird. She's dressed in full, hair woven into intricate braids. Standing before the window, she's cast in shadow, a dark thing not unlike my image of her in the dream—the nightmare—which comes back in flashes, yanking at my innards like grasping fingers.

"Yes, you look unwell, love." Lorelei rises from her crouched position where she'd been inspecting Chester.

"Fine, I'm fine." I swipe at a bead of sweat as it rolls down my collarbone. "Just a frightening dream." I regret the admission the moment it leaves my lips.

"Bad dream?" A quick glance at Viola tells me she's delighted at the thought, but happily Lorelei doesn't see this, her eyes fixed on me as she makes her way to my bedside.

"Something troubling you?" She holds the back of her hand to my forehead, checking for fever.

I grasp her wrist, lightly pressing her palm into my cheek and nuzzling against it before letting it fall. "Nothing I can remember." I say it so convincingly, I almost believe it myself. Who am I becoming? What sort of harlot am I now, who can lie with such ease? But my relief that Lorelei has not yet discovered the true nature of my indiscretion is enough to let the guilt of my deception melt away—at least until her emerald eyes go wide with alarm.

"What's happened?" She pulls back the blanket, running her fingers over rusty stains on the patterned linen. "Have you scratched yourself?" She moves my head this way and that, checking the skin of my neck, then searches the length of my arms, finds nothing.

I remember Viola's blade. How it opened my flesh. How it danced inside me in a dream.

"You'd do better to keep track of your cycle," Viola offers, cutting the tension in the air.

"Aw, come on!" Chester's face is contorted in boyhood disgust, and with all the drama of an actor at Loew's American, he folds both hands over his eyes.

"Here," Viola continues. She slides open her nightstand drawer and tosses me a Lister's Towel. "Get yourself cleaned up." With consideration befitting a more respectful woman, she excuses herself onto the balcony and makes a show of staring out at the waves.

Lorelei has a slight look of confusion, but finding no injury on my flesh, she seems to dismiss the unusual timing. "I'll take Chester for some breakfast. When you've freshened up, I hope you'll meet us."

"Of course." I put on a smile.

Chester is already at the door, thoroughly repelled by even the brief mention of feminine woes, and Lorelei turns to meet him. I glance toward the balcony, and see through the sheer curtain that Viola has given up her faux fascination with the choppy sea and is poised to rejoin me.

My pulse quickens.

"Adele?"

I snap my neck back to Lorelei, flush with worry that she's read something in my gestures.

"I heard talk of whales off the starboard side."

True happiness eases me. This reminder of ordinary wonder, normalcy. "Sounds wonderful."

When the door has settled on its hinges, I pop out of bed, eager to lock myself in the bathroom before Viola can corner me with some fresh wickedness. I make it there, flick on the light, and begin to shut myself inside when a hand adorned with silver rings catches the door.

"That's no way to thank me."

I step further into the washroom, and she tosses the door open all the way, resting her weight on the doorframe. My eyes pass over her neck, searching for the silver chain, thinking she might cut me again. But it's bare, wherever she's stashed the amulet it's not between her—

"Eyes here, dove."

I roil with humiliation. Viola cocks her head in amusement. She reaches for the towel rack, removing a perfectly white hand towel and running it beneath the tap. "Heard a story about a boy in my hometown." Her fingers roll beneath the stream of water, as if she's waiting for it to warm. "He saw a whale, aways off shore." Cutting the tap, she wrings the excess. "Swam out to it." She approaches me, pushing all the hair off my neck. "But do you know what he found?" Viola presses the towel against my skin, rubbing purposefully but with care.

I shake my head.

"Wasn't a whale at all." In rhythmic circles she scrubs away the evidence of her violence from the night previous. It's very nearly a comfort. "What do you think would happen to you?" She moves behind me, turning me so I see us both in the mirror's reflection.

"I'm not sure what you mean."

Eyes on mine, she reaches between my legs. "If I threw you to the sharks."

My body goes taught as she presses against the fabric of my nightdress. I push off her, and she stumbles back one step, catching herself against the wall. I'm whirled around. A smack lands across my cheek, sending ringing through my ears. I lift my arms, but Viola's hands grip each wrist like a vice.

"If they tore you apart," she goes on, "would you wake the next day, healed as you have today?"

I want to pull away, in fact, I command my limbs to move, but they do not. Once again, I find myself stiffened to stone before her.

A whisper in my ear, "Did you dream of me, Addie?"

Finally, my limbs abide me, and I get myself free from her. "I really must be getting ready. Lorelei is expecting me." I grab the first dress hanging in the closet, collecting undergarments from the dresser in a flurry.

"And here I thought she had no expectation of you."

I don't look at her, determined to dress and be gone from her company as quickly as possible.

"Is that not why you were so quick to taste me? Your tongue eager for work and the woman you love uninterested in the prospect?"

My outfit chosen and the pieces gathered, I'm forced to either dress in the open or make my way past Viola, now blocking the washroom entrance. My cheek still stings where she struck me.

"I would appreciate some privacy, please, so I might dress."

She tips her head. "Of course." In a mockery of respect, she does a half curtsey and waves me inside, where I shut the door and turn the lock. Attentive to every sound should Viola try to force her way in, I clothe myself and fix my hair into something passable for style. One final check in the mirror confirms the blooming redness where her palm landed, but where last night Viola dug trenches in my flesh, not a scratch remains. I cannot help but wonder about Viola's question. What *would* happen if she threw me to the sharks?

I emerge from the washroom to find our cabin empty, an initial relief. But a creeping dread lingers. For at least when a dangerous creature is within your sights, you might see its attack coming, might gain half a moment to brace or prepare. Unseen predators pose the most lethal threat. Scheming from shadows, they spring at the most vulnerable moment, dealing the damage before the victim has time to be afraid.

Chapter 15: No Hard Feelings

Lorelei

"If you don't slow down, you're going to make yourself sick again," I say as Chester takes the bacon from my plate, having cleared his own in less than seven minutes. "And for god's sake, Chester, chew."

He makes a show of nibbling daintily at the bacon whilst I sip at tea gone cold too quickly. I close my eyes and see spots of rust before them. Twice Adele has been gone from my sight for a night, and twice blood has clung to her the next morning. Even if Adele had somehow met someone and took them to bed, I doubt Viola would be able to contain her glee at it. The temptation to goad me with the knowledge would be too much for her to resist. Yet … I know Viola has a taste for women, but surely not one as passive as Adele. The ferocity with which she had me fuck her is testament to this. Not to mention their being relations. It simply must be Adele's time.

"You look so far away."

"Excuse me."

"I said, are you alright?" Adele has sat down at the table. "You look so far away."

"I'm better now you're here."

Adele smiles at me. A little of her color has returned and she looks more herself.

"What would you like to eat, my—"

"I rather fancy something I can sink my teeth into." Viola sits down next to Adele, picking up a fork as she does. She presses the tines idly into her thumb. "Something with a bit of substance. Something sweet maybe. Suggestions, Adele?"

Adele looks down, but I can see her ears are tipped with red. "Perhaps toast with a fruit preserve," she says, still not looking up.

"Yes." Viola puts the fork down. "Raspberry, I think, there's something so pleasing to the eye about the color."

"I think I'll just take coffee, my stomach feels unsettled," Adele says.

"Some toast might—"

"You don't want coffee," Viola interrupts. "Far too bitter a liquid. You want a milky tea."

Adele nods. "Yes, perhaps you're right."

"Toast would—"

"I don't want anything to eat, Lorelei." She pauses here, apparently feeling the cut of her own sharpness. "Thank you," she adds. I try not to let her cold civility towards me, done as an afterthought, ruin what we recaptured last night.

"I think I've had enough, Lore," Chester says as he swirls his finger around his plate and licks the grease he finds there. "Can I go explore?"

"Are you going to drink from random bottles?"

"No."

"Go." I put a hand on his shoulder and draw him in so I can whisper, "You may think this is a very large ship, but it's really not. Keep yer fingers in yer own pockets."

He nods. "I promise, Lore."

"Off with you then."

Viola is looking at me, brows raised.

"Yes?"

"That accent keeps rearing its head."

"And?"

"Nothing. There are many who prefer a bit of rough. What do you prefer, Adele? Kind and refined or rough and ready?"

"I …" Adele's tone trembles slightly before she smooths it. "I think Lorelei has a lovely voice," she says, Viola's double meaning lost on her.

Still, I'm unsettled to think Viola would speak so crudely in front of family. A beat passes, Adele twiddling the lace tablecloth between her finger and thumb. I think of when I was rough with Adele. I sank my teeth into her, marked her as mine, or, rather, I'd been so sure I'd marked her.

Viola's eyes flick to Adele's lips. "All this talk of voices reminds me of something. I understand you are a talented mimic, Adele." She turns to address me. "Must be wonderful to have someone with such a talented tongue. I hope you put her skill to good use, Lorelei."

Excuse me? I bite the inside of my cheek to keep myself in check as Viola continues talking.

"I myself could think of a dozen or so things."

To anybody listening, her words are innocent enough, carefully chosen to needle me and me alone. The dining room is thinning out as breakfasting hours come to a close, but too many patrons remain for me to say what I want without recourse.

"I know I said I felt better, but I may just have to go lay down a little while longer," Adele says, getting up from the table.

Is it her shame or mine she tries to save with her exit?

"I'll come with you." I push back my chair.

"It's alright." She halts me with her palm. "You enjoy the morning. Maybe I'll be up to eating something later."

Viola's lip curls into a sneer once Adele is safely out of earshot. "I'm sure she'll be ravenous later. In fact, I may join her, that beautiful cousin of mine. I'm feeling a little worn down myself."

"Don't—"

"Lorelei." Viola tuts. "You must be mindful of the other guests. They didn't come here to listen to you."

"I think I'll go and get some air, then." My jaw aches, a gift from Viola. "Perhaps a walk on *deck* might serve to wake you up and bring you to your senses."

I turn away but I can hear the smile in her answer. "Perhaps I'll join you."

***

In our short time on board, and after having found my equilibrium, I have come to love the salt-laden air, it has the marvelous effect of not only clearing my lungs but my mind as well. Deep breaths, cleansing breaths. Breaths that temper the temper Adele has so long wished would be quelled. It won't be quelled today, however. It's spitting, the droplets cool and welcome on my skin, but the dark clouds indicate that heavier rain will soon fall.

"Lorelei, Lorelei, Lorelei. Inviting me on deck as though we are children about to embark upon a playground scuffle." There's a distant rumble of thunder as she leans against the railing. "We both know who'll win if you try to come between me and my cousin ... I'd be able to convincingly plead that it was you that lost control, with that violent streak of yours I think Adele—"

"Tell her." The deck starts to clear as the heavens are torn asunder, and the rain falls in a torrent. "She knows I'd never do such a thing."

"Does she?"

The rain, whipped up by the wind, stings as I nod. "Unequivocally."

"Perhaps a different tack is in order." A flash of lightning, dangerously close, lights up her amber eyes. Her tone is low, but even with the peal of thunder I hear her perfectly. "I will destroy her."

My nails dig into my palms as I close the last foot between us, our lips so close a sheet of paper could scarcely be slid between them.

"You know how fixated Adele is with social propriety. One well-placed word would be all it would take to—"

"You wouldn't."

"Perhaps you're right. But Chester—Chester has found himself in so many scrapes already. It's only a matter of time before—"

I glance about, making sure only Viola and I have been foolish enough to stay out in this weather. We are alone. The sound of my open palm making contact with her cheek rivals that of the storm, and though my hand stings with it, she does naught but smile.

"Is this how you want to play, Lorelei?"

Her first blow lands just above my eye. The second is on my mouth, mirroring that night in Lovers Walk when I first tried to warn her off. Blood streaming down into my eye, I strike out blindly. Blood pours into my eye, filling my vision. I hit her through more luck than judgment.

She doesn't flinch; it's as though I've done nothing more than caress her.

"You never learn." The words are calm, measured as she brings her fist to my cheek effortlessly but effectively. "But I haven't time nor inclination to teach you."

I reel backwards but I am not done for yet. I ready myself to strike again, raising my fists.

"Oh Lorelei, I know you desperately want to hurt me, but not like this."

She stands still before me, wide open for me to land another blow, but I find myself rooted to the spot, arms heavy as lead.

"You're boring me now." Viola puts one hand on my shoulder as her other jabs upwards into my stomach. I double over, but I'm determined I will not go down. My resolve is soon ended as she punches the back of my head, sending me onto the cold, hard wood.

I curse the mewl that escapes my lips, the weakness I have shown.

She kneels down beside me, reaching out to grasp my face with one hand, forcing me to look up at her. "Tell Adele about this and I'll kill the boy."

She lets my head drop back down, sending a fresh jolt of pain through it. She stands and starts to walk away before turning around and administering a swift kick to my stomach.

"No hard feelings though."

I close my eyes and listen to her retreating footsteps.

When I open them again, the rain is still falling, leaving no hope that a passerby will find me and offer aid. I draw my legs to my chest and shiver. Maybe if I just close my eyes and rest a little longer, I'll be able to get up.

I don't know how long I've lain there before a small voice brings me back to myself.

"Lore, Lore. Please get up."

I open my eyes to find Chester, inches away from my face, eyes wide with fear.

"I'll go get Adele."

"Don't. Just help me back to the room."

Chester pulls at me, and it takes great effort on my part to get up so he won't believe his help is ineffective. On unsteady feet, with Chester doing his best to prop me up, I make my way to the stateroom and collapse on its sorry excuse for a bed.

Chapter 16: The Damage of Her Mouth

Adele

To call this place a *stateroom* is more a trick of verbiage than description, for—put simply—there is nothing stately about it. The stink of infection permeates its thin, peeling walls. Maids seem to have forgotten it entirely, leaving old stains to stiffen the linens and carpet. Close to the engine room, the mechanical roar is punctuated by hacking coughs from the neighboring suites, but despite my many attempts to encourage Lorelei to utilize the luxury cabin we've been sharing, she insists on recovery here, *in private.*

Sprawled upon the slim mattress, cool rag pressed to her head, Lorelei inspects me through narrow lids. Whether this look is one of suspicion or simply the result of swelling, I know not, but it sets me on edge.

"Please tell me what happened," I try once more.

"It's nothing to concern yourself with." Her tone is brisk, the true message clear: *do not ask me again.*

Now that the cloth has absorbed some of the gore, I notice the depth of the split in her brow. "Perhaps I should call the physician."

"No need." She casts the cloth into the bedside table, a wobbly thing marred by watermarks. The chasm above her eye fills quickly with blood which trails to her cheek, stark red against the bruise's greenish hue.

I go to her, snatching a handkerchief on the way, and blot at the wound. She scoots over to accommodate me, and I sit in the curl of her midsection, her flesh radiating heat despite being soaked in the storm.

"You really must work to reign in your temper."

A pause in her breaths.

"I only mean, I don't wish to see you hurt." I reach for her hand, dab the cloth on her busted knuckles, raw but already beginning to clot. While I didn't mean this as a chastisement, a strange expression tells me I must have insulted her, implied that she somehow brought this upon herself.

Like a wheel spinning in mud, I stumble on, deepening the trench. "Perhaps you might soften your manner of approach. Take Viola, for example, she manages to command authority whilst maintaining a certain air of …" I stop myself.

Lorelei's teeth dig into her split lip; she's seething. "If you desire a more aristocratic lover—"

"It's not that!"

"I've had actual aristocrats, they're not all they're cracked up to be," she mutters.

Though I have, on many occasions, suggested changes to her demeanor or inflection of speech which might more closely align with the type of company around which I was raised, I restate that truth I've repeated so many times, the truth she seems simply unable to hear. "It's your resourcefulness, your resilience that drew me to you."

Her sour expression tells me I've picked at an old wound, added insult to injury.

I must right the wheel.

I circle my fingers around the frame of her ear, lean in. The scent of rain, salty sweat, and copper are a potent reminder of her toughness. What I want to say—what I mean to say, but can't, is: *I wish you'd save it. Wish you'd save all your violence to lovingly disburse upon me in our bedroom.* So instead, I press a small kiss against the damage of her mouth.

I pause. Check her eyes.

There's no wince of pain, and the sharpness of her glare has dulled somewhat, so I go on. I kiss the length of her lips, from one corner to the other, and as I make my way along, she begins to return my affection. Straddling her, I move to her jaw, where drying spatter has escaped her cloth. I ignore it, kissing my way to her ear where I catch the lobe with my tongue and lightly press down with my teeth.

Her moan spurs me on.

Down I trail, and she tips her head back, permitting me to access the sensitive space where her neck meets her shoulder. There I become frenzied, nipping at her in rapid succession as her breath becomes heavy. My palm finds its way between her legs, and I press between them, causing her hips to roll and meet me.

"It's been so long," I whisper.

She says nothing in response, but her battered hand pushes my shoulder, and I eagerly catch her meaning, descending her torso and lying between her spread thighs. My ache grows, possessing me like some demonic thing, and in a flash, I've hiked up her skirts—still cold and wet from the rainfall—and slipped off her undergarments. I'm surprised when her fingers dig into my hair, when her nails scrape my skull, directing my movements.

I'd meant to tease, to kiss and lick and play. But she allows for none of that. Both hands wrap around my head, blocking sound so all I hear is my racing pulse. There's naught to do but open my mouth, extend my tongue. Firmly she presses herself against me, rocking her body to create the rhythm as she sees fit.

Lorelei has never used me this way, as a sort of prop in her own game of pleasure, however, the degradation of it, the objectification, sends me reeling. Her pace quickens, and I think to reach down and touch myself, but she's too tight a grip on me, so I'm left to writhe against the bed, enough to torment but not reach my own end.

Breaths now deep and even, she rolls herself in a circular motion over my tongue, arching her back as she draws closer to a finish. I strain to glance up at her, a visible flush in her cheeks around the bruising. And her eyes! Only a sliver of green swallowed by hungry black. Saliva runs down my neck and pools beneath me. I must look—

But her mouth cracks into a smile, and she handles me with such ferocity that I have to wrap my lips over my teeth to keep from harming her accidentally. Incisors slide into the lining of my upper lip, pain sharp and brilliant, my little yelp drowned out by her cry of ecstasy as she topples over the edge.

She releases me.

My face drops into the soaked place between her legs, a mess of spit and desire. When I glance up, her eyes are closed and her stomach rises and falls as she catches her breath. I linger a moment, thinking she might move to reciprocate, but her eyes remain shut and she lets out a deep sigh, relaxing into the filthy bed.

"Just a moment," I say, rising, thinking surely now she will object to my leaving, but she simply gestures *okay*, so I step into the washroom. There's no mirror in which to correct my appearance, so I splash a bit of water on my face and smooth back the errant hairs by feel. Taking my time, I expect her to call to me, but she does not.

Have I done something wrong?

I peek around the corner. Still, her eyes are shut, and in spite of the cuts and bruising, her face carries an easy satisfaction. The anger has dimmed, leaving the wounds to focus on.

No, I've done nothing but act as her puppet.

Perhaps I bore her. Could this lead her to stray? Or to find squabbles as some source of entertainment? Surely many have done worse with less cause?

"Lorelei." I approach her bedside. "I wonder whether you've given fresh consideration to the notion of Spiritualism of late, requesting the tarot reading and all." The temptation is palpable. I could show her exactly how unique I am, that no other Lady could fascinate her the way I—

"Flesh and bone, Adele." She sits up, peeling at the fresh scab on her lip. "That is what I believe in. Let's not rehash this." Crossing the room, she replaces me at the sink basin.

I shrink. It's no use. She would think me mad.

She thinks of another. The thought gnashes at me. So distracted I have been with Viola's malevolence, it would have been simple for Lorelei to court some highborn lady on the ship, to sneak away to some other balcony suite.

I know you, Lorelei. I think it hard, as if I might inject the thought into her mind, causing a twinge of pain. *It's a pastime you only think you hide. The evidence has shown itself in a hundred conversations, countless furtive glances in the wealthy parts of town.* I allowed guilt of my indiscretion to drown out any clue that Lorelei may be indulging in one of her own.

To think of her pleasuring some treacherous woman while a clueless husband smokes cigars in the—Hah! Of course. The simplest solution is often the correct one. Is that not what they say? She was caught! Beaten by the brute and has now retreated to the poorest part of the ship to evade any further altercations. It's no wonder she's been so evasive about the source of her injuries.

"What were you thinking of just now?" *Who,* is what I mean. *Who were you thinking of just now?*

Tossing a bit of water on her face, she takes her time in responding. "Just relaxing. Is that not what you wanted? To relax me?" Blotting her face with a hand towel—one I wouldn't dream of touching without a glove—she adds rust to the palette of stains upon it.

"Of course, but …"

She moves past me, unfastening her wet dress.

"Why didn't you—"

"More evidence that I should work on my manners."

Retching coughs sound from behind the wall. I make no attempt to hide my frustration.

It is one thing to struggle financially, but to choose squalor when finery is available, to rebuff guidance on how to avoid being beaten like a criminal, to use me as Lorelei has then think of another whilst reveling in the afterglow!

"If you're going to scowl at me, Adele, why don't you join Viola, who you seem to admire so much. We both know you'd sooner throw yourself from the deck than sleep in this room anyway."

"Very well then." I'm gone from the room before the neighbor can finish his coughing fit, moving at a brisk enough pace my skirt is swept up from around my ankles.

The thought of Lorelei's lips on another makes me pulse with exquisite pain, as if a swarm of angry wasps has struck a coordinated attack, sinking thousands of stingers through every inch of me. My body hums. I strike at my arms, but, unable to dislodge the sensation, I wind faster through the halls of *Challenger.* Silent tears flow freely when I climb the stairs, my hearing gone. Weaving through the crowd near the dining hall, my body slams into glaring men, frightened children, women who wear expressions of shock but whose eyes tell me they understand.

I see her once more, the *Woman with a Parasol*, or the reproduction of her. Before her gilded frame I pause, bat the tears from my eyes to get a clearer look. Lord Harrington had spoken of a trip to Paris to see her—the real her—during his attempted courtship of me, and I cannot help but wonder where I might find myself now had I not run across the seas, had I allowed the tendrils of my birth to firmly grasp me. The painted boy stares from behind brushstrokes, dares me to consider that he might have been mine, had I chosen differently. A noble marriage. A husband. A child. All scattered to the wind, and for what? A shame so deep it burns, a lover I cannot claim—who does not claim me!

I can bear to look at her no longer, this specter of a forsaken future. So, down the steps I go, following the blurred lights which hang upon the walls. Faintly, I'm aware of my fingernails biting into my flesh, but already at the height of pain, the leaking half-moons only serve to focus my attention. I need to be alone, and with any shred of mercy from a God above, the suite will be empty.

Hand trembling, I blink back the tears enough to position the key in the lock. I fumble once, twice, and finally turn the knob. I don't think, don't breathe as I lock myself in the washroom. There, I allow myself to crumble.

Sobs wrack my chest, and there's an honesty to my strangled cries which offers a fleeting respite. Fleeting, for as my mind turns back to the present, unseen insects bury their stingers into me once more. My shame is a vice.

I gasp.

Take great sucking breaths.

But all land shallow.

I glimpse at where I've marked myself: four little crescents, one smaller than the next, each offering the tiniest portion of blood. Beside the deepest, a layer of skin is slightly raised, and I have a sudden and steadying thought.

It is pain I need.

I pinch the translucent bit of myself between my forefinger and thumb, and gently, carefully, like a mother lifting a newborn, I tug. I watch it separate from the length of my arm and pull further. Beneath I am red, raw.

Pain without drowns the pain within.

I continue pulling. A long thread of me pulled taught, revealing the truth of myself beneath. The ugliness, the wrongness that has always resided inside me.

I feel it, but not in the way I might have expected. Rather than a line of sharp stinging, I carve a linear piece of solitude from my own flesh. I grip the ribbon closer to the base so it doesn't snap. I pull and I pull and I watch, hypnotized. Heartbeats happily push my blood forth. It runs down the length of my arm, warm, soothing.

It whispers, *release me.*

A hand mirror stares from its place on the sink. I am not myself when I snatch it, when I smash the glass against the porcelain tub. Or I *am.* I am most myself when I grip the shard so tightly in my palm that it slides through the flesh of four fingers and the base of my palm. More pouring blood, more invitations.

You are so close.

Let me out.

The immediate sting has gone, but I have waded too deep to stop. I slide the jagged glass over the skin of my wrist. I dig in the point and lift, and like an ill-fitting bit of clothing, my forearm is ready to be parted from its beauty, *its lie.*

I should be trembling when I wrap my fingers around the severed parts of myself. My stomach should roil when I see the glimmer of white bone, when my foot slides on the mess I've made against the slick tile. But instead, I am steadfast.

I rend myself. From arm to arm, then leg to leg. The shattered mirror is my accomplice as I slide it across my collarbone and open like a sack of grain. Hardly do I have to pull now. This disguise I've worn too long, this lie I've told too long, drops from my shoulders like a costume. When I've plucked the last little bit of stubborn flesh from my ear, air finally reaches the depth of my lungs. The coppery scent of me is thick in the air, but my pulse is even.

Weak, but even.

And I am not afraid.

For the first time, perhaps in the entirety of my life, I am not afraid.

I think of that woman in the white bodice, spinning her parasol with an expression of cool satisfaction. And then I rise to my feet. I am ready to see my truth. Bracing myself upon the sink, I avoid slipping in the burgundy puddle. I smooth my hair back. Once ashen, it is stained red with discovery.

I take in my reflection. Angry, twisted musculature stares back. Tendons, joints, white lines of fat nestled between like contented lovers. The laugh comes from my torn lips, reaching a fever pitch as I lean in closer. So many layers of me.

I think again of the woman in white. Of what she might say if she saw such a ghoul as me. Eye to eye with my disfigured form, I imagine she's just on the other side of the mirror.

I lean closer, the cool glass pressing hard against the shreds of my lips.

I kiss her, the imagined version of her, and when I open my eyes, they're not blue but a pale green.

I step back.

My jaw elongates, the gore disappears from my hair and, strand by strand, it takes on her dark tones. Glancing down at my hands—*these are not my hands.* Freckles I don't recognize, fine hairs a shade too dark over tanned flesh, proportions beautiful but not quite right, not for me. My breasts turn from torn meat to full curves, nipples tinged with brown, not blush pink like my own. I heal—not heal—but transform. I am becoming. Becoming *her.*

Beneath my feet, the puddle of blood I spilt shrinks, then disappears altogether, and when I glance back to the mirror, it is not my own pitiful face staring back at me, but the woman in white, the woman spinning the parasol. She is beautiful.

You are beautiful.

I take another step back, admiring the smooth curve of her hip. My finger—her finger—traces the line from the slit of her bellybutton to the silky tuft of hair at her center. I watch myself—her—as fingers slide between the folds of her skin. Warmth meets me.

Another invitation.

I cannot look away as she dips her finger inside, rounding her back to sink deeper into herself. An electric sensation makes us pull in a quick breath and push another finger inside. I press against the firm spot I find. She is more sensitive here than I, and I draw forth delicious pressure, a pressure I derive from a place a bit higher, swirling in a rhythmic motion.

Her skin gooses over the length of her shoulders, but her nipples don't harden as mine would.

This difference, this thrill, drives me onward. I press my—her—thumb into the most sensitive place at her center, working her from within and without. She cries out from my throat—her throat—so long and delicate. Her wide eyes staring back at me build the pleasure to a climax that rocks her body. Every muscle clenches and I—she—emits a deep moan, an octave lower than any sound I've made wearing my own flesh. Her knees weaken. Black spots invade my—her—vision, and I, in her skin, collapse back onto the clean tile.

Once more laughter erupts from a buried place as wave after wave of pleasure rolls through this new skin.

"I suppose I'm done with you now," I say to the empty washroom. I run my fingers over those tanned breasts once more, and before my eyes the shade lightens, warms.

All my flesh restitches, rearranges, returns to its prior pallor. I twist a length of hair around my familiar finger, still coated with the slickness of her desire, and find it ashen once more. Shards of mirror glitter like diamonds on the floor, the only evidence of my misadventure but for the scent of her still ripe on my hand.

Chapter 17: She Took All I Had to Give

Lorelei

I suppose I ought to be ashamed of how I treated Adele, but it's the most fulfilled I've felt since I fucked Viola. More so, as it was with someone I love, someone I should have held afterwards. Had I done that, though, I risked letting it slip that it was Viola that had beaten me, and as much as it pained me, going cold was my only option to keep those I love safe. It's been three days since I last saw her, the longest we've ever gone in our three years. I miss her. I miss waking up with her hair in my face, the scent of her enveloping me, the warmth of her body.

I've spent the length of that time in this room. Chester brings me food, though I have no idea where he is obtaining it from, for he refuses to dine with Adele because of Viola's perpetual presence. To Chester, she very much encapsulates his idea of a witch with her strange dress and manner. But despite his fear, he follows them at a distance, giving me constant and, quite frankly, unwanted updates on their movements around the ship. Apparently, Adele looks happy in her company. *Happier than she's looked in months*, Chester tells me with all the candor of childhood.

Though it has never been said out loud, Chester knows that Adele and I have lived together as a man and woman might, and he recognises Viola as a rival for Adele's affection.

"She's not even that pretty," Chester says, with a vehemence that makes me love him that little bit more. Though I'd argue that this is very much not the case. Viola has an unearthly beauty, strange and sharp in contrast to Adele's softer, more welcoming look. "I mean, you don't look as good as you normally do, but you're not totally unfortunate."

"If you expect to have any luck with the ladies when you're older, Chester, we need to work on your sweet talk."

"No, I don't want a wife or anything like that, naught but trouble and for what? A kiss and a cuddle in bed? Doesn't seem worth it to me."

"You'll understand when you're older," I mutter.

"What?" Chester picks at the peeling paint on the wall.

"Nothing."

"I might go out. Sure you don't want to come? I hate leaving you alone." Even as he says the words his hand is on the handle, but he looks to me for permission.

"It's fine," I say. "I think I'll feel up to taking a walk in the morning."

He almost rips the door off its hinges in his enthusiasm. "Thanks, Lore!"

"Just keep out of—" The door slams shut behind him. "Trouble."

I settle back into bed. Chester's words about my not looking my usual best still ringing in my ears, I'd hate to walk about on deck and be subject to whispers and speculations about my personal life. I shift, trying to find a little comfort. I'd love to take off my clothes, having always preferred to sleep in the nude, but even I don't trust to have these sheets against my bare skin. I close my eyes and think of Adele. Has she been alone in that big soft bed, or has Viola crossed the room to fill it? Would she settle between Viola's legs as she did mine? Or would Viola be as desperate to please her as she did me? No! How could I even think such depraved and disgusting thoughts? I ought to be ashamed.

The rattle of the door disturbs me from my thoughts.

"Back so soon?"

"What a dump!" Viola's lips are curled in disgust as she looks about the room. "Why did I bother paying so much for a room big enough to accommodate all three of us just for you to retreat here to dwell amongst the vermin?"

Anger swells within me. I'd done what she asked of me, leaving her and Adele to their own devices in exchange for Chester's safety. I don't fear another beating from Viola, it's my pride that can't take another blow.

"If you've come to mock me—"

"And if I have?" The sneer has been replaced by a look of wry amusement. "Lorelei, do you really think you can demand anything of me?"

"Why are you here?"

She drags a chair to the side of the bed. "I've come with a proposition, though if you'd rather stay …" She gestures around the room. "You're a scavenger by nature, feral and vicious, but you're also cunning and adaptable. Why sulk? Hide away here in your little fox's den when you know it makes much more sense to submit to the situation? Why deny yourself comfort?" She reaches over to trail a finger along my jaw and over my lips. "Deny yourself pleasure?"

An involuntary moan escapes me.

"You'd like to come home to Adele?"

I nod.

"As I thought." She snatches her hand away and reclines back. "You want to do to Adele what you did to me, no?"

The memory of Viola clenched tight around my fingers rushes forth, followed by the sting of my palm after I had slapped her, the way she looked on the desk as she took all I had to give.

"Yes." The word catches in my throat. "I want that."

"And more?"

I think of Adele spread out before me, bound. Mine to do whatever I please with.

"And more."

"I can make Adele more receptive to your … shall we say, proclivity."

She could not possibly mean …

"You would speak so indecently of your own cousin?"

"Distant cousin," she says, fingers twiddling the door frame. "By marriage."

"Adele would never—"

"Wouldn't she?"

Viola's arched brow drives me to consider Adele in ways I have never dared to, assuming her upbringing and sensibilities precluded her from a certain level of … depravity. Up to a month ago, I hadn't been aware of the full extent of my own tastes, though the signs had been there all along: my need to take charge, to push whoever I was with to their limit. I'd put so much of who I was away when I met Adele, so sure she'd be unable to handle anything more. And I suppose I put parts of her away too. Things she might be capable of, might even enjoy. So the bites I'd bestowed upon past lovers became playful nips for Adele, fingers entwined in hair guiding my lover's movements became brushing back the wayward lock that always fell upon her brow.

"You and Adele are on the brink," Viola says, interrupting my rumination.

"Adele and I are fine."

"Are you? You've locked yourself away in this room but Adele hasn't come knocking on that door, has she? She prefers to stay with me. Why did she run into the arms of another that night, Lorelei? Because she needs something more than you were giving her. You saw the muck on her knees, the blood on her gown. She craves what you can give her. Even if she doesn't know it yet."

"How do you know about …"

It occurs to me; it was only Viola's word that convinced me Adele had gone willingly with that man. I'd been so quick to believe the worst of Adele because it meant I could indulge the worst of me. Had Viola been involved in some way? Viola certainly has a violent streak and an obsession from the beginning with Adele, one not entirely explained by lineage and matrimony.

Still, I can't be understanding her correctly. She would never suggest what I think she might be. "What exactly are you proposing?"

"Lore, may I call you that?" I shake my head but she continues regardless. "Lore, Addie is positively bereft without you and I am positively annoyed. The way she mopes about, though the moping is preferable to the bouts of hysteria, is quite frankly ruining this journey for me. I can act as a medium between the two of you so that you can get your …" She bites at her bottom lip as she thinks. "Bedroom activities in synchronization."

Viola may have some sway over Adele, but not in this area. Adele would never discuss her wants in the bedroom with anyone else; I can't even get her to articulate what she wants. She'd say it was too *coarse* a topic. And with a relative, no less? She'd find it unthinkable.

"She would never agree to chat so openly, she'd rather die than suffer the embarrassment of it."

"She already has, was her idea, in fact, that I should arbitrate."

"Agreed to talk about her sex life with her cousin?" I don't hide the incredulousness in my voice.

Viola sighs. "You are making this difficult. Perhaps *cousin* was a bit of an overstatement."

"Overstatement?"

"*Family friend* might be a more accurate summation."

"Hah! So, you lied to me, the both of you?" I shake my head, a desperate attempt to sort the thoughts flying through like a moving picture.

"Enough semantics!" Viola touches her fingers to her forehead as if she is getting a headache. "What do you say to my proposal, hm?"

I think again of the power I wielded over Viola that day, imagine Adele in her place, my pulse racing in my ears. Viola must take my silence as a yes as she continues talking. "Come by the room tonight. Adele will be waiting." She gets up with such force that the chair tips over. "Just one more thing, Lorelei."

"What?"

"Wash up first, you fucking stink."

***

My hair is still damp at the nape of my neck when I arrive at Viola's door. Washed and with fresh clothes on, a single rose liberated from the dinner table's centerpiece in hand, I'm ready to face Adele. I don't know what to expect on the other side, but at least Viola has spurred me into leaving the room and, for the first time in days, I feel human.

Viola opens the door wearing nothing but a white silk shift, made all the more blinding by the contrast with her olive skin. "I thought I better open the door lest you stand there all night."

Adele sits on the bed wearing her own shift of off-white cotton, staring blankly ahead. I wonder what Viola has told her about me to persuade her to agree to this. Viola sits down next to her, slipping an arm around her waist.

"It seems we are somewhat ahead of you. Why don't you catch up?"

Adele doesn't lean into Viola's embrace but she doesn't recoil from it either. Pain bites at my palm. I look down at the rose held too tight in my hand, the bead at the bead of blood between my fingers. I let the flower fall to the floor.

"What's going on?"

Adele swallows and says nothing, eyes trained on the floor.

"Talk is cheap, I thought a more hands-on approach was in order. Undress," Viola says, running a hand up Adele's back.

"I don't understand."

"Come now, I know this isn't your first time with two women, or more for that—"

"Adele, tell me what's happening."

She folds her hands in her lap.

"Tell me that this isn't what you want."

"Viola's right, we need—it's not working as it is."

I turn to Viola. "Lay one hand on Adele and—"

"Oh, but I'd like to see Adele's hands on you." She nods toward Adele, who pads over to the dresser, retrieving a sheer scarf which she rolls self-consciously around her wrist.

"You don't trust her," Viola says to me.

"I tru—"

"You don't!" Adele interrupts. "You never have."

The arguments of our past reverberate between us and I know better than to challenge her further. I look to my own hands, filling with terror at the thought of being bound and powerless in the presence of this awful woman.

"Will you let me?" Adele asks, her voice so fragile even a too strong breath could shatter it. She crosses the room, holding out the scarf like an olive branch, and against my better judgment, I accept it, offering my wrists and sitting at the bed's edge.

"We can leave right now," I whisper. "I know I can't give you what she can but—"

"The silence between you has had a high price. You and Adele need to rebuild your trust, and it starts with compromise. It starts with telling the truth."

"I don't know if she …" Adele drops her voice to a whisper, glancing to me as if seeking approval. I try to get up but my limbs will not obey me.

"Walk away, Lorelei." Viola reaches over and pushes my arms up above my head where they remain. "Walk away if you don't want this."

I struggle within but am fused to the spot.

"Look, no resistance. For the first time in her life, she is being compliant. Bind her."

Adele wraps the scarf around my wrists. I try to protest but my voice has been stolen. All I can do is meet her gaze and try to tell her with my eyes, *please don't.* When she's done, she looks to Viola.

"Very good, well done. But she can still move them about. Take another and attach it to the headboard."

Adele does as she is instructed, digging another scarf out of the dresser and securing it to the first, then the headboard with a series of knots. It's only once she is finished that I am able to move again. I try to free myself but Adele has done a fine job with the ties, for they only tighten with each tug against them.

In an instant Viola is on me. Hand entangled in my hair, pulling my head back, she looks at me a moment, and I brace myself for a strike, but she does something I never would have expected. She kisses me. Her lips are soft and sweetly spiced, a harsh contrast to the acidic horror of knowing Adele looks on.

"It's time you told the truth," Viola says, the amulet around her neck dragging across my torso as she sits back up.

"Lorelei, what is she talking about?" Adele's voice trembles slightly, and she folds her arms across her chest, trying to hide herself, from myself or Viola I do not know.

I turn to Adele. "Nothing, darling, she wishes to tear us apart. That's what she's wanted from the beginning—"

"I brought it with me, you know. It's just over there in that trunk. I'm sure Adele, lamb that she is, would fetch it for you. Is show and tell in order?"

"Lorelei?" Adele blanches, waiting for me to explain.

Panic threatens to choke me. I struggle against the binding. "Viola, I'll fucking tear you apart." The words come out as a snarl, and when I look back at Adele, tears have collected in her eyes. Have I scared her? She's seen me in rages fiercer than this one before.

"Promises, promises, Lorelei." She fiddles with a silver braided ring, a ring which looks strangely familiar to me. "I'm going to do something no one else has ever been able to do." She grasps the silver amulet from round her neck and, from it, draws a glistening blade before pushing Adele's shift up, exposing her stomach.

Adele, who makes no move to fight. Adele, who must be as similarly paralyzed as I was. Viola drags the blade lightly across Adele's skin, leaving a red welt in its wake, before settling on a spot. "I'm going to make you believe in magic."

A drop of blood wells where Viola's blade pierces her skin.

"Stop, please!"

Viola looks at me with wry amusement as I tug at my restraints.

"I'll do anything." The scarf digs painfully into me now, but I don't stop. "Please Viola, hurt me. Do whatever you want to me but please don't hurt—"

"You had your chance."

Adele doesn't scream as she drags the blade across her stomach and back again, forming a rectangle, but I do. Her eyes bat a silent apology, sending tears streaming down her cheeks.

She doesn't scream as Viola peels it back and away from the yellow fat beneath, depositing it on the bed where it curls like a ribbon, but I do.

I only stop screaming when the flesh starts to knit back together before my eyes and Viola turns to me to ask.

"Do you believe in magic now?"

Chapter 18: Wasting Precious Breath on Apologies

Adele

The binds around Lorelei's wrists are so tight I crack a nail loosening them. If she hears it split, she doesn't let on. She stares unwaveringly at the leaking window in my belly. We both watch the wound seal, Viola's eyes upon us all the while, until only a pink shape remains on my abdomen. I am reminded by the distinct tingle that shortly, smooth flesh will take its place, and I will once again be Lorelei's Adele, whose unblemished pallor suggests innocence, naivety, prudishness.

"What …" Lorelei's word dissolves in the darkness as Viola sits back, leaning against a stack of pillows, hair tumbling over her shoulders.

What can I say? I say nothing.

Lorelei scrambles to her feet. In the dim light of the draped lamp, her hunched form could be easily mistaken for some wild beast.

I right my shift, clinging to me where my blood has soaked through, realizing that I can no longer be *Lorelei's* Adele, no matter the state of my flesh.

Lorelei looks to Viola. "What is this parlor trick?" And back to me. "Have the two of you conspired to mock me?" Ligature marks of red deepen to purple around each wrist.

"I would never—" I start, but Viola is quick to fan the flame.

"A plan to mock you would be the least of our conspiring, to be sure."

Lorelei freezes. "Adele, what does this witch imply?"

"The truth," Viola says.

I am unable to swallow the lump in my throat, and I think for a moment I must look like a snake attempting to consume a too large egg. A snake, for serpentine I have been.

"I fucked her, yes," Viola says, gazing at the rings on her left hand. "In more ways than one, in fact."

Lorelei lunges, grabbing Viola by her jaw with such force that her mouth cracks open. "Watch the lies you form with this tongue, Viola, or I shall cut it from your mouth."

"What troubles you most, Lorelei? The thought of Adele coming for me? That she is even more rare than you realized? The way I've carved her to bits, or that she let me—"

Lorelei strikes her, spraying my arm with a mist of blood.

"Tell her, Adele." The words are warped from the odd position of Viola's jaw, but still they land like a punch to the gut. Viola's teeth are stained rusty. A wet trail, black in the low light, dribbles down her chin.

"Is it true?" Lorelei unhands Viola, choosing instead to circle to my bedside. Her breath hitches, and there's a look upon her face I have never before seen. She is vulnerable. I know she would give anything to have me deny it, to call Viola a treacherous woman with a mind for hurt and disarray, but I cannot. I lack the fortitude to maintain the ruse.

"It's true."

Something leaves her then. A ghost within her eyes. I'd expected her to rage, or to argue, or to sob, but none of the stories I fabricated in my hours of worry prepared me for the truth.

Lorelei turns to stone.

The curves of her face are unchanged; the features themselves remain. Imperceptible to anyone else, I watch the lines of her forehead disappear as she releases her care for me. Her neck has straightened, perhaps the result of a lessened burden, and she breathes deeply as if she finally has room enough in her lungs without me burrowed inside her, taking up residence in her heart.

Lorelei stops loving me, right then and there.

I reach for her. "I am so sor—"

"Wait, wait, wait, little dove."

Fury rages at the interruption, and I think of throttling Viola. My hands could wrap around her fragile neck before she knew I had leapt for her.

But then she says, "Before you waste your precious breath on apologies, I believe Lorelei has something to say."

I seek Lorelei's eyes but cannot find them, for they are fixed on Viola and wide enough to hold a heavy secret.

"Do you require a bit more time to revel in your hypocrisy?" Viola crosses her arms over her chest. "Here, I'll help you start." She clears her throat and, with a mockery of Lorelei's coarser accent, says, "That's quite alreyt, Adele, because I—"

"Stop!" Lorelei goes a shade paler.

"—fucked Viola in ways your sweet, privileged mind could scarcely imagine." She drops the tone. "Except you can imagine, can't you, Adele? You can think of the things I've done to you, and use your darkest fantasies to fill in the blanks."

I clamp my eyes shut and shake my head. *No. No, it's not true.*

"Oh, not sure you can imagine? Quite alright, I'm happy to show you." Viola moves toward her trunk. "In fact, your education in these illicit matters has become a favorite hobby of mine."

The crack of a hand on flesh jolts me.

Viola cradles her cheek in her palm and Lorelei tears a fistful of clothing from a drawer before making her way to the door. "Enjoy one another," she says, handle turned. She steps, and when I think she will disappear behind the door, she pauses and turns back. "No one else would bloody well 'ave you, after all. Seems ole Beatrice was right about you fucking Satan." Lorelei slides through the opening and a final word is hushed by the door's whoosh of air. But in my most fragile heart I hear it. *Freak.*

I still hear the pad of her steps down the hall when the feeling comes rushing out of me. "Is it true?" I grab Viola's shoulders. "Is it true, Viola? Have you … with Lorelei?" This close, her cinnamon scent stings my already watery eyes.

"Have I what, dear?" Her signature sneer returns, and I know she wants me to say it, to humiliate me further, as if she has not trampled over my life enough for one night.

"Have you …"

She takes both my cheeks in her hands, runs her thumb along my bottom lip. The blanket falls, exposing her breasts, olive skin kissed by a darker shade where they crest into her nipples. Scooting forward, she presses her body into mine.

"Come on, little dove."

I cannot say it, and the absurdity of this does not escape me. Here I sit in sheets still dampened from an affair of the most illicit sort, a feminine lover—not even my own—presses her naked form against me, and yet the crass word feels a bridge too far.

"Say it. Say it aloud or I won't tell you." She collects my hair and spins it into a cord behind my back.

"Have you been with her, as you have with me?"

At this, she chuckles. Chuckles! "Oh, it is nothing of the sort. Lorelei does not contain your sweetness nor your obedient nature. She is a wicked and wild one. Some might say feral. I've saved you from a great deal of depravity, in fact. The things she did to me …" Her eyes wander the room with memory. "And wanted to do more still."

I hear the words, understand what they mean. And yet I fail to thoroughly process them, as if their implication is too big and stops up somewhere in my mind. Lorelei? Wicked and wild? I think of the afternoon when she sank her teeth into my shoulder and how she worked herself against me when we last were intimate. A bit rough, but wicked? I find myself unable to conjure the image of it, and perhaps luckily so, for to imagine Lorelei and Viola together …

A chill creeps down my spine, and, as if sensing it, Viola runs her palms down my back.

"I am glad to be rid of her," she says. "It was clear from the moment I happened upon your shop that I am a more suitable lover. In no time at all I parsed out your secret desires, and I have brought them to life, have I not?"

Absentmindedly, I rub at my knee where it was mangled during our first dalliance in the park. "You have."

"Do not mistake me, I have no intention of replacing Lorelei as your partner, but I shall keep my word and deliver you to Aleister."

"Aleister?"

"You still wish to be cured, do you not? Aleister Crowley is the spiritual master I have told you of. Do you not recall pestering me until I gave you my word?"

"Of course."

Viola rises, leaving cold in her absence. I do not follow her movements, my mind reeling between Lorelei's parting words and the painful idea of her lips on Viola's.

"I've a home in Lily Dale. Do you know it?"

The mention of this infamous town rips me from my mind's wandering. "Lily Dale? They say it is cursed, no?"

"Hah! Cursed. So like people, isn't it? To speak ill of what they do not comprehend. Lily Dale is far from cursed, rather the opposite. It is something of a spiritual center. I think you will find it quite healing."

"You intend to bring me to your home?"

"Adele, do try to follow." Viola cups something in her hands, but in the dark, I cannot see it. "We sail to New York. Our aim, as it ever was, is to meet Mr. Crowley and see about a cure for your … condition. Lily Dale is where we will find him, as well as my home. I'm supposing you should like somewhere to sleep at night? Or would an empty barn do you just fine? Just say the word, there are plenty about."

"No, no." I am eager to put that notion to rest. Viola has shown time and time again that she is not above treating me like an animal. "I would be happy to stay with you."

"Good girl."

"But first you'll take me to my family's home? I'm in need of money." Of a *familiar face*. "It's not far off from the city. Shouldn't be too much—"

"We shall help each other, yes?"

I nod, and the thing in her hands catches the light, reflecting it with a mirror shine. I recognize the shape at once, and my gut sinks.

Viola draws the blade from her amulet. "It's somewhat unfortunate that Lorelei left us in such a huff. I had high hopes for how she might handle me tonight." There's a twinge of pain as the metal enters the flesh at my collarbone, but I hold her gaze. "Luckily for me, a mimic such as yourself will make a passable replacement." Sliding the knife down to my shoulder, the sharp rip turns to a warm flow as my layers of skin and sinew melt downward. She repeats this same cut on my other side, and I grit my teeth to take it.

"There's a simpler way, you know. No need to pick apart every bit of yourself."

I come to understand what she means as my lacerated flesh pours over me like warm syrup. I come apart like an unfastened blouse, down to the hip. And when I stand, I'm stripped further, my legs surrendering their flesh to a viscous puddle on the floor.

"Think of Lorelei, Adele. Lorelei!"

I shut my eyes and remember the day we met. The journey to Liverpool had been full of excitement, possibility. But standing at the port with naught but my trunk and vague ideas of European life, Lorelei's aid had spared me much turmoil and distress. For it was only then, I think, that I truly understood the privileged nature of my upbringing, that I was quite useless without the assistance of more worldly others. She'd beheld me as no woman had prior and, trapped in the intrigue of her gaze, I felt, for the first time, less alone. It's a blissful place and time, and I'm hesitant to leave it. But curiosity gets the best of me and I open my eyes as Viola says, "Good, good. Well done!"

When I look down at myself, I find Lorelei's torso: her breasts, the curves of her waist, her long legs. Red hair falls in soft waves around my face.

"Beautiful." Viola sits on the bed, then leans back, spreading her knees and exposing herself to me. "Now fuck me as I've fucked you. Let us hope I've taught you well."

I am not inside my body as I do what she asks. Rather, I feel like an adornment of the wallpaper, looking on without feeling, while some withered form crosses yet another threshold, leaving the last bit of pride she has on the floor to be carried off by rats. When she affixes the strange contraption to my hips, I can hardly look at it, wobbling forth from me like an unwanted appendage. The weight, the feel, the burn of my muscles from the thrust—it's all wrong.

Viola makes no secret of her fantasy, calling out Lorelei's name time and time again.

A perversion.

A corruption.

I bury my face in the pillow beside her shoulder to hide my tears, thinking they might shatter the illusion, interrupt Viola's imagining, and draw out the encounter even longer.

It must not last more than half an hour, but when Viola finally reaches the depth of her pleasure, I am desperate to return to my own skin, my own voice, my own manner of being.

Afterward, I run the water as hot as it will go. I rub my skin raw in the bath, finally understanding the nature of the burns I once spotted on Lorelei's hips. The pain of the realization dwarfs that of sting as I scrub the area again and again, until a wisp of pink stains the water like so much smoke. Still, I feel filthy when I emerge from the tub.

It seems an odd distinction, good shame and bad. For while it was thrilling to be debased in the course of illicit play, it feels entirely different to be pulled from my true and natural inclinations (though perhaps *natural* is not the right word), and forced to act out the role of another. The role of Lorelei, no less.

When I return to the room, I see Viola has laid clean nightclothes on the bed for me, and the simple kindness after so much cruelty sends me into hysterics.

"There, there."

I pull on the nightclothes and she embraces me, stroking my hair as I cry into her shoulder.

"It's quite alright."

Viola tucks me beneath the blankets, much as she had some nights previous after doing her work with the amulet knife, but this time, she lays beside me. The lamp glow lights her irises like honey. A quiet calm settles upon us as we watch one another, close enough to touch but not to kiss.

I am glad for her, then. Damn me, I am glad for her. Despite everything, her soft breaths in time with mine provide much needed comfort.

"You said something earlier," I say, speaking in the hushed tones usually reserved for Lorelei. "You called me a mimic. Didn't say that I mimicked, but called me such, as if it was a thing one could be. And you knew—"

"At last, you listen well." Her words have an edge, but I push on.

"So what did you mean? Is it something to do with my … affliction?"

Viola runs her finger along the healing seam at my collarbone. "Yes, little dove. You might say it is your diagnosis, though one of the spiritual sort, rather than the medical."

Her touch should not send a shiver. Perhaps one of pain or fear or distrust, but not of pleasure. I know this even as cold travels down my legs. And yet, in her own strange way, Viola has been a constant. She worries the fabric of my hem as if checking for quality, and I cannot help but think that for all the harm she's done me, I find myself grateful to her, for her.

Had I not reveled in such harm, after all? Had I not welcomed it? Dreamt of it? If she pushes me, then perhaps I must be pushed. I have always been thought of as prudish and naive. Surely a woman who can show such tenderness now, as she twirls my hair between her finger and thumb, could not harbor ill intent within her deepest heart.

"A mimic," I repeat, rolling the word over my tongue.

"A rare gift."

Gift?

"I understand why such a thing might trouble you, but I would encourage you to think on whether you truly wish to part with such a rare ability, and one with such endless potential."

I think only of the distasteful show I've put on her for her tonight and my expression sours.

"You must be generous, Adele," she says, as if reading my mind. "As I have been with you. I've shown you not only how to access your power, but a sliver of how you might use it."

Framed this way, I suppose she is right. "You have."

"My word is good." She nestles herself deeper into the blankets. "I will take you to Aleister, should you desire it. But do consider the alternative."

She goes to turn away, to settle on her side, but I grab her arm.

"Adele?"

I do not know what comes over me, but I turn instead, curling into her body and placing her arm over me so I might feel her warmth.

"You are a very good girl." She whispers this into my ear, "A special girl."

I allow myself to relax into her, and my only thought of Lorelei is how little I think of her. The sting of the knife is not so sharp. I wonder whether I could become accustomed to such a thing, should this comfort steadily follow it. Sleep comes upon me, so swift and heavily that even the soft glow of the lamp does nothing to keep me from its hold.

***

Viola and I pass days in the room, ordering food to be delivered when our appetites demand it. She compels me to repeat the act as Lorelei twice more in that span, and each time it feels again like I am a passenger on the journey, watching myself while some alternate version of me drives.

In the quiet moments between, I think of Lorelei and Chester. I wonder whether Chester's gotten himself into any more trouble and whether he feels the fracture of our makeshift family as I do. Viola seems to have a sixth sense for when my mind turns to Lorelei, regaling me with stories of her travel: India, Egypt, Stockholm, places Lorelei and I couldn't dream of traveling. She tells me about a woman she heard of, another mimic, who used her ability to thieve 91kgs of gold from a South Eastern Railway Company train in 1855. To think of it! Others out there like me, not bemoaning their oddity but embracing it.

On the fourth day, Viola draws the curtains and indulges herself in an afternoon nap. Under the guise of exploring the library, I go looking for Lorelei. If nothing else, she owes me an apology for her hideous parting word, an acknowledgement of her hypocrisy. I first check the stateroom, where I find Chester with a heap of items spread over the dingy mattress: a string of pearls, a few American dollars, a pair of spectacles, and—most puzzling—a single leather shoe.

"You look well," I say as he ferrets his goods into an empty pillowcase.

"Can't say the same for you! Though I don't s'pose anyone'd look well after days starin' at the devil's arsehole."

"Chester!" I near gasp. Though familiar with his forked tongue, he has never turned it on me.

"This is a private room, ma'am." He gesticulates toward the door accompanied by a mock bow.

"Please, just tell me where I can find Lorelei."

My plea seems to incite him, as he crosses the room and reaches across me to open the door and show me out with his eyes. "Four days gone, Adele. My Lore's got more pressing things to tend to. She won't be just fuckin' about, waitin' on you to pick her, would she?"

I dip my head. "I'm sorry, Chester." If he hears me, he doesn't let on, closing the door promptly once I've stepped over the threshold.

Next, I check the dining room, the upper decks, which remind me of the Jubilee bridge—the way the lights reflect off the walnut stain of the wooden planking, somewhat like lantern flames dancing across dark water. From there I work my way back down, even sneaking past the entry to the infirmary to venture a glance inside, but I find the beds empty, save a twenty-something man with a bandaged finger.

My ideas of where I might find Lorelei exhausted, I start course to return to my suite. Winding through the quiet halls, I realize I must have made a wrong turn, for the decor grows sparse and industrial, and where I passed hanging art and wainscotting on my way, I now find steel barrels and coils of spiny rope. I walk faster, intent on returning to the fairer areas of the ship. Through small, hazy windows, workers eye me with distaste. A light sweat has broken across my back and my shoe leather chafes at my ankle. I search for any sign of how to return to the passenger areas, but find myself deeper and deeper in the belly of *Challenger*, and a prickle of fear turns to panic when a firm hand grips my shoulder.

"Lost?"

I spin on my heel, expecting to find a rough man prepared to take advantage. When I see Viola's face instead, I embrace her with both arms. "Thank goodness you found me."

She thrusts me away, my head meeting the wall with a dull thud. "It was not me you were looking for."

For a moment I am stunned, and await a throbbing ache at the base of my skull.

"Do not lie to me." She squares her shoulders with mine, advancing so I'm pressed against the wall completely and must turn my head, becoming as flat and still as I can be.

"I just wanted an apology, and perhaps—"

"Perhaps what?" With the p's come a fine mist on my cheek.

Is she jealous? Does she feel herself challenged by my desire to seek out Lorelei? "Nothing."

"Nothing indeed." She grabs me by the wrist, fingers digging in hard enough I expect bruises to form overnight. "I have gifted you with a fine room, pulled you from the jaws of poverty, brought to life your most depraved desires, and you repay me with sneaking treachery."

Treachery? "I'm sorry, I didn't mean to … I thought only—"

Viola's patronizing stare confirms her view of me as a mewling child, and the climbing pitch of my tone flushes my cheeks with shame.

"You will abide me." She leans close enough for her breath to warm my lips. "If I have caused you confusion, that error is yours alone. Let me be clear: you are mine." Her fingernails dig into the flesh of my wrist and I feel the skin begin to loosen and soak the surrounding fabric. "From the moment you eagerly dropped to your knees, suffering the bramble to heed my command, you were mine."

Though humiliation radiates in my core, I cannot help but recall the night at Lover's Walk with a twinge of lust.

"You will do as I direct you, and do it happily." She pauses, and for the next bit, whispers into my ear, so close I feel the flick of her tongue on my lobe. "I would ask you to bend over as every deckhand on this ship assembles in a line to have his way with you. Have your ruined form crawl on hand and knee like a dog for my amusement. And you should thank me for the honor."

Viola lingers there, her cinnamon scent intoxicating. Though the acts she describes are the furthest thing from what might bring me pleasure, what I might imagine for myself, the *possibility* of them, the fantasy that another could hold such unwavering command over me, unleashes waves of lust and fear so strong I feel as though I might collapse in on myself. Relieved of my desire to find Lorelei, who wishes not to be found, I allow Viola to lead me back to our room. Once there, she unleashes her retribution for my deceit in ways too delicious to speak of.

Chapter 19: I Made You

Lorelei

I spent less than a day locked away in that bloody awful stateroom, thinking about Adele, before I came to my senses. Loving her had made me soft, vulnerable. No matter her reassurance otherwise, I always suspected she would grow restless with someone of my station. And, foolishly, I ignored my better instincts and opened myself to her anyway. Never shall I make that mistake again.

Viola's marks upon my face have yet to fully heal, but they are not serious enough to mar my looks too much. Combined with my charm, I should have no problem finding another to warm—well, not that bed. I couldn't bring anyone back to that room. But there are plenty of lonely ladies onboard whose husbands are too busy drinking port and talking business to think too much about what their wives might get up to in their vacant suites.

Viola and Adele seem to have shunned the dining room, no doubt being unable to tear themselves away from their bed. This suits me just fine. The upper decks of this ship are now my hunting ground, and the last thing I need is for them to sully my mood by flaunting their new relationship in my face.

I've engaged a particularly buxom blonde in a suggestive chat about where one can find the most succulent oysters when a tap on my shoulder disturbs me.

"Lorelei? Lorelei Keyes?" I turn around to find a woman who, though in her middle forties, looks the same as she had when I'd last seen her over a decade ago, save for the streak of silver in her otherwise raven hair. "My God, it is you. Though I must say I never really doubted it; I'd recognise that hair anywhere."

"Lady Harrington, how wonderful to see you." I lean forward to place a kiss on her cheek. "What business takes you to America?"

"I could ask the same of you. I thought it time to visit my wayward son, he's been over there burning through his trust." She touches her hand to my brow.

My buxom blonde rolls her eyes and leaves, muttering something about rudeness. I don't care, for I know for certain what delights my new companion can offer.

"Has your wandering eye finally caught up with you? Or have you finally run out of English women to bed, and so must start afresh in a new land?"

"I fancied a change of scenery."

"I hope that's not all you fancy." Her gray eyes flick down to my lips.

The obsession I felt from seventeen to twenty-two returns full force. I may have chased other women when Lady Rose Harrington didn't have time for me, but I'd always come back, chained and bound to her as I was. I rub the fading marks around my wrists.

"Do you travel with Lord Harrington?" I ask, hoping that she will tell me he is no more. The smarmy git seemed an ancient thing ready to keel over at any moment when I met him fifteen years ago. Surely, he can't still be hanging on?

"No." Hope rises in my chest. "He passed last autumn."

"Such a shame!" I say, with all the fake sincerity I can muster. "So Maxwell has inherited his full title?"

"You know better than to say such utter bollocks to me, Lorelei. You couldn't care less about the fact he's dead. You hated the nights where I had to make my presence in his bed known." She leans in, the scent of rosewater filling my nostrils. "I know you better than anyone. Remember, I made you."

My heart skips as I remember the first time she took me to her bed, and all at once I'm as destabilized as I was at seventeen. She was as old then as I am now, so beautiful, so experienced. I worshiped her. The way her skin, covered in a sheen of sweat, glinted in the candlelight as she lay atop the sheets. Her ebony hair, free from its usual braid, fanned out in gentle waves beneath her. She'd been so vocal, directing me in every movement. Patient but firm in her lessons, she'd taught me all the subtleties of feminine pleasure.

Viola once said that I needed a woman, not a girl, and here she is.

"May–maybe–I can keep you company for the rest of the voyage?" I curse myself, as the shyness of my youth, thought long conquered, takes hold of me. But I've learnt so much in the eleven years since I was last in her bed, maybe she'd let me teach her this time.

"I've grown bored of this place, Lorelei. There's a rather fine bottle of whiskey in my room. I had intended it for Maxwell to enjoy, but what he doesn't know ..." She places a hand on the small of my back to direct me. "Would you like that?"

I swallow hard. "I'd like that immensely."

***

"Tell me, Lorelei." Rose reclines on the bed, a tumbler of liquid the honey hue of Viola's eyes in her hand. "What have you been up to?" As she speaks, she taps the side of her glass with her ring finger, her wedding band causing the crystal to ring. It's a pleasing sound, gold on crystal. It's quality and wealth. Warm beds and full stomachs.

"Nothing of interest."

"Still in the seance game?"

"No." I take a sip of whiskey. "Not anymore."

"Have you even a plan? When you get to America?"

"No." I take a deeper draft.

"Thought you could get by on charm alone?"

"Something like that." I drain the glass. "Anyways, I didn't think we were 'ere to talk." My step forward turns into a stumble. The heat of the liquor radiates from my chest into my shoulders. It's been years since I've drank anything of strength, and I partook of it rather too quickly. I manage to deposit myself on the bed next to her.

"Who is she?"

"Who?"

"The woman who's broken your heart."

I scoot up so that I'm sitting next to her and pluck the glass from her hand, finishing it, before setting it down on the bedside table.

"She's nothin' to me." *She's everything to me.*

"Come here." I let her arms close around me. It feels nice to be held. When I shut my eyes, I can nearly pretend … I crane my head upwards, placing a kiss on her jaw, then another and another, moving along until I reach her lips.

She turns her head away.

"Don't you want me?"

She looks at me as though I'm a petulant child, and I suppose I am. "Yes, but not like this."

The rejection, though kind, stings, and my eyes drift to the bottle with its Viola-coloured contents. They'd be in bed by now. Would Adele curl into her as she did me? Allow herself to be enveloped by her warmth? I settle in beside Rose.

"You know that you're your own worst enemy, don't you? The way you keep everything bottled up. Maybe you should try telling the truth, if not to me then to yourself."

We lay in silence for a few minutes, her hand rubbing up and down my back whilst I fiddle with her pendant. It feels strange beneath my fingertips, like a plait of hair plated in silver. Would it lessen the pain to finally tell the truth? I take a deep breath.

"I did a bad thing." She doesn't respond or push for elaboration. "I betrayed her." She doesn't ask who "her" is. "I f—went with another, while I was still with her."

"Not the first time you've done that."

I tense in her arms. "First time I done it t' someone I love."

"And it's too late to set right?"

"She 'as some other tart."

"And when did you ever let that stop you?"

We fall silent again. Once Rose's breathing slows into that of deep sleep, I carefully extract myself from her and pull the covers over her.

Yes, when did I ever let that stop me?

***

It's more luck than judgment that I make it to the stateroom without getting lost or doing damage to myself. The bottle clutched in my hand is down to the halfway mark, lighter, and I continue to make it lighter still. I stumble in the near dark, tripping over some unknown object, causing me to lose my grip on my bottle.

"Bloody hellfire!"

Someone bangs on the wall. "Quiet out there."

"Oh, hush your gums," I retort as I pick up my miraculously unbroken bottle. Resoluteness has damped the anger of the previous days. I *can* and *will* get her back.

I will get down on my knees and beg if need be. Aware of the late hour, I knock softly. Scarcely a minute passes before Viola flings it open. Her usual sneer is absent tonight, replaced by a previously unseen weariness.

"What do you want?"

"Just to talk to Adele, nothin' more."

"Then talk." She glances down, examining her nails.

"You need to clean your tabs out. I want to talk to Adele. Not you."

She sighs. "You're the last person she wants to talk to after your ever so loving parting word to her."

Freak. Shame fills me, that I could ever have uttered so vile a word to her is incomprehensible to me now. "Please, will you ask her?"

"Fine." She closes the door in my face, leaving me to wait. I hear hushed tones, but cannot decipher their meaning. I take another swig from my bottle, just in time for Viola to open the door and catch me. "She doesn't wish to speak with you. I suggest you leave. Take care not to stumble overboard on your way back to your hovel." She moves to shut the door again, but I quickly put my foot in between it and the frame.

"Will you tell 'er something, please?"

Viola rolls her eyes before nodding.

"Tell 'er that I'm sorry, for everythin'. I—I was wrong."

She presses on the door, that bloody sneer on her lips, no intention of passing my words on to Adele. No, I won't leave without speaking to Adele myself. I push past Viola and tumble into the room.

Adele jolts upward in her bed, the sheets beside her mussed. A quick glance to my right confirms that Viola's bed is flawlessly made.

"Adele?"

"Lorelei, what are you—"

Viola tosses her hands into the air, door slamming behind her. "She insisted."

"I had come to tell you I missed you, hoped that you were missing me but now I'm not so sure. You 'aven't missed me at all, have you? Got that slag to replace me already. Tell me, Viola, would you be so quick in my grave as you were 'er cunt? Both of 'em still warm with the memory of me."

"Lorelei!" Adele gasps.

Viola leans backward against her vanity, eyes darting between us.

"You've got quite a bit of gall forcing your way in here, hurling venom." Adele throws the blanket aside and scrambles to her feet. "A poor memory too, it seems. Have you forgotten your new lover already? Forgotten that you too fu … laid with Viola." Stomping across the room, she throws open Viola's trunk, grabbing the harness and whipping it in my direction. "Look familiar?"

"Yes," I put a hand to the back of my neck as I take another drink. "Maybe if you'd excited me more, I would have fucked you with something similar."

Viola chuckles, biting at her lips to seal in the sound.

"Well." Adele clenches her jaw and smooths her shift. "I'll just add that to the list of apologies I'll never receive from you." She advances, grasping me by the shoulder and leading me toward the door. "I trust you can find your way back to your hovel. Just follow the stench."

I plant my feet. "You ungrateful little bitch, do you know what I gave up for you? Do you even bloody care?"

"What *you* gave up? What *you* gave up, for *me?*" Adele shrieks.

"I sold the last remnant of my life before you, for that *hovel*, and don't think I didn't notice that you used her word. I sold it for you. Regardless of what you might think, Adele, I 'ad a life before you. A life where I didn't have to worry constantly about you, a life where I had fun." I wish this bloody ship would stop swaying for just one fucking second.

"Then I encourage you to return to it." She grabs the handle, ready to usher me out.

No, I can't go yet, not after having let my temper get the better of me once more. I have to fix this.

"I'm sorry, I didn't mean it. You're my life." I try to grab at her wrist but my hand closes around empty air. I adjust my aim, reaching out a foot to the left of where I thought Adele was standing the first time, this time finding solid flesh. "Yer coming with me. I can make you feel things she never—"

She twists away. "Viola!"

A firm hand grabs the back of my neck, and I spin to find Viola leering down at me. "That's quite enough." My quick movement makes the room sway, but I feel the rush of air as Viola pushes me out the door, feel the lights in the hall beat against the back of my eyeballs.

As the stateroom door eases shut, I catch one last look at Adele, her cheeks beetroot red, shoulders rising and falling with anxious breaths, and Viola's arm encircling her. *You're alright,* I think I hear Viola tell her, before the latch clicks and lock turns.

***

The last thing I remember is collapsing, fully dressed, on the bed. Yet I'm naked and beneath covers when I awake. Rose sits on the edge of the mattress, sipping from a fine china cup.

"I thought you might have saved a little more for me." She indicates the bottle on the nightstand with a smile; only a quarter of its contents remain. "I'm not a young woman anymore, Lorelei. Getting you out of those clothes and into bed properly near killed me. All the while you muttering about 'that bitch' and how it's 'over'." She finishes her drink and sets the cup down before lying beside me. She brushes the hair back from my brow and places a kiss there. My whole body shivers.

Adele isn't the only one who can find solace in another. I said I was sorry, tried to get her to come with me, and yet still she closed the door on me, on us.

"I'll look after you," Rose says, trailing her fingers along my jaw and down my neck.

Maybe it would be nice, for once, to be looked after by another. "Promise?"

"Always and forever. You know what I'll expect in return." She pulls her shift over her head and settles back onto the pillows. "But I think you'll be more than happy to provide it."

I place myself between her legs, my palms either side of her ribs so I hover above her.

She runs a hand over my right bicep. "So strong."

It takes all my being not to tremble at her words. "Yes?"

"Yes. Why don't you show me what you can do with it?"

I hook an arm under her, bringing her with me as I sit up, so she straddles me. Her hands are everywhere as she kisses me: entwined in my hair one moment, clawing down my back the next. I'm sure there was a time when Adele kissed me like this, as if the world might end at any moment. When Rose nips at my earlobe and whispers, *"I need you inside me,"* I growl.

"Tell me more."

"I want you to put me on my stomach, take those skilful fingers and fuck me, hard."

Adele never wanted me like this, only made nagging suggestions as to how I might become more like the women she wished I was. Viola can have her.

But Rose, Rose knows the game well, she taught it to me after all. She'll tell me exactly how she wants me, and I will always oblige her.

***

"I didn't realize how much I missed this, missed you," Rose says, her head on my chest as her hand makes lazy circles on my hip. "Why did you disappear, Lorelei?"

My jaw tightens. "You know why."

"You weren't the only one who was scared. When I found you … I'd never seen so much blood."

"Well, you weren't the one it was puthering out of." I push her away as I sit up. "You loved passing me around amongst your friends, and their friends. Your little bit of rough that you picked up off the street. It was only a matter of time before you let the wrong person play with me. Do you even remember who had me that night?"

"I think you exaggerate somewhat, Lorelei. You went to their beds quite willingly. You liked the gifts and the money, but most of all you loved the power it gave you. Ever since you discovered the ability to make women shatter beneath your fingertips you've chased the thrill of it again and again."

I settle back down on the bed and close my eyes against flashes of silver and amber. One thing I can remember from that night is a blade cunningly hidden within a piece of jewelry, a thick copper cuff adorned with silver braidwork.

Braidwork very much like Viola's ring. Braidwork very much like Rose's pendant. I reach over, moving my hand over Rose's breasts until I find the metal braid nestled betwixt them. I pick it up. "I like this."

"I liked what you were doing a moment ago a lot more."

"Where did you get it?"

"It was a gift." She catches my wrist, bringing it to her mouth. Her tone is feather soft, but her eyes are steel. "Why the interest?""No reason." I drop the pendant and move my hand down between her legs. "No reason at all."

Chapter 20: Any Sign of Love

Adele

After the incident in the lower deck, I find it prudent to keep to the room. For the first couple of days, I'd half-expected Lorelei to turn up, or, at the very least, slip a note beneath the door. But she has not, and I no longer suffer the delusion of her spending nights wide-eyed, staring at the water-stained ceiling, thinking of me.

Viola tells me the truth. She mentions it in passing, as if remarking on the weather.

"Quite the dark-haired beauty Lorelei has found herself." She stirs her tea and sucks droplets the color of her eyes from the spoon. "Do you think our last encounter left her seeking closure, as it did me?"

I am numb to the prod. It joins with the ocean of hurt already frozen inside me, just one more layer of thickness. What difference can it make now?

"Or perhaps I am vain, and it's nothing to do with me at all. Perhaps she simply wanted a change of …" Her gaze passes over my pale hair. "Scenery."

I've learned better than to show emotion.

My face holds perfectly still. I make a game of keeping my breath even.

In, I breathe, and out. "I should think she would struggle to replace you." Arching my back, I fill my chest with air, and relax when she curls her lips into a satisfied smile.

"Struggle indeed." Viola turns her body toward the window and sips her tea, steam enveloping her jaw.

As tension thins, I allow myself to relax. I have passed this small test. Many times a day she tempts me, digging at me with or without her small knife, searching my body and spirit for any sign of love for Lorelei.

"I prefer to watch you struggle." She rewards my coolness with a wink.

It brings me no pleasure, too many barricades between her words and my heart. But I inscribe the sentiment in my memory to return to later, when her testing has ceased and I open myself to her.

"Thank you," I say.

"Such a lucky thing that I found you. Let her leech off some other unsuspecting fool." With this she crosses the room and stands before the edge of the bed where I sit. A caress of my cheek draws my eyes to a close, and I nuzzle into her palm. "Never knew how good she had it, did she?"

I reach for her hip to pull her closer, but she recedes like a parting tide.

"A fine treasure, you are." She sets her cup and saucer upon the silver serving tray and sits before the vanity, smoothing an errant strand of hair and securing it with a pin.

"Very kind of you to say." I must make myself strong. I know not whether Viola can truly care for me, but I suppose I will never find out if I cannot make myself worthy of such a thing.

"What's the use anyway?" Viola sighs, a long, drawn-out thing.

"The use?"

She motions toward the window. "Of beautifying oneself in such tumultuous weather." With a quick swing of her arm, she clears the vanity of all products and tools, causing me to startle.

"You might join me in bed." I invite her, leaning back onto my arm.

"What do you think will disturb our neighbors more?" Viola moves to the opposite bedside, and when I turn my head to hold her gaze, she turns it back with a rough grab at my chin. "The chop of the sea? Or the way I shall make you scream?"

I feel the scarlet flush of my cheeks, but dare not look back at her as she unfastens the top button of my dress.

"Tell me about your family, Addie."

Button after button pops from its clutch as I consider whether to let this slight pass. "I wish you wouldn't—"

A snatch at the fabric of my already tight bodice pushes the air from my lungs. "And why is that? Who called you Addie, and how did they so thoroughly disgust you that you shudder at the sound?"

I must choose my words carefully. "There was a man to whom I was promised, an Englishman living in New York until, I suspect, he inherited some nobler title and familial wealth."

More buttons loose. The fabric slacks, enough that I might take a deep breath.

"And?"

"And he had this scent about him, slick and chemical. From the oil, you see." I'm not making sense, and I know it. Viola's hands have moved away and my thoughts fix on where they will next land.

Hot breath lands in the crook of my neck. "The oil?"

"It stained his fingers as well, great black divots around the nail. The thought of those hands burrowed beneath covers on our wedding night, his greasy hair staining the pillowcase … He called me Addie."

Viola tugs at my bodice, then at the shift beneath, exposing my chest to the cool air. "Enough horror to cross an ocean. Is that right?"

Thoughtlessly, she pinches at my right nipple, tugs, releases it, then pinches again.

"That's right." The words come out uneven, but I try not to squirm.

"And your mother?" She reaches for my skirt, hiking it up over my knees.

"I cannot think of—"

"Your mother, Adele." She pinches again, and this time twists.

I cry out despite myself. "My mother thought it a fine match." The explanation races from my lips. "And my father as well."

"That wasn't so hard."

I shake my head, eyes cast downward. Seemingly pleased with the position, she grips me by the root of my hair, holding my neck in place, and with her other hand sinks her claws into my thigh above the knee, raking them upward and stopping just short of my center.

"Are you an only child, Adele?"

The circle she traces over my hosiery is hard to ignore. If this is some new test, I've not devised its purpose.

"It would explain your spoilt nature."

"I have a brother—" My breath comes heavy as she begins to stroke me. "George."

"And what was the man's name? The one who intended to fuck you with those filthy fingers?" Dipping beneath the fabric of my undergarments, she plunges her own inside me.

"Lord …" It's a whisper. She presses against me and I try again. "Lord Harrington."

I hear my slickness as she makes quick work of me. Releasing her hold on my hair, I crane my neck and land a kiss on her cheek before the intensity of the strain forces me to turn back and face the window. A crack of thunder reverberates over the sea as she pries my knee toward her, fully opening me for her taking.

"If I had a gift such as yours …"

The pressure firms. My belly clenches tight, pleasure forming a knot at my center.

"And remade myself now in the image of Lord Harrington …"

Do not speak his name, not now when I'm so close.

"Would you let him fuck you?"

Pushed by the coarse word or detestable notion, I shatter, my moans covered partially by another roll of thunder. Yet still she thrusts inside me. I move to close my legs, in case my cry was not sign enough that I had finished, but she jerks my knee back, rubbing even more quickly and with more force.

I twist my body up and away from her, then curse myself for the reflex, for I know she will despise it.

"Imagine it's him inside you now, his black nails in your most sensitive place."

Without seeing her eyes, I sense they are aflame. Such strength she has, clutching me at all sides. Unable to move away, I've no choice but to suffer her, bleating like a wounded animal.

"Can you smell him, Addie?"

"Viola, please!"

"Address him properly."

Tears gather behind my eyes. "Please!"

"Properly."

"Please, my lord."

"Now look at me."

The sensation is unbearably strong.

"Look at me when you say it."

I pivot, twist my back and neck, but can't see her eyes. I flail in the other direction, a shooting pain snaking down my spine as I meet her gaze long enough to shriek, "Please, my lord!"

With that, she stops. Her slick fingers slide from my undergarments, leaving a damp trail over the curve of my hip and stinging the friction burn she will not let heal. Coils creak and the angle of the mattress changes. I follow Viola's movements by the rustle of her skirts and lie on my side. The first drops of rain give way to a torrent, driving sheets that bounce off the waves.

"What do you say?"

Swirling thoughts of my family mix with the sharp scent of pleasure. A kick of nausea.

Viola clears her throat.

"Thank you." My voice is as small as a dormouse.

"What's that?"

I ball my fists, digging crescents into my palms where she cannot see. "Thank you," I say more firmly.

"Better," she mutters. "I'm going for some air. Stay here."

A quarter of an hour passes while I lay dormant, undergarments still hiked to the side where Viola left them. When finally I rise, I move straight to the washroom and strip myself of all evidence of the tryst. I right my hair, rebraiding the band that moves from my left ear to the dip of my neck on the right side. This was my mother's preferred hairstyle for travel, though her locks were stained a dirtier blonde, made ashy by age.

How I craved her attention and approval! So seldom did I see her, mere glances between trips with my father. I knew better the portrait of her, hanging above the mantle. I whispered to it on many occasions, but stopped when George caught me and mocked me tirelessly for weeks on end.

The thick oaf had skill only for tyranny. He failed abysmally in his studies, his attempts at French sounding more like the slurring of a drunken street urchin than the language of romance. "George, son, you'd make a better horse than accountant," my father said to him once after eyeing his arithmetic. And there was something to that, perhaps, as George spent the better part of his time at the races, throwing good money after bad on thing after 'sure thing'. He was hundreds in the hole by the time I left.

I rub the spot on my arm where his bookmaker grabbed me on my way to ship, hard enough I dropped my trunk. I'm sure he thought I'd gone white as a specter for fear of him, but it was fear of being stopped that struck me. I hadn't cared much about his threat to chop my hair and sell it to pay George's debt, only that he didn't ask after where I was headed or how I'd procured my ticket, and when St. Louis cleared her port, I harbored a secret hope he'd find George and cut off his ginger locks to sell as a merkin.

Hours of solitude lead me to wonder about my family. How might they receive me after I left them without a word? Allowed years to pass without so much as a letter confirming my health? Would George still be cross with me for stealing the ticket? Had he ever even noticed it amongst his stash of winnings?

I've time enough to imagine all of them: Mother and Father returning from trips to ask after me, 'Any word?' George shaking his head, pleased to continue his reign as favorite child until he's shackled in irons and hauled away to debtor's prison. I wonder about the small burial plot on Mornington's grounds, and whether they've erected a headstone and inscribed my name, thinking me dead. Surely Lord Harrington has taken some other hostage in matrimony, so I must be safe from that.

***

When Viola returns, dusk has fallen and the storm has cleared. She is in unusually good spirits, moving about the suite with light steps as if floating. I've changed into evening wear, though I'm quite sure she will call for dinner rather than taking me out, and I needlessly press down about the audacious, scarlet fabric to draw her attention.

It doesn't work.

She rifles through drawers of her own vanity, and I begin to feel silly standing and waiting for her praise.

"You were quite right about the dress," I say, trying something less subtle. "It fits like a dream."

"Wonderful," she says without looking.

I take two steps toward her. "A generous gift."

Finally she turns, giving my outfit a quick glance. "Could be tighter in the waist." Her still-swollen mouth twists into a frown. "We'll see to that when we get to New York."

I cradle her hips and pull myself close, suddenly desperate for the smallest validation. She grants me a kiss, for which I linger too long and feel her lips slacken and go cold.

"You smell of rosewater," I say.

"Do I?" She turns from me, grabs the book at her nightstand and flips to the earmarked page.

"Where did you go?"

"For air." Her finger glides along the paper, though I know she is not reading.

"And it took all afternoon to find it?"

Her brows raise in annoyance. "A needy one, aren't you?"

"It's just …" I curl the fabric of my skirt around my hands. "You asked me to wait for you."

With a sigh, she drops the book to her lap. "Did I? Or did I tell you to stay here? Tell me, is it poor memory or a propensity for lying that drives you to twist my words?"

"I—"

"Need I remind you, I am not your beau. You had a lover you could call to task over too long wanderings, but you tossed that out the moment you had a more alluring alternative."

My shoulders drop.

"Don't fret. You've traded up by ridding yourself of her. I pass no judgment on your clinging to her as you did, desperate times and measures, as they say. In any case, she looked quite happy tonight, parading around with her brunette. You needn't feel guilty."

It is not guilt I feel, but a stab at my chest like sucking in icy water. "And you? Were you with another woman tonight?"

"Take care not to pester me, Adele. You remain here on my dime, and you'll do well to remember that."

I sink to the bed. The thought of cowering back to that hellish stateroom and begging Lorelei to receive me between visits with this new woman is enough to turn my stomach over.

"If it comforts you to know," Viola adds, "I was not with a woman."

It does comfort me, more so when I hear her pad over to my bed. "Do you swear it?"

She stands over me and has never looked so tall. "Your mind is full of the worst possibilities, little dove." Taking a seat beside me, she strokes my hair. "No need to punish yourself unnecessarily."

Her lips meet mine, soft and warm once again. I ignore the cloying scent of rosewater and take her tongue into my mouth. Intrusive flashes of Lorelei's hands woven into dark hair, my mother's back as she drags luggage, George rifling through my things, make me hungry for distraction, for something akin to love.

"You finished me," I say between breaths, "but not yourself."

"Would it please you to prove your worth to me?" Viola lies back, parting her legs enough for me to slip between them.

"It would."

She hikes up her skirt, pressing her hand to the back of my head to guide me. "Then let me put your mind at ease."

Chapter 21: No Fault of My Own

Lorelei

Rose has kept me busy these last few days as we fast approach America. She is insatiable, only allowing me to leave her bed to tend to my basic needs. Day and night have merged; I doze between bouts of servicing her, paying no heed to clock or sun. Time always did come undone in her presence.

"As much as I hate the thought, you're going to have to remove yourself from that bed soon," Rose says as she sits at the vanity, putting on a pair of diamond earrings.

I burrow my head under the cover in protest. Leaving the safety of this room, this ship, would mean having to face that Adele is not coming back to me. I want to stay in this remnant of the past, remain forever in limbo.

"You must have some things to attend to before we reach port. A change of clothes for example."

Chester! I've left Chester to fend for himself, as he'd been left to do all his life by his mother. "Yes, I do have things I need to do."

I dress quickly. Just as I'm about to leave, Rose grabs me by my wrist, pulling me to her. "Don't disappear again, Lorelei. I meant what I said about looking after you. Whatever you desire you can have, so long as you continue to please me." She lets go and turns away, so smug in her certainty that I will return to her.

***

Guilt and panic ease when I find Chester on the deck, moving seamlessly through the crowd, liberating watches and money from pockets and handbags as he goes. He is quite amazing in his skill, but to tell him such would only serve to encourage him and I want him to do better, be better than this.

It's several moments before he twigs to my presence, bounding over to me with a wide grin. I suppose my disappearance hasn't bothered him as much as I thought it might.

"Alreyt, Lore?"

"Yes, I'm alright. Won't be long until we reach land, so we need to think about what we're going to do when we get there."

I consider taking him back to Rose's room and explaining that, through no real fault of my own, I'm his guardian. I don't think she'd like that though; she's happy to take care of me, but a child would be unthinkable. I've never asked Rose just how long she'd planned on staying in New York. Maybe if I arranged a place to stay for Chester until she was ready to go home … I'm sure he'd be happy enough, running around the city. I could visit him every other day or so, and he has always harbored a fascination with 'city life'.

We go back to the state room and it's only then I realize I've left my clothing and meager possessions in Viola's room. With hesitant steps and balled fists, I make my way there, steeling myself for the worst. I run through every scenario: hearing Adele's moans through the walls, Viola's wretched name coming from her sweet lips, the pair of them answering my knock naked, barely stopping their kisses when they see me. But as I turn down the hall, I'm relieved of my worst fantasies. My bags have been packed and await my pickup just outside the door.

***

My heart pounds as we disembark the ship. I don't know what would happen to Chester should he be caught without papers, though he assures me he has a plan. I've told him Rose and I will be staying at the Astoria on Fifth Avenue and to come find me there. The line moves quickly for First Class passengers, their papers only getting the most perfunctory of glances. The queue shortens, and my worry for Chester intensifies. As Rose's papers are examined by the customs officer, her status as a lady evidently of great interest and novelty to him, an object hits him square in the face, and a short, brown haired blur races by. As I approach the officer who, while rather taken aback, is unharmed, I spot a single leather shoe on the ground.

Chester is going to be just fine.

***

New York is so easy to navigate, set out in little squares as it is, and Chester wastes no time in finding me. Though Rose would bestow upon me anything my heart desires, she will not allow me to have cash. That would give me too many options, too many chances to strike out on my own.

So, with Chester unable to stay with me at the hotel, we'll be forced to make our own coin. During his time on board, he managed to procure a few American dollars. We'll quadruple and then double it again in an afternoon.

We wander a few blocks down away from the hotel, where finely dressed men and women rush to their destinations. We find a street vendor selling salted knotted bread and purchase one before inserting ourselves into the throng of people. I hold Chester's hand as he clutches the pretzel. It isn't long before, with a slight angling of his body on Chester's part, a man bumps into him, knocking his treat to the ground.

"Sir!"

The man glances briefly down towards Chester, but does not stop.

"I say, sir!" He lets out a *humph*, and turns around to face Chester who, with a wet gleam in his eyes, is pointing at the ground. "Knocked it right out me hand."

"And?"

"That's the first thing I've had in days."

"Get your mother to buy you a new one."

"Sir," I say, drawing Chester close to me. "My husband, David's father, came to America some months ago on the promise of work and a better life. We left everything behind to come out here to be with him, only to find that he's set up home with some …" I cover Chester's ears. "With some tart. We've no money left for the boarding house or food, let alone the passage home and—"

The man digs into his pocket, producing a dollar bill, which he thrusts violently into my hand. "Buy the boy some food."

Once the man is safely out of sight, Chester picks the pretzel up, dusts it off, and we start again.

A few hours later, as Chester eats the pretzel, despite my telling him we could buy him a new one which hasn't been on the ground a hundred times over, we count our earnings.

"Waste not, want not," he says, stuffing his cheeks. "How much we got?"

"Enough to keep you off the streets and fed for a fortnight."

"Who's that woman, Lore?"

"Who do you mean?" I know full well who he means. His silence presses me to continue. "She's just a friend, from a long time ago."

Chester regards me with eyes that are far too knowing for a lad his age. "Friend?" He says the word so strangely, as though unsure of its weight and meaning.

"Yes." I have to turn away from him. How is it he has the ability to strip me bare?

"Like how you and Adele were *friends*? Like her and that woman are now *friends*?"

"Yes."

"Lore, you're a bloody idiot. Even I can see that you miss her, that she misses you."

I shake my head. "She doesn't miss me."

"She, er, came looking for you."

"What?" I turn to look at him so quickly I feel a twinge in my neck.

He looks downwards, shuffling his feet. "I was so mad at her for hurting you. I thought you didn't need her, but I think I was wrong."

"And why do you think that?"

"Your eyes." He says with the honesty that only small children are capable of. "They're sad."

I'd given up too quickly, believing that the door had not only been shut on us but barricaded as well. But she came looking for me.

"And did she … When Adele came, did she look—"

"Sad." He nods, biting at the skin inside his cheek.

Fuck. I have to find her. I have to explain, to apologize properly. I shake my head, recalling in bits and fragments the night I went to the stateroom. If there's a chance I could make things right … I will find her. And I will tear New York apart, if need be, to do so.

Chapter 22: Return to Mornington

Adele

The city of New York invites me into its great mouth. Honking horns and hollered solicitations of all manner of goods, towering buildings I could so easily slip between, and the flurry of people, smartly dressed and beggars alike; enough movement to drown in. The last thing I want to do is trade one ship for another.

"Steamboat's the most expedient route," Viola reminds me. I suppose she has taken notice of how I stare into the chaos of the city. Deeply, I breathe its fumes. Couldn't be further from Matlock in distance or disposition. "We can hail a cab or …"

A gull spirals down, snatching a loaf of bread from an open-air stand.

"Adele!" She stamps her foot as she says it, the combination enough to steal my attention.

"A cab sounds just fine," I say, not having heard the alternative.

With a wave she summons one, driven by a man who, seeing the fine silk of her gloves and delicate embroidery of her skirts, is far too eager to pander for a tip.

"Lovely day, ladies!" He scrambles from the driver's seat, tripping over himself to open the trunk.

I peer over top the wall of industry. Slate gray sky, nearly the same shade as steel.

"If you say so."

"Adele, watch your manners. A fine day, to be sure. We are headed to the docks with a mind to catch the next steamboat to Lloyd Neck."

"Ah, Lloyd Neck!" There are dollar signs in his eyes. "Of course, ma'am." He scuttles to stow our trunks and makes a show of opening the rear door to grant us entry. "First time in the city?"

Viola ushers me past her with firm pressure on my hip. Only a last-minute duck keeps my head from hitting the door frame. "Hardly," she says.

With the doors shut, one shoulder touches the window while the other touches Viola's. The driver babbles on about the weather, taking turns at a speed which knocks me into the window, and attempts to ask after our plans for the evening, but Viola ignores him, directing her attention to me.

"A long-awaited reunion, *hm*?"

"I wouldn't say so." I flush, wishing she would keep her voice down.

"How will dear old Mom and Dad receive you after all this time?"

I spot an arch in the driver's unruly brow through the rearview mirror, and hold my hand at an awkward angle so he can't easily see my face.

"I suppose we will find out together." It's a harsh whisper. Viola takes my meaning enough to back off the subject, yet cares little enough for my comfort to broach an easy one.

"Did you spot her?"

"I don't follow."

"Lorelei. I assume that's who you were craning your neck to see as we disembarked the ship."

I press my chin to my chest. If I could climb completely into my dress, I would. "No."

More loudly, she says, "No, you weren't trying to spot Lorelei? Or no you didn't see her?"

"Neither."

Viola leans close; these words are just for me. "Liar. Ungrateful liar."

Ungrateful?

"You should be relieved."

"Relieved?" I no longer care whether the driver hears me.

"I spared you the indignity of confessing your ruse. You must realize she would have left you anyway, when she discovered there was no uncle, no fortune, no further pennies she could squeeze from you. I'm sure you're not that dense."

I fold my arms and press my forehead to the window, conceding that she is likely right: Lorelei would have left me one way or another.

The remainder of the ride is much the same, as is the steamboat trip to Lloyd Neck. Only when we reach the dock does Viola ease up on me, perhaps sensing my trepidation around returning to Mornington. The air is not salty as I remembered, but laden with the stink of fetid shellfish. As Viola waxes on about finding us a coach, making no secret of the cost of our extra travel on my behalf, I study the shoreline.

Clams lay open, rotting where the tide laps in. Movement in the shallows, which at first I clock as fish, turns out to be no more than slimy lengths of abandoned rope, a rusty, forgotten crab trap. My head is heavy with travel fatigue, and when I slide beside Viola in the coach, I rest it on her shoulder.

"Rest while you can, little dove."

The clopping of hooves on packed earth nearly lulls me to sleep. I suppose the journey has wearied Viola too, for she doesn't shrug me off or prod me with questions for the length of the ride. It's peaceful. Calm and still as an empty sky before a summer storm.

The storm arrives, however, when the clang of Mornington's gate sends a jolt of anxiety, waking every one of my nerves. In something of a daze, I clutch Viola's hand, expecting at first to find Lorelei's. Her cold rings—or the looming prospect of confronting my family—chills me. I have a fleeting thought that I might enact my ability, transform myself into someone they wouldn't recognize, and avoid the ordeal altogether. But it's foolishness, I know. For the whole point of this detour is to ask after whether they'd be willing to extend a loan while I …

While I what?

The realization creeps at first, like moss over a stone, then inundates like I'm falling through a frozen lake: While I find a husband, of course. There are no other terms they might find agreeable. While Mother and Father's pockets are deep, they would not 'throw good money after bad', writing endless blank checks without the promise of some future stability, even to their own daughter. On my own, I've no prospects. Only a suitable marriage would grant my independence from them, a fact they have long known, and so endeavored to marry me off years ago.

Viola runs a finger over the goosed skin of my forearm. "Ready?"

The driveway is long, winding around a fountain at its center, but not nearly long enough. Once calming hoofbeats now pound away the pumping of my heart, counting down my last seconds before I step back inside the high society world of my birth, the expectations therein. Arched windows and wrought iron terraces glance down from their high places. Behind the sheer curtains, at any one of them, could be my father, or mother, or brother. Any or all might already be planning a new betrothal, might already be poised to run me off the property—I cannot figure which would be worse.

The coach pulls to a stop, horses stamping their frustration at the change in pace.

"Adele?"

Great wooden doors clad in the same gaudy adornments: iron hinges, a cherub seemingly holding the door-knocker in her feet.

Lorelei would've poked fun at the—

Lorelei would've …

Quiet.

A swirl of black.

I'm only aware I've slumped over when Viola pushes me back upright. Her hands are hot against my cheek and forehead, and I'm coated in damp. A shiver jostles my shoulders.

"Get her some water."

Footsteps fade, then a smack of flesh on wood.

I remember where I am and nearly swoon again, but Viola bats my face with her palm. A minute or so passes, Viola content to let me close my eyes so long as I return her squeezes of my palm.

Cool glass touches my lips and water dribbles down my chin until I push its bearer away. Fuzzy vision clears enough to see Viola and a figure behind her peering into the cab. His ginger hair is trimmed, his beard tamed into a gentlemanly shape.

"George?"

He's less rugged than I left him, wearing a tailored suit and holding himself in a manner which might have me believe him noble, did I not already know better.

"Your sister has had a trying journey," Viola offers. "Are you well enough to walk?"

"I'll get your things." George doesn't move to take the bags, rather he motions with his arm, and two men I don't recognize come to retrieve them. "Your old room has been converted to guest quarters, but the house is quite vacant and I trust you will still be comfortable there. As for ..."

"Viola. My travel companion." My voice is thin but my mind is steady enough to offer up this explanation.

"Viola. We have an additional guest suite which should suit you."

Viola steadies my hand as I move from the cab to the great wooden doors of Mornington. George trails a few feet behind. I feel his ire upon me, await the sparring questions. We are nearly to the staircase when finally they come.

"What great fortune has returned you to us, sister? We feared the worst, years without so much as a word."

"Can a daughter not simply wish to visit her family?" The foyer is deathly quiet, not so much as a distant, echoing footstep on the marble. "Where are Mother and Father?"

"Traveling, I'm afraid." There's a smugness to his voice. How it must delight him to know I've come such a great distance only to be disappointed.

"Traveling."

Viola must sense the impending spat, for she intercedes. "We apologize, of course, for turning up unannounced. It was most unseemly.

Had the trip been better planned, we would have sent word far in advance. As it stands, I am sure a man of your position must have business to attend to. I trust a member of your staff can show me to my quarters."

"Quite right." George nods, replaced by the two men weighed down heavily by our baggage. The seemingly older man, shocks of gray streaked through his auburn hair, speaks first.

"This way, Miss—"

"Marwood."

"And Miss Hughes, Robin here will escort you with your luggage, though I am sure you know the way."

The men lead us up opposite sides of the twin staircase, an exercise in pomp, as they both lead to the same landing. From there, Viola and I part ways, I to my room in the east wing, and Viola to her guest quarters in the west.

It's a strange thing, returning to my childhood bedroom. One would never know a child slept here, though I suppose my parents were never the type to adorn their home with dolls or anything else that might interest a young girl. It is changed, nonetheless. My once yellow walls have been papered with a tropical pattern, deep green palm fronds the color of Lorelei's eyes. The wainscotting's been stained a deep walnut, and the bed is dressed in beige linen. The effect is something of a sad replica of tropical paradise. I can almost picture my mother, jazzed from a trip to Grand Cayman or Belize, insisting on bringing a bit of it home with her.

Robin offers to unpack my bags but I shoo him away, eager to rest after the long and arduous voyage. Happily, solitude comes easily. Viola must be equally tired of company, for no one comes to call on me all evening. The only disturbance is a gentle rap at the door, after which I find a plated dinner. Mother and Father would never allow me to eat in my bedroom. George must be telling the truth. They are gone after all.

I lie in my bed, both familiar and strange, and wonder where Lorelei and Chester sleep tonight. Imagining them swatting roaches in some hovel makes my stomach twist with guilt, but they are resourceful. They could have so easily procured money through one scheme or another. And perhaps they had no cause to. If Lorelei was as happy as Viola said with her new beau, maybe she's not asleep at all. Maybe she writhes against her, sweaty, fingers tangled in brunette strands of hair. The thought makes my skin hum with dull pain. Briefly I consider making my way to Viola's guest suite, stripping my clothes and climbing beneath the sheets beside her.

For revenge? No. That's not it.

I don't realize I've dug my fingernails into my forearm until a bead of blood appears. The sight of it, a vermillion pearl against my fair skin, calms me. Once more I grate at my flesh, clawing three ragged lines. The sting silences the torment in my heart. But I can only do so much; pain by my own hand is limited by my strength of spirit.

I sit up. Viola would be happy to lend her expertise. She seems to find as much elation in giving me pain as I do in receiving it. More. For she doesn't suffer the fear that it may go too far, cause some permanent damage or surpass my limits. But, ultimately, I decide to stay put, exhaustion ushering me into a deep sleep.

***

A quiet night is followed by an equally quiet morning, breakfast left at my threshold the same as dinner the night before. Without much of an appetite, I pick at a biscuit before padding my way out of the house, using the backdoor to give myself the best shot at remaining unseen. My efforts are rewarded. While I hear staff in the kitchen scrubbing at pans, I am not seen, and find myself in Mornington's gardens, even more impeccable than I remembered them.

Through rows of roses, red, pink, and white, I spot the barn, knowing its familiar scents and a morning ride will do my heart good. Hay, sweat, and molasses. When I close my eyes inside, I can nearly forget my troubles. Jinx, a chestnut gelding approaching the mature age of ten, *harrumphs* to see me. I stroke his white snip, the hair there fine and soft as fur.

Trixie is less impressed with my return, pinning her ears and spinning a quick circle in her stall to show me her ebony rump. My boots have stiffened from lack of use. I strain against both boot pulls to get them over my calves, and they dig into my ankles near the heel, a quiet chastisement for abandoning them. Ordinarily, I'd have the groom saddle Jinx, but I find it a comforting practice, stripping the dust from my tack, running a thumb over my nameplate, selecting the proper bridle from memory.

Its leather is dark from years of oiling, the bit curved at the center to accommodate Jinx's tongue. Not a speck of grime here. He's been ridden in my absence. I am both glad of it and fretful, hoping it hasn't been George upon him, getting happy with his long, thin whip.

I'm startled by a smacking sound, leather on flesh, and startled further when I look up to find a long, thin face, eyes like George's whip.

"Lord Harrington." My tone is hushed, as if speaking to a ghost.

"Adele Hughes." He cracks the jumping bat in his palm once more, glances casually about the barn before his eyes settle on me.

"You took me by surprise." I rest the bridle on its hook and clasp my hands at my front.

"A happy surprise, I hope." Tensions ease a bit as he places the jumping bat on a nearby trunk. "I thought your parents would have told you. I've been boarding my mare here until our new barn is raised. A dreadful, costly process. Workers seem to lack the initiative they once had. Wouldn't you agree?"

I cast my eyes down as he steps closer. "My mother and father are out."

"Of course." He reaches for Jinx's bridle, fingers strumming over the bit. "Terribly old thing." Narrow lips scrunch into jagged lines. "Ah!" Throwing open a forest green trunk, he says, "I've something for you. Not much of a welcome home present, I confess, but …" He draws a silver bit with brassy embellishments from the dark space inside. "Brand new. What do you think?" That chemical scent overtakes me as he draws closer, the saddle oil he smothers his tack with, settled in every nail bed, every fold of skin.

I take it, letting it hang awkwardly in my palm. "It's very nice. Thank you."

In my periphery, I watch him eye me up and down. "I could've given you more, you know."

I step back.

"Much more. Why did you run from me, Addie?" He takes an accusatory tone, as if I'd not wounded his heart, but his ego.

"I—" I move to step backward once more, but feel a saddle rack press my shoulder blades and know I am pinned where I am.

"I know about you, about your preferences. A lesser man may balk at that but I know. I know that once you've had a real cock and not just whatever a woman might try to substitute, you'll forget about those silly notions. You don't know what you're missing. I could do things to you that no—"

"That's quite enough," Viola says.

The bit drops like a stone, clanging against the concrete floor. "And who might you be?" Lord Harrington asks, turning his attention to her.

"Viola Marwood, pleased to make your acquaintance."

I move quickly across the tack room, putting space between Lord Harrington and me as Viola scoops the bit off the ground.

"Though it does not appear that Adele is glad to see you," she says, inspecting it and rolling the center piece with a flick.

"Oh!" Lord Harrington scoffs. "Addie and I are old friends."

He winks at me.

I don't hide my disgust.

"Intended to be more than just friends, in fact. Weren't we, Addie? We were just discussing that very thing."

I draw my arms around myself and take my place beside Viola.

"And who are you to her, might I ask?"

Viola steps in front of me. "We are travel companions. It is important for a woman traveling great distances to have company. So many unscrupulous men in this world might take advantage of a woman alone. Wouldn't you agree?"

"I don't care for your insinuation, Mrs. Marwood. Or, is it Miss?" A knowing gleam illuminates his pale eyes.

"I've no meaning but the plainest one, I assure you."

"I'd encourage both of you women to think less on what harm a man might bring, and more on what protection he might offer." His mouth twists into a sneer. "I'll be going. Do enjoy your ride, Addie. And please, let me know if you *need* anything." Lord Harrington moves through the aisle between the rows of stalls, his dark jacket blotted with dust from the scuffle.

When he's out of earshot, Viola says, "You were right. The nickname is quite detestable coming from his forked tongue."

Chapter 23: For My Sake

Lorelei

Between Chester and I we've asked after her at every one of the city's fine hotels. The Hughes are well known and it takes only asking the right Waldorf Astoria bellhop to ascertain they are not in their New York townhouse. They must be at their estate in the country, could that be where Adele has gone? I'd always had the impression that she would rather die than face her family. Rose has insinuated we shan't be long in New York; her son resides elsewhere and we must be moving on soon. I wonder how she'd react to my saying I wish to stay in the city? She'd ask me why, why I had changed my mind so abruptly, and I can hardly tell her I need to stay where Adele could find me.

Would she still wish to find me? After how I've acted towards her; and with my continuing to warm another's bed, how could she forgive me?

Rose has taken control of my life once again, and I have not uttered one word in protest. She gives me freedom enough to take walks by myself around the city, my heart leaping at every flash of blonde hair only to crash once again when I realize it is not Adele. She knows how restless I'd become if she didn't, but my mornings are spent dutifully trailing after her as she visits fine store after fine store. My nights are dedicated to her pleasure.

I come back from one of my walks, to find Rose has thrown all my clothes and possessions away and replaced my entire wardrobe with outfits more suited to her taste.

"This is a new beginning for you, Lorelei. You've spent far too long living in squalor." She removes the pins from her hair, her ebony locks tumbling down her bare back, and cups my cheek. "If you hadn't been so silly and ran from me you could have had all this and more years ago."

I entwine my fingers in her silver streak and pull her into a kiss. She tastes of whiskey and peppermint. Everything about this woman intoxicates me and I wish I could break the chain that binds me to her but …"Take your clothes off and get on the bed, Lorelei."

I obey her like the obedient puppy I am and lay down on the soft cotton sheets. Going to the vanity, Rose retrieves a silk scarf that she'd left casually nestled amongst jewelry and expensive toiletries.

"Do you remember this game, Lorelei?"

"Yes."

"Would you like to play?"

"Please."

She blindfolds me, plunging my world into darkness. I feel the dip of the mattress as she lays down beside me, the scent of rosewater filling my nostrils as her hair brushes against my face. Rose straddles my thigh, the wet heat of her against my skin causing my own flood. She starts to rock against me, moaning in time with her movements. I push up against her, the extra pressure causing her to gasp before we fall into a rhythm, her languid moans turning into rapid sighs. She takes my nipple into her mouth, grasping it lightly between her teeth and flicking her tongue. I long to reach out and touch her, but the rules of the game say I can't. Rose can use any part of me for her own pleasure, whilst denying me mine.

"Do you remember when we first met, Lorelei?"

When seances had been in vogue, the Harringtons had held them regularly, inviting all their society friends to partake in the novelty. I would help Rose set up, ever her dutiful apprentice I would sit in the corner. Watching, learning.

"Even by the light of a single candle I could see your eyes were always on me."

"You were—are—so beautiful."

"Thank you, Lorelei." I hear the smile in her voice as she slows her movements, drawing out her pleasure. "I spent years molding you into what I wanted, only to be disappointed by you."

"I'm sorry."

"Are you? What, exactly, are you sorry for?"

"I'm sorry—" For ever loving Adele, she would have been far better off had I not drawn her into my life. I'm sorry for not being open with her, for would she have run into the arms of a madwoman had I shared my feelings and fears with her? I'm sorry for being weak when faced with temptation. "For leaving you."

"To whom do you belong?

Adele.

"You, I belong to you."

Rose goes quiet as she bares down on me. Her climaxes have always been marked by silence, as though the ecstasy within her is so much that it creates a bottleneck, leaving it unable to escape. She collapses onto me, shuddering slightly as she rides the last waves before stilling.

Her breath is hot on my neck as she whispers, "I value my possessions and will always take care of them." Her hand moves between my legs. "You're so wet." She presses at my entrance. I take a deep breath; I can do this. She pierces me; I can't do this.

"Please stop."

She plunges deeper, her fingers brushing against my inner walls.

"I said, stop!"

"Shhh, it's alright," Rose says softly as she withdraws from me. She removes the scarf and wipes the tears from my eyes. "You should have said something."

"I did."

"Well then, I didn't hear you" She envelopes me in her arms. "Come now, darling. There's no need for tears." I melt into her. "I'm hurt that you don't trust me enough. Lorelei. There are many people in this world who want to hurt you, but I won't." She entwines her fingers in my hair, turning me to look at her. Gray eyes bore into me. "I am all you need."

***

Maxwell Harrington was always an odious little shit. Two years my junior yet utterly convinced of his innate superiority, he could never understand why his mother lavished her attention on me. It would enrage him that, when he returned from boarding school for the holidays, I was there in *his* house.

I can only imagine that he saw me as some sort of sibling rival, that I was the daughter Rose always wanted. Had he known (and I was tempted to tell him on several occasions) I spent the nights warming his mother's bed, the cold cruelty he kept under the thinnest of veneers would have been unleashed full force upon me. The idea of having to spend ten days in a coach with him is abhorrent.

Everything is packed in trunks and waiting in the lobby for our imminent departure.

"You'll like it upstate," Rose says as she tugs a pair of gloves on. "Wide open countryside, greenery, all the things you love about home."

I can only nod in agreement. Adele has not sought me out, and I certainly can't afford to remain in this room indefinitely. There's a knock on the door, brisk yet polite.

"Come in," Rose calls.

"Your carriage is here, Lady Harrington." The bellhop nods once in farewell before closing the door behind him.

"I suppose we better get going." I say before following Rose down to the lobby like the coward I am.

Our luggage has already been loaded by the time we reach the carriage.

"Now, Lorelei, I know you and Maxwell were never the best of friends, but try to be good." She lifts my chin up with one gloved finger to look at her. "For my sake."

The bellhop opens the carriage door and the only thing I can focus on is a shock of blonde hair.

CHAPTER 24: FOR WANT OF A COACH

ADELE

Though I would have preferred to ride alone, taking in the stillness of the summer woods, Viola's company is some assurance I'll not be hassled again by Lord Harrington. And for that, I welcome it. She trails me on Trixie who, reliably ornery, is remarkably compliant under Viola's command. The quiet on our worn trail is broken only by crunching leaves beneath the horses' hooves and a smattering of birdsong.

"You're quite the competent rider," I say, noticing the ease with which Viola guides Trixie over a fallen tree. "Did you grow up with horses?"

"I've learned by watching." That familiar smirk crosses her lips, and I feel a twinge of embarrassment, though I don't fully take her meaning.

"You mentioned a home in Lily Dale," I say, eager to change the subject.

"I did."

"Considering my parents are away, perhaps we should set course there sooner rather than later."

"Have you money enough to cover your part of the journey?" Viola raises a questioning brow, though she must know I do not.

"I'd hoped to ask for a loan from my parents, but seeing as they're away …"

"No matter. I should've guessed I'd be footing your half of the bill. I'll work something out," she says.

Sweat foams at the edges of our saddle pads when we return to the barn, glistens where the reins stroked our mounts' necks. A groom greets us. He's hasty in relieving us of the horses, no doubt concerned for his employment at the realization we had to tack them up ourselves. When he's taken them to be cooled, Viola says, "Wash up."

I'm suddenly aware of the chestnut hairs coating my boots, the silhouette of dirt inside the thighs of my breeches.

"You smell like a barn."

She walks me through the property, follows me up the stairs to my room and inside, and I think for a moment she intends to watch me strip, but mercifully she takes her leave, closing the washroom door behind her.

It's a luxury to stand beneath the streaming water of a shower once more. Of course, Lorelei and I could not afford to have one installed, and I'd so missed the way the steam fogs the mirror (another thing we couldn't afford), and how the scalding water reddens the skin where it bears down. My lavender soaps have been replaced by gardenia scented ones in glass bottles. The foreign smell is unusual on my skin, but preferable to the stink of the barn.

Viola is already knocking when I emerge in my towel.

"Just a minute!" I call.

She turns the knob nonetheless and steps inside, looking me up and down before saying, "You'll have to dress quickly. Much as I'd like to explore your current state, our carriage awaits."

I pull the towel tighter around me. "Already? How have you—"

"Dress, Adele."

She slams the door behind her. I select a comfortable dress, suitable for traveling. Unsettled at the idea of being seen with my hair wet and undone, I make only a cursory attempt to find George and bid him goodbye. Relieved when I don't find him, I pen a simple note expressing my gratitude at the brief opportunity to see him and my regret that I missed Mother and Father.

Robin totes my trunk to the door. I linger in the foyer a moment, a half-formed notion that I might stay. Viola's cruelty is difficult to endure. But how might I survive at all if forced to marry Lord Harrington or someone like him? How long until my curse was discovered? It strikes me I've not had an incident since leaving Matlock, at least not one uninvited by the slice of a blade. What might that mean?

Viola clears her throat. She opens the door and gestures Robin outside. He hobbles under the strain of our stuffed trunks, and I resolve myself to follow him. My companion might be wicked, but am I not also wicked, for how my body responds to her? I don't deserve the comfort of kindness. There's something evil in me: in my skin, my blood, nestled deep in the marrow of my bones. I wonder, when I meet Viola's friend, and he cures me, whether the sickness that beckons me to yield to another will be healed along with the strange abilities of my flesh. I do hope so. If I could be riled by a simple kiss rather than grating teeth, by the caring stroke of a hand rather than the sting of it, then I needn't live in fear of my partner taking liberties with my submission, as Viola so often does.

The ebony carriage is drawn by two gray mares, old enough that their dapples have faded. In the midday sun, they appear ghostly white beneath their harnesses. Our bags have already been secured when I draw back the curtain and step up to the cabin. My heart drops at what I find—who I find.

"Lord Harrington happens to be traveling in our same direction," Viola says from somewhere behind me. "He was kind enough to welcome us along."

His pale eyes leer at me from his seat where he's struck a relaxed pose, spreading his knees widely and resting his weight between them on a black cane with some silver embellishment, peeking out from between his oil-stained hands.

"Someone had to ensure you had safe passage," he says, tapping the seat beside him.

I refuse the invitation and sit on the opposite side. "How generous of you," I say through gritted teeth as my eyes flash back to a sliver of Mornington still visible through the curtain, but Viola closes the space and sits beside me before I can make an exit.

Lord Harrington clears his throat, an obvious bid for attention. "It's not a short journey to Lily Dale, about ten days, I expect. And we'll need to stop in the city to fetch my mother. I hope you're agreeable—"

I'm about to decline when Viola speaks over me,

"Of course. Four will be quite comfortable in a cabin of this size. And it would be difficult," she eyes me at this, "to secure any other transport for such a great distance."

Lord Harrington taps the roof with his cane, and I discern the silver tipping to be a braided design, similar to that of Viola's ring.

"What's—"

I'm cut off when the driver lashes the horses, who lurch forward at the crack of the whip. My head smacks the board behind me, and stars wink in my vision.

"Are you alright?" Viola does a cursory check of my skull, and when her hand comes away with no spots of blood, says, "You really must be more vigilant, dear."

I stare out the window to indicate my lack of interest in discussion. Viola seems to take the hint, drawing a book from her bag and flipping to a dog-eared page. Lord Harrington, however, doesn't take his eyes off me, scrutinizing me from toe to tip. I want to ask how Viola arranged this trip. She was hostile to Harrington in the barn, not an advisable way of securing a favor. But I cannot very well ask her in front of him, and to whisper in her ear, well, what would he think? I was not ignorant to the rumors about me before I left Lloyd Neck. Something so intimate would surely get them started again—if they ever ceased to begin with. I content myself by deciding to ask her when we reach the city.

It's a sleepy ride and would be peaceful if not for Harrington's eyes grating me, his chemical smell burning my nostrils. Grasses grow thick from summer rainstorms, and I spot the odd rabbit and squirrel darting about the fields. I hold my nose when we pass the shore, the air still ripe with the scent of rotted shellfish. This seems to amuse Lord Harrington, who chuckles and adjusts himself in his seat.

"Tell me about your travels, Addie," he says as we reach a stretch of gravel road. "It's been, what? Three years since you've been home? What kinds of adventures—or misadventures—have you found along the way?"

I hope Viola might intercede, but she licks her thumb to flip a page.

"No adventures, I assure you. I worked in a shop in England. All very drab."

"England! In which city?"

"Matlock."

He presses me for details, so I recount the inane steps of inventory, stocking, tidying up. Perhaps if I bore him, he might doze off and leave me be. I make no mention of Lorelei, who intrudes on my memories with painful jabs. It goes on this way for some time. Tips of buildings break through the cloud cover, then seem to rise up all around us as we draw closer to the city. The sky turns from pale blue to smoky gray, and the gravel turns to pavement. While the roads were empty in Lloyd Neck, here they buzz with activity. A thousand voices echo off the buildings and the roads, and honking horns fill any gaps between them. I cannot help but search the crowd for Lorelei's loose, red hair, her impossibly straight posture. Is she still in the city? Perhaps her new lover has whisked her away, set up somewhere with Chester as a family. Lorelei has always been a charmer, she'd have no trouble—

"It's just up here," Lord Harrington says as we round a corner, narrowly avoiding a collision with a taxicab. "The Waldorf Astoria."

Viola stows her book and folds her hands across her lap.

The driver stops the carriage in front of The Waldorf, a grand building I know well, for it's just a few blocks from my family's townhome. Today its highest turrets are obscured by smog. Arched windows seem to wink at me. The bellhop is at the side of the carriage in a flash, stumbling over himself to find out how he can be of assistance.

"Please inform the Lady Rose Harrington that her carriage awaits."

The bellhop scuttles off, disappearing inside the double doors.

"She shouldn't be long."

My body flushes with fear, and I embrace the instinctual urge to find the source of danger, drawing back the curtain all the way to get a full view out the window. Normal street traffic, but nothing more. A finger runs across my arm, and I glance down to notice Viola's ringed finger running over goosed flesh.

"And here I thought you would be too warm," she says, pulling Lord Harrington's folded jacket from the seat beside him and placing it over my shoulders. I draw it tightly around me, unsure why my heart races. I peer out the window once more, again finding nothing. But then, a voice—which might as well be Viola's blade—cuts clear through my spine.

"Adele."

Chapter 25: Eggplant or Aubergine

Lorelei

"Lorelei!" Adele turns to look at me, brow raised, voice little more than a squeak.

"You, it's always you!" Maxwell's words drip with disdain and grease, much like his hair. He always did overdo it with the pomade.

"Maxwell," I say, keeping my tone even.

His gaze bounces between Adele and I. "You know one another?"

"Your old business partner, is she not?" Viola intersects.

"Yes." Adele looks at the carriage floor. "Business partner."

I step aside so Rose may alight first. She sits next to Maxwell, barely acknowledging his presence. Instead, her eyes are firmly on Adele. She's no fool. Rose knows that Viola's words are a screen designed to hide the truth. I climb in after Rose, glad to have her as a buffer between Maxwell and I.

"Mother, this is Miss Hughes and Miss Marwood. They'll be making the journey to Lily Dale with us."

Rose holds out her hand to Adele. "Delighted to make your acquaintance."

"And yours, Lady Harrington." Adele takes it, holding Rose's hand a respectful amount of time before letting it drop. "It must be wonderful to be reunited with Lord Harrington—" My snort of derision earns me a look of utter rebuke from Adele. "Something funny?"

"Only the obvious." I nod my head in Maxwell's direction.

The corners of Adele's mouth tug, ever so slightly, up. Hope leaps in my chest; I still have the ability to make her smile.

My eyes fix on Viola's dress, a rich dark purple.

"What color would you call that, Adele?"

She looks at Viola, her brow furrowed. "Eggplant, I suppose."

"Eggplant?" *Please remember.* "You're making it up. It sounds made up." I look about the carriage, raising my voice in mock astonishment. "Does it not sound made up?"

Her smile widens. "All words are made up. They're not mined from the earth, you know."

"No." I feel that my own grin must make me look quite the idiot, but I don't care. "I suppose they are not." Our joy is short-lived though as Viola's eyes narrow and the amber fire within them ignites.

"And how," Viola's lip curls, "is it that you know Lady Harrington, Lorelei?"

"My long-term patron."

"Yes, I'm sure the lady has *given* you a great deal over the years. I hope you remember to show your gratitude."

Adele's smile fades as realization dawns, and the true nature of mine and Rose's relationship becomes apparent to her. *How did it come to this, my love? So close together yet oceans apart.*

"Lorelei has done nothing but please me. I suppose you could say that she's the daughter I never had, but she's so much more than that." Rose pushes a lock of hair back from my brow. "She's always been such a good girl."

"I'm sure she can be most amenable, when handled correctly."

Heat rises to the back of my neck. There was a time where these kinds of exchanges might have passed Adele by, but she is no longer the sweet naive girl she once was. An uneasy silence falls upon the carriage when Lord Harrington declares he has *business to attend to*, drawing a ledger from his bag.

We ride, Adele staring intently out the window as if she might witness something spectacular there, Rose sneaking glances at Maxwell's ledger, and Viola with her nose buried in a book, a grimoire bound with cracked, maroon leather, embossed with an emblem I recognize. I search my memory, reaching back in time and working forward to discern where I might have seen that emblem before, and half an hour passes before I place it: it's the same emblem embossed on the text I spotted in Rose's library. A few hours without anyone uttering a word, my thoughts racing with the possible meaning for this similarity, until Maxwell bangs on the roof with his cane.

"I don't know about you ladies, but I'm in need of relief."

The carriage pulls to a stop and we all disembark, grateful for the chance to stretch our legs. Rose and Viola move away from us, having suddenly found some common thread of conversation whilst Maxwell removes himself to a wooded area some distance from the road.

"You look well," Adele says, looking at anything but me.

"So do you." She's a little thinner than last I saw her.

"Such a small world, isn't it? Though I suppose New York society is insular, a few families inter—"

"Adele, please listen."

"—secting. Lord Harrington was so generous to offer—"

"Maxwell is nothing of the sort. He doesn't do anything unless it stands to benefit him."

"You should show some respect, Lorelei, addressing him by his given name like that. Titles—"

"Mean nothing. Respect has to be earnt, and believe me, Maxwell has never done anything in his life to garner it. He is not my better, nor is he yours. Just because he happened to be born to the right people. I'm more deserving of that title. And is—is that his jacket you're wearing?"

She fiddles with the cuffs of it, as though ascertaining just who it is it belongs to, before choosing to ignore my question all together.

"And does this same line of reasoning apply to Lady Harrington? You seem more than happy to defer to her, to be her 'good girl'!"

"She's done more for me than anyone. I …" I what? Love her? Am fixated with her? "I respect her." The memory of Adele looking to Viola for approval the night she bound me rises like bile in my throat. "And what's more, she respects me."

"She's very beautiful."

The change in subject throws me off balance. "Yes, she is beautiful."

"I could … I could … I can change, be like her in every way. Would that please you?"

That Adele could think it would please me for her to be anyone other than herself horrifies me. That I made her feel that way … "Gods no! I don't want that, the very thought—"

"I see." She turns and makes her way back to the carriage, leaving me to wonder what I said wrong.

Chapter 26: Mine to Kill

Adele

The carriage ride leaves me more confused than before. I'd nearly resigned myself to the idea Lorelei had given up on me, moved on to some faceless woman. Now the woman has a face, a lovely one at that. Not only that, but deep pockets and deeper family connections. The Harringtons are an older family even than my own. There is nothing a Harrington couldn't offer, as was so well ingrained in me by mother and father at the time of Lord Harrington's proposal. Rose could burn down the Matlock shop and rebuild it ten times over.

And yet Lorelei latched onto my smile. Her playful words dare me to hope. So why was she so quick to rebuke my advance? Surely our love could not fade so thoroughly in such little time? She must still love me. If she ever loved me, she must.

And Viola has noticed my wondering. Worse than that, she spotted my brief conversation with Lorelei outside the coach. I know from the deep black of Viola's irises the extent of her fury with me, and yet I trail her to our room at the inn, hoping very much this sign of fealty will abate her anger. She is careful in closing the door, gentle. When she turns the lock, it's as if she wants no one to hear. And I think, for a moment, that she has calmed. But when she faces me, I feel the slice of her blade at my collarbone already.

"Come here." Her voice is a growl.

I plant my feet in their spot. My eyes drift to the window.

"Go ahead, try it." She's crossed half the room by the time I look back at her.

I shake my head. *No.*

"You humiliated me."

Heat radiates from her flesh to mine, so close now her cinnamon scent burns my eyes. "I'm sorry."

"You think you can flirt with her and come to rest in my bed at night? Travel on my generosity?"

I wouldn't be in this mess if not for you. The ember of resentment pushes me to speak swiftly without forethought. "Lorelei and I would—"

Her palm cracks across my cheek, a hot burn that brings tears flooding to my eyes.

"Would what?" She balls her right fist, holding it at her side.

I shake my head and cast my eyes down.

"Say it, whore."

I move to back away but she snatches the hem of my dress.

"Say it!"

Without looking at her, I do. "Lorelei and I would still be together."

She raises her arm, and I block my head.

"Don't worry," she says. "I wouldn't mess up that pretty face." The blow lands in my gut at an angle. There's a crack within, and I instinctively grab my lower rib cage before blinding pain forces me to withdraw. Lungs empty, I gasp for breath, stumbling to my knees.

"You are mine, Adele. Mine to fuck. Mine to cut. Mine to kill, if I wish it."

I feel like a fish flopping on shore, Viola a fisherman watching me struggle until it's time to gut me.

"Say you understand."

Mouth wide as it will open, I suck at the air. Only slivers make it down my throat.

Viola yanks my head back, sending hairpins flying across the floor. "Say you understand, Adele." She raises a fist before dropping it. "I think I've a better idea, Adele. You need rebreaking." Viola goes to her trunk and, from it, draws the bit she recovered from the barn at Mornington. "See this piece in the middle." She indicates metal rollers affixed in horizontal lines. "It's meant to busy the tongue."

Her fingers close around my jaw and I pull away, but her grip is firm.

"A similar piece helped to break my mare. Keeps the mind occupied during the training process. Lessens resistance."

I step back despite her hold on me, my balance shaken.

"Open wide, Addie."

Her fingers pry into my cheek at the space between my molars. I've no choice but to open to relieve the pressure, just as a horse would. Gently, she eases the bit over my tongue.

"Very good."

The metal is cold and tastes of copper, of blood. A cinnamon flavored finger wedges its way between my lips and flicks the hardware. "Go on, test the rollers."

The weight of it drags my expression to an exaggerated frown. Humiliated, I whine and struggle against her, but my torso is angled such that any hasty movement would cause me to fall face first.

I've no choice but to hold my body still and hope she doesn't notice my shaking. Grabbing the bit by its rings, she pulls it taut against the edges of my mouth, forcing it open further. Saliva leaks onto my cheeks, dribbling down, out of sight.

"I'll repeat myself one time and one time only."

Metal clanks as the bit's components jostle against one another. Viola pushes further, stinging the corners of my mouth and forcing my head to tilt backward.

"You are mine. To do with as I wish."

A wet trail slides down my neck and into the space between my breasts.

"Do you understand?"

"I understand!" I nod, as best I can with my head cranked back in this unnatural position.

Viola unhands me, and I drop to the ground, a sobbing heap.

"Oh, good." Viola removes the bit, wiping the spittle gently from my cheeks. "Good girl." I've gotten to my hands and feet when she says, "You embarrass yourself as well, you know. Lorelei doesn't want you. Why would she? A woman like Rose has real wealth, real power."

"My family—"

"Lady Rose Harrington doesn't rely on Mommy and Daddy to balance the checkbook."

The pain at my side is near unbearable as I move to stand. I wipe a bit of blood from my lip, a rusty stain across the back of my hand, when the room spins. I catch myself on a nearby chair to keep from falling over. "She loves me," I say, then brace for the impact.

But none comes. Instead, she says, "Loves you? There is nothing left of you to love."

I feel Viola at my back. She grips my waist, hands sliding upward until she reaches the aching spot at my ribcage and I cry out.

"That won't heal as easily as the other wounds I've inflicted. That one is more than skin deep." She whispers in my ear, "Watch your tongue, girl," then digs her hands into my slides. I collapse from the pain, my vision strobing black.

"Torture me if you must," I say, curled up on the floor. "Nothing will convince me otherwise. Lorelei *loves* me."

"Hah! A romantic. I'm sure that, up until recently, Lorelei has been very careful not to hurt your feelings. But I shudder to think of how she speaks about you to others. To Rose!" Viola begins hanging her garments in the small closet, one by one. Her steps have lightened, anger abated for the time being.

She's right. How has Lorelei explained our relationship to her new beau? It strikes me then, a way to finally use this curse to my advantage.

"I can find out," I say, a bit louder than necessary, distracting her from her task.

"What do you mean?"

"I can change. Become Lady Rose, go to Lorelei, and see what she says." Hearing it aloud, the fear creeps in. What if Viola is right?

She spins around, eyes alight at the idea. "How wonderful. Yes, you should. I'll even occupy the real lady, make sure you have Lorelei all to yourself—well, in a manner of speaking."

The idea is madness. Madness and yet … irresistible. As Lady Rose Harrington I could surmise the nature of their relationship, how deep or shallow it might be. I could ask questions, questions Lorelei may not answer honestly to my true face. And though she's seen me heal, she hasn't seen me change. So, she would never suspect …

"Okay, I will."

Viola beams. "Excellent. After dinner, then. I'll make arrangements with the Harringtons. They never have been able to resist a betting game."

Chapter 27: What Game Shall We Play?

Lorelei

I shouldn't be surprised that Rose wanted to spend time with Maxwell. Despite inheriting nothing but her gray eyes, he is her son after all. So when, after dinner, Viola suggests a game of cards, it stands to reason she would want to go. What is surprising is the rapport between Viola and Rose, developed in such a short space of time. The tap of the door reverberates in my chest, making it pound in time with the knocks. It must be Adele! This is what we need, a chance to talk. Just the two of us, free from the influence of Viola or anyone else. But instead of cornflower blue, it's dove gray eyes that greet me when I open the door.

My disappointment turns into puzzlement. "Why did you knock? This is your room as well."

"Politeness." She casts her eyes about the room. "And I wanted to be sure you're alone."

Why would she think—Adele. She's come to see if she's here.

"Of course I'm alone. Why would I not be? There's no one I'd want here."

"No one?" A flash of disappointment.

"Present company excluded." My words seem to have no effect. Her eyes fixate on a point somewhere behind me as though she is afraid to meet my gaze but daren't show it. Rose never cared in the past who I had dalliances with, encouraged them in fact. There was always someone else to warm her bed when I wasn't there. Is it a symptom of the passing years, this new found insecurity? I pull her to me and capture her in a kiss; she stiffens before melting into me, her hand snaking up my back to the nape of my neck.

"I've missed you," she murmurs against my lips.

"I've not been anywhere."

"I—I meant since dinner. Lo—Maxwell is ever so dull."

"And Viola?"

"What about her?" She backs away from me.

"Just that many find her fascinating." I can't keep the bitterness from my tone. "I'd be careful of her, is all I'll say for now."

"You don't know her well—"

"You met this morning, you don't know her at all." The ease with which they fell into conversation? Not impossible for a first meeting, but given their characters, highly unlikely. "Do you—"

"I …" Rose puts a hand to her temple. "I don't feel well. I must be confusing her with someone else." She stumbles forward and, for a horrifying second, I think she's going to hit her head on the dresser. I manage to catch her just before she makes contact with the heavy wood.

"Rose, darling. Are you okay?" I guide her to the bed and pour a glass of water from the carafe. She takes the glass with unsteady hands and drinks deeply from it as I sit down beside her. "Better?"

She nods. "I don't know what came over me."

"It's okay. I think we need to get you out of that dress and into something less constrictive." I turn her gently around and pull the pins from her hair. "It's been a long day," I say, raking my fingers through her hair, combing the tangles out. "I think some sleep will do you a world of good." I unbutton her dress, pushing it aside so that red satin pools around her waist.

"I don't want to sleep, Lorelei."

"That's good." I place a kiss on her shoulder. "Neither do I."

She shivers when I stand in front of her and start to undress. "Let me help you." With trembling fingers she strips me and though no sound escapes her lips, I'm sure the word upon them is gorgeous.

I push her dress down so we stand breast to hip. "I'm going to make you feel better."

"Promise?"

"Promise." I lay her down on the bed, pressing my body on top of hers. My soul is a tinderbox and she radiates a heat that sets it aflame. Our kisses are leisurely and deep. Every so often I'll break away to bestow a kiss on her jaw or a nip on her neck, only to return to her lips with a renewed ferocity. "What game shall we play?" I whisper.

"I …" She turns her head to look at some spot on the wall. "No games, I just want you."

"As you wish." I slide down her body, peppering kisses along the way until I come to rest between her legs. I lay for a moment, breathing in the scent of her, my right hand brushing along her inner thigh, until a hand on the top of my head pushes me with gentle insistence downwards. I nuzzle her folds, and as she spreads her legs for me, I employ a gentle pressure just hard enough to keep her on edge but too soft to offer any real satisfaction. She arches her back, lifting her hips up to meet my tongue. I trace wide circles around her clit before taking it between my lips, sucking, gently at first, then a little harder. I alternate between licking and sucking until her mewls and the tugging of my hair tells me she needs more. I slip a finger in, delighting in her gasp as I do so. I don't move within her, I don't need to; my filling her combined with the ministrations of my mouth will be enough to please her. Minutes pass and though she skirts dangerously close to the edge, she never tumbles over.

"Stop." Her voice is thick with emotion and when I look up her cheeks are wet. I've never seen Rose cry before, the sight both pains and disconcerts me. She wipes her eyes. "I'm sorry, I just don't think I'm going to—to …"

I crawl up to lie next to her. "Shh, it's okay. You must be feeling rather unwell, this isn't like you." I cuddle up to Rose, putting my head on her chest and draping my leg over her. She winces. "Have I hurt you?"

"No, you didn't hurt me." She takes a deep breath, wincing again. "You asked me what *game* I'd like to play earlier. What would you have liked to play, Lorelei?"

This feels like a trap. Rose always chooses. "Whatever would've pleased you best."

"Will you hurt me? Tell me what to do?"

There was a night, so long ago, when Rose allowed me free reign to do as I willed. And though I am always allowed to be rough, should I choose, it is not the same as being given control. I swallow down my excitement and keep my voice even as I answer.

"Yes, whatever you wish, my lady," I whisper softly, placing a kiss on her temple before straightening my back and making my tone icy. "You think you're so high and mighty, don't you?" I wrench her head back so she has to look at me. "Don't you?" Her nod is barely perceptible. Such is my grip on her. "You need to learn your place."

"What's my place?"

"On your hands and knees, begging me for release."

"Yes?"

"Yes!"

"And what if I don't want to beg?"

I push her off me.

"Hands and knees, now."

She obeys as I kneel behind her, pulling her against me.

"How does it feel being subordinate to your piece of rough?"

She doesn't answer, just bucks against me.

I lean forward and grab her hair. "If you think you're too good to answer me, then you are sadly mistaken. So." I pull. Hard. "How does it feel?"

"It thrills me."

I enter her with two fingers. "It does?"

"Yes, I've always wanted this."

"You could have always had it."

"I didn't know how to tell you."

I let the movement of my hips drive my fingers into her. Hard, fast, deep. It doesn't take long for her to near her climax; the slight twitching around my fingers and her rapid breaths tell me so. I close my eyes, delighting in the feel of her all around me.

"Tell me you love me."

My heart clenches, my mouth goes dry. I pretend not to have heard her, thrusting faster in the hope that she'd forget about her request once the moment of rapture has passed.

"Please, tell me you love me!"

"I …"

"Please." Never have I heard that word said with such desperation, such heartfelt yearning. It shatters me.

"I—I love you, Rose."

I thought my saying the words would make her happy, would keep me in her good graces, instead she goes cold, pulling away from me.

"I'm sorry, I …" She leaves the words suspended in midair as she bends to gather her skirts from where they lay, unceremoniously tossed upon the floor. "I need …" She hastily dresses. I go to her to help with the buttons, but she bats me away. "It's fine, I'm fine. Go to bed, Lorelei. I'll be back later."

"Would you like me to—" The slamming of the door slices my words off. I crawl beneath the covers and let the tears flow.

***

The dip of the mattress and a kiss on my bare shoulder wake me from dreams of amber, silver, and red.

"I'm sorry I'm so late," Rose murmurs into the back of my neck. "I had to help that idiot son of mine win back the deed of a rather lovely little cottage in the Cotswolds." She draws me closer. "Perhaps we'll have a fortnight there when we get back home."

No mention of earlier.
No mention of how she fled the room close to tears.
No mention of the *words.*
“Did you have a good night?” I whisper into the darkness.
“Oh darling, I had a wonderful night. Thank you.”

Chapter 28: Cracked

Adele

I love you, Rose. The words play on repeat, warp and take on new meaning. Does she love Rose? Or could she have somehow known, deep down, it was me she spoke to?

No. I've indulged enough foolish, girlish notions, done enough rationalizing, enough hoping, enough waiting. She loves *her*. And if not, cares about her feelings enough to pretend to. Either way, a night spent tossing and turning has left me tired, and not only in my body. Solitude in the dark hours has fortified my pain, turned it from slush to hard ice.

I am tired in my spirit. Tired of being the kind one, the polite one, the easy one, the one cast aside and trampled upon. I know the truth of Lorelei now: a user, a seductress, a liar. And as I watch her spread jam over toast, I plan the sweetest way to impart the truth of me.

If I am kind, polite, and easy, it is because it serves me.

If I am cast aside, it is because I tire of being held.

If I am trampled, it is because I throw myself beneath cloven hooves for the rapturous pleasure of their brutality.

Lord Harrington dismisses himself from breakfast, muttering as he takes his leave and bumbling with some documents, trying his best to look important. It's just as well. The innkeeper set up a small table draped with powder blue linen, a simple vase hosting a pale carnation in the center. We've paired off, Lorelei beside Rose and I beside Viola. In Rose's form, the pain where Viola struck me disappeared, but now the aching of my rib nags at me. I find that if I angle my body just so, the throbbing subsides. Oil pops in a pan in the next room, the innkeeper bustling back and forth to play host.

"What are you in the mood for?" Lorelei asks.

To cause you pain.

"Toast will be just fine for me as well," Rose answers. "I've never had much of an appetite in the morning."

Lorelei flashes her a look and she giggles.

"Viola is voracious in the early hours," I say, grasping her thigh beneath the table.

"Eggs for me," Viola calls to the innkeeper. "Voracious at every hour."

"Of course, ma'am," the innkeeper responds.

"It strikes me that a woman of your poise does not hold a title," Rose says, blotting her lip with a cloth napkin.

I clear my throat. "Lorelei once told me that titles hold little meaning. Respect is earned, is it not?"

Any trace of congeniality drops from Rose's face as she looks to my former paramour.

"I don't recall—" Lorelei starts.

"Just yesterday, in fact." I press on. "But you must forgive her, Lady Harrington. I am sure you can see why a woman of her"—I eye Lorelei up and down—"*circumstance* might feel the need to tout such a conclusion."

Unseen by all, Viola's hand grazes from my knee to my center. She is pleased with me.

I sit straighter, do not try to contain my smile. "It was so good of you to take on a case such as hers, Lady Harrington. I am sure Lorelei would agree that she learned much under your tutelage."

The innkeeper sweeps in, carrying a plate of steaming eggs, and sets it before Viola, then turns to me. "Anything for you, Miss?"

"I am quite sated, thank you."

As the innkeeper dips back into the kitchen, Viola grasps a fork in one hand and my sex in the other. The shock upon Lorelei's face and the confusion on Rose's spurs me on.

"If only she had continued under your guidance, perhaps our business venture might have seen better success."

Lorelei drops her toast, crumbs still speckling her chin, and storms down the hall toward her room.

"Your companion is testy this morning," Viola says, scooping scrambled bits of egg onto her fork.

"So it would seem," Rose says, grasping the jam jar.

"We would take no offense if you'd like to go to her." Viola chomps on the fork, teeth clicking against the metal.

"None whatsoever," I add. "And do extend my apologies if I caused offense."

Reluctantly, Rose follows Lorelei's path to their shared room. With sinister hope, I strain my ears to hear whether I've caused a rift between them, but the innkeeper chooses this moment to soak her pans, water against hot oil hissing loudly enough to block any sounds from their room down the hall.

Our company gone, Viola releases her hold on me, finishing her breakfast with only the odd word. We are told the horses have been harnessed and to gather our belongings to continue the trip west. I'm loath to share air with Lorelei, understanding, finally, the depth of her deception. I was a placeholder. A pocketbook. A thing to be toyed with—though not to my full satisfaction—while she awaited the return to Lady Harrington's good graces.

In the room, I make a vain attempt to delay the awkward carriage ride. "Won't you play with me?" I ask Viola, bending over the bedside while she clicks the locks on her trunk.

"We haven't time," she says, dragging it to the door.

One more try. "You've made swift work of me before." I toss my hair with a flick of my neck, deepen the arch of my back.

At this, Viola crosses the room and stands behind me, pulling my hips into her. "Did Lorelei leave you wanting?" Her words have the curl of a smile.

"Yes," I say, bucking up against her.

A smack lands on my rear and I startle.

"Good," Viola says. "A timely reminder of why you cut ties with her. Come now." She grabs my bag and drags it to the door beside her own. Begrudgingly, I follow her to the main room, where the breakfast table has been cleared away. The innkeeper rushes behind us to grab our bags, and I greet the fresh, summer air, letting a hot breeze billow through my red, satin skirts.

The same skirts I wore last night.

They may have gripped Lady Harrington's hips more firmly, but my bust is unquestionably more lovely in the bodice. And I think Lorelei would agree, should she be sharp enough to notice.

***

Lord Harrington and his mother take up the length of the day with talk of raising their barn. Lorelei and I offer intermittent compliments on their description of design choices, and Viola makes sympathetic overtures at complaints of lengthened timelines and unscrupulous contractors, but largely the ride is quiet. All the better to allow the tension between Lorelei and I to fester like an infected wound.

I hope I hurt you, I think when I catch her staring. *I've chosen another as well and I let her do things to me that …*

Do I enjoy them? What should be a simple question circles round in my head for miles. I watch hills roll by as I consider it, yellow wildflowers billowing like an ocean swell. I must enjoy Viola's torments. I return to them time and time again. And yet, so often, I wish she knew some limit. Is it the fear that thrills me?

"Another two hours," the driver calls from his seat.

Sun hanging low in the sky, I catch Lorelei's eyes on me once more, their green distant and faded like a scuffed jewel. *Do you recognize me now?* I ask with furrowed brows.

"Such interesting embroidery," Lorelei says, her gaze narrowing on my skirt.

This catches Lady Harrington's attention, but Viola remains absorbed in her reading. "Fine stitchwork," the lady says, reaching across the cabin to draw it closer to her face. "Gold thread, so very regal."

"Why, thank you." There's no warmth in my tone. "Viola was kind enough to help me choose it."

"Excellent taste, she has," Lady Harrington says.

Viola rewards this with a flick up from her book and a curt smile.

"Do you not have something similar?" Lorelei asks her companion.

Locked onto their faces, I do my best not to gape.

"I should think not," Lady Harrington says. "Red is such a forceful color, I find it blanches me."

Lorelei swallows away some look—confusion or suspicion.

"Though it's quite lovely on you, Adele."

"Must we pass our remaining hours on such a feminine topic as fashion?" Lord Harrington asks, making a hacking sound.

Silence falls over the coach as night encroaches. Rhythmic hoofbeats and the occasional snap of the driver's whip are the only sounds as we close in on the next inn, slightly larger than the last, built of stone rather than wood, with arched windows emitting a warm glow from inside.

When the horses are halted before the door, Lord Harrington offers to settle the rooms, to which Viola argues, an obvious clamoring for status. They hurry inside, Lady Harrington tailing them to settle the faux dispute over who is most generous. I think Lorelei would have followed dutifully behind her, had she not caught the look of challenge in my eyes.

"I see you've rid yourself of Chester. Better that he not witness your … affair. Sent him back to England on his own?"

Lorelei scoffs. "Of course not, I'd—"

"So much like a mother you are to him, so much like his mother."

Her jaw trembles as she restrains the urge to spew venom from it. A sharp inhale and she says instead, "What is the purpose of this cruelty, Adele? You've made yourself comfortable at Viola's side, so you must not be too upset about my traveling with Rose."

I lock my stare on hers. "At her side, beneath her, abo—"

"Enough!" She throws her hands into the air and rises, but I am a beast with the taste of blood on my tongue, and I chase her from the cart.

"Is it? Is it enough, Lorelei? Would you not like to hear how she takes me?"

I don't realize how high my voice has risen until she places a palm over my mouth. "No! And quiet, please. They'll hear you!"

Her fingers press into my cheek. I lift my chin and she lets them slide down my throat before pulling her arm to her side. "What do you care if they hear?" But I say it in a whisper, for should the Harringtons learn of my predilections, all rumors about me would be confirmed.

"I care." Her eyes drift over the ground, to no spot in particular.

"Would you silence me then?" I have grown too bold in my anger, and the challenge alights that familiar green fire.

Lorelei grabs my throat, just firmly enough to feel the pressure, still allowing me to suck in breath. Crickets trill in the dark, surrounding fields. A faint murmur of voices presses through the thick wooden door. Moonlight bounces off the red curl at Lorelei's temple. She leans in.

My eyes ease shut, and with the press of her lips on mine, she grabs my side.

I buckle. A strangled cry and a stumble to my knee separates us.

"What is it?" She tries to make her voice small, but there's urgency in it.

I clutch at the injury, shielding it from further contact. "It's nothing," I say.

"It's something!" She steps closer, but how could I explain?

I could not. So, I spin on my heel and straighten. I toss open the door of the inn, using the ears of our travel party to keep me from having to tell her. Having to tell Lorelei how Viola beat me. How I chose to stay.

***

I manage to avoid Lorelei's searching looks as the innkeeper, an older woman with a grizzled face, explains the timing of breakfast and checkout. Once we are shown to our room, Viola excuses herself to wash up. I use the opportunity to undress. Unfastening my bodice on my own is difficult under the best of circumstances, but the stitching pain makes it all the more difficult and slow. When I've finally got it removed, I trace the bruise with trembling fingers. It's spread since this morning, reaching now from beside my navel nearly to my breast. An angry thing, it is dark at the center, shades of red and purple fading toward the edges. I press my finger to it and clench at the instant shock of pain.

"It's cracked," Viola says, rounding the bathroom corner, beads of water rolling from the tip of her chiseled nose. "It will heal."

"You broke my rib?" I'd thought it just a nasty bruise, but to hear it said—

"Cracked," Viola corrects. "I *cracked* your rib, and I truly wish you'd remembered your manners yesterday. It brings me no pleasure to watch you hide your wincing."

I pull my bodice over my breasts. "Doesn't it, though? Not even Lord Harrington has laid hands on me."

"Would you like to warm his bed? I'm sure that could be arranged."

I think of his tack oil smell, his brash advances, rough, masculine hands all over me. "No."

Viola selects a nightdress from her trunk and laces her arms through the sleeves. "I hope you don't plan to pester me much longer. I'm exhausted."

I'm exhausted, too. The stress of the day has caught up to me, and after the spat with Lorelei, I've not the energy to go back and forth with Viola as well. I retire to the washroom to strip, poke and prod my cracked rib a bit longer, then run the tub as hot as it will go until steam hangs overhead like a cloud. Leaning against the porcelain, I shut my eyes, trying to think of a time and place other than now and here.

My mind floats. I tell myself to dream up a meadow: long grasses, the trickle of a waterfall, and skies all the colors of a pansy. But intruding upon my would-be peace are images of Lorelei and Rose, all the more vivid now I know how Lorelei handles her. Still, I hear the echo ringing, *I love you, Rose.* I shake my head, lodging a bit of water in my eardrum.

Admitting the bath was a failure of an exercise in relaxation, I dress and join Viola in our bed. Again, she is reading. Always reading of late! "Must be a fascinating story to capture you so."

"Fascinating, yes." The hint of a yawn cracks her jaw.

"Would it interest you to hear about my night—"

A dramatic sigh as Viola lets her book fall into her lap. "You would like my attention, that much is clear."

Is that what I want? Viola's attention? Her affection? Her love? "I'm just feeling a bit …"

"Unwanted." Pulling three pins, Viola's hair topples from its updo and lands about her shoulders.

I nod

"As I already told you, I'm exhausted. Perhaps tomorrow night."

A sinking feeling. "Please, Viola." Another imagining of Lorelei's tongue dancing between Rose's legs makes me yearn for escape. "I can do the thing you like." I jump from the bed and go to Viola's trunk, unfastening the small compartment where I know she keeps that phallic belt. "I can be her," I say, holding it aloft. "Use this."

"Your eagerness is dull."

I toss Viola's toy back into the case, roiling with a potent mixture of shame and disappointment. But I'll not be spurned by Viola too. "What is it then? What might hold your interest, invigorate you?"

She considers this a moment, and, when her mood seems somewhat improved, I know some devious thought has occurred to her. "I've tired of your imitation, but perhaps if Lady Harrington was willing to loan Lorelei to me—just for tonight ..." She says it as if it might bring some comfort. "Yes, I feel energized already. I could see if the lady might enjoy your company while I entertain Lorelei, if you'd like."

"No."

"Suit yourself."

The illicit idea breathes new life into Viola. She takes her nightdress off, discarding it before pulling on a robe, slips her ever present book into her pocket, and leaves me alone in the room. Will she really be so bold as to make such a lurid request? Of a lady, no less? Curiosity drives me to press my ear to the door, and a few minutes later I hear snippets of her conversation with Lady Harrington.

"Late to be ..."

The rest is muffled, but I recognize Rose's crisp accent.

Viola must speak in hushed tones, for I hear only Lady Harrington's response.

"Your list of favors grows long ..." *List of favors?* "No interest in Adele beyond the obvious."

Finally, I hear a phrase from Viola's lips. "Serve the highest order."

And Rose's response, "You serve only, as you ever have, yourself."

There's a rustling and a quiet before steps approach the door. I flee back to my bedside, expecting Viola to enter, but instead hear three light knocks.

"Who is it?" My voice cracks, pulse thumps. I've not overheard the words of two acquaintances. They speak as if they've known one another well, long before this trip.

"Adele, it's Rose Harrington. Would you open up please?"

I pad over to the door, opening it a crack and hiding my sparsely clothed body. "Lady Harrington." I dip my head. "What can I do for you this evening?"

"You may suspect my intention."

No. Viola cannot simply lend me like a carriage horse. I will not debase myself—

"Dress. I'd like to speak with you privately. Years ago our families intended to merge, and I would like to see that through."

Chapter 29: A Favor of Violence

Lorelei

"Late to be knocking on my door, Viola."

Rose's voice lulls me out of my whiskey induced slumber; I'd needed something to numb my senses after the incident with Adele. She'd looked so fragile, so beautiful, bathed in moonlight with my hand at her throat. Rose steps out into the hall, the door clicking softly shut behind her.

They must have moved further down the hall as all I can hear are muffled voices with the occasional word coming clear.

Favour? What possible favor could Viola be so bold to ask of Rose?

Another moment passes before I hear footsteps approaching the door. I bury my head in the pillows, pretending to still be asleep.

"Lorelei, Lorelei, Lorelei."

Viola strokes my hair as she sits down on the bed beside me. "Little fox hiding in her den, is she? Afraid to come out and face me."

I lift my head to look at her. "What do you want?"

"You didn't think that Rose would be eager to share you? You know that's how she gets her thrills." She brushes her thumb against my bottom lip. "Don't you want to frolic and play with me?"

Play?

I think of Adele clutching at her ribs, lies about it being nothing spilling from her lips. *Like you play with her, Viola?*

"Yes, I'd like to play."

"Good girl." She undoes the belt of her robe. "You'd do anything for your lady, wouldn't you?"

"Yes, I would."

Viola leans back on the pillows, her robe falling open, exposing herself to me. So beautiful, but oh so vulnerable. The belt of her robe snaked out beside her.

"How would you have me please you?" I know what the answer will be. Viola likes it both ways. She has Adele to cater to one side of her, and she expects me to sate the other.

"Just be yourself, Lorelei. I'm more than capable of taking it."

She is far too arrogant to realize just what it is she asks.

"As you wish." I kneel beside her, taking her in; from the soft hollow of her throat to the hard muscle of her thighs.

"Well, are you going to do something? Or are you just going to sit gawping?"

I smile; she means to rile me, to make me lose control. I won't give her the satisfaction. "You'll speak when I tell you to speak," I say.

"I do love that fire, but I think you need to show me what you're prepared to do to get me to listen to you."

I lean over her, cinnamon breath hot on my face. "You don't want to push me, bitch."

"Don't I?"

She tries to capture me in a kiss, but I pull away from her.

"As if I want those vile lips and tongue on me."

Her amber eyes seem to glow. "We're more alike than you care to admit, Lorelei. You'll see that one day."

On a surface level our tastes may seem similar, but Viola does not care for such things as limits and consent. And tonight, neither will I.

This isn't me making love or having sex. Nor is it me fucking.

This is me enacting revenge.

This is for Adele.

"Turn over." I keep my voice low, little more than a growl.

"Make me." She settles back into the cushions, that smug sneer on her face.

I don't hesitate to slap her, the crack resounding through the room. Her sigh of pleasure and the buck of hips thrill me despite myself, but I push it down. This isn't about that.

"Turn. The fuck. Over."

She complies, wriggling her buttocks as I strip the robe from her. When I pull the belt from its loops a slim leather volume falls from its pocket. The same book Viola has been reading in the coach, the same book that looks so much like the ones in Rose's possession. I quickly tuck it away beneath the mattress.

"Would you agree that you're a very bad girl, Viola?"

"Oh, the baddest." She rolls her hips. "Are you going to punish me?"

"Yes, I am." I bind her wrists behind her back tighter than I would for anyone else, but Viola is special. Satisfied she'd be unable to work herself loose, I turn her over and sit her back up. "You truly disgust me. Do you know that?"

"Tell me more," she moans, eyes closed, her bottom lip between her teeth.

"Sincerely, truly disgust me. I didn't think myself capable of such hatred until I met you. But I guess we've all learned a lot these past few months."

I push on her collarbone, slamming her head back on the headboard. "I can't make Adele do anything she doesn't want to, including leaving a vile piece of scum such as you. She's a grown woman, after all. But what I can do …" I grip her shoulder, bringing her towards me so I can slam her back once more. "What I can do is make you aware that if I ever see so much as a hint of pain on her face, I will make you feel the same, tenfold."

Her eyes snap open as the realization dawns that this is not a game. I trace my fingers over her ribs until I find the same spot that had been so tender on Adele. "Understand?" She nods her head. "Good." I ball my fist and hammer it down onto her ribcage. My strike lands true, and I feel a slight crack and pop.

Her scream is a silent one, contorting her beautiful features so they are a true reflection of her foul and twisted nature. *What's the matter Viola? Never felt real pain before?*

I get out of the bed, pulling Viola with me. I march her to the door and throw her out into the hall, naked and bound. After a few seconds though, I grab her robe from the bed, tossing it so it lands upon her shoulder. It drapes down, covering her right breast. It won't afford her much dignity as she makes the walk back to her room, but she doesn't deserve dignity after repeatedly stripping Adele and I of ours.

"Goodnight, Viola."

I put my back against the closed door, willing my heart to slow. I can feel her out there but it's some moments before Viola finds her voice, her scream of rage reverberating through the wood, and I just pray I haven't made things worse for Adele.

***

Rose could be back at any moment. If I'm to get a look at this book I must act swiftly. Though its binding is no more than a year or two old, the pages within are yellowed with age. The text is densely packed and long sections are in some strange language that I do not recognise, but it's clear this is a tome of the occult. There was a time I'd think little of it, it being such a fashionable subject, but now …

I think back to that night on the ship when Viola cut Adele, and I watched her skin heal before my very eyes. I'd convinced myself that it must have been a trick, a clever illusion made possible by the dim light. I flick through the pages until I find one with its corner folded down.

Restorative powers.

Did I not watch as a hole in Adele's belly stitched itself back together? I'd been so sure I'd sunk my teeth into her in Matlock, and yet, after no time at all …

Transmogrification.

Rose's strange behavior the night before in bed, how she had returned later that night and spoke not a word about it. The red skirts she denied possessing, yet had me strip from her body.

The words leap off the page. As much as I'd tried to convince myself otherwise, I'd seen Adele do one of these things. Was it really so outlandish to think her incapable of the other?

But surely Adele would not trick me like that. Would she? The Adele I'd always known would never do that, but I suppose I, too, have done things of late which I did not deem myself capable of.

I read for hours, barely stopping to wonder where Rose is. Once I've exhausted the volume, I make my way tentatively to Rose's trunk where I had seen the similarly bound books. I doubt I'll have time to read so freely and long again though. I go to my own trunk and, after finding another book of similar proportions, tear it from its spine, doing the same with Rose's. I swap the bindings before carefully placing it back where I'd found it. I'd managed to time my activities well, as I hear the closing of Adele's door down the hall and light steps closing the distance between. I dim the lights and dive beneath the covers with only seconds to spare before Rose enters the room. She undresses and slips under the covers with me, pressing herself against my back.

"Oh Lorelei, what am I to do with you? You used to play so nicely with others."

I say nothing, hoping she'll think me sleeping. Eventually she turns away from me, and I hear her breathing slow as she drifts into sleep.

I wonder if Adele is safe in her bed with Viola, or if the violence I doled out on her behalf has been returned to her.

Chapter 30: Nothing is Happenstance

Adele

Rose pours a glass of water and offers it to me, as if my stomach could accept anything through the clenching of my nerves.

"At a certain level of society, nothing is happenstance."

I bat away the glass, and Rose rests it on the wicker table beside her.

"It was kind of your mother and father to offer you the illusion of choice, though I imagine now this must all be quite jarring."

She is mistaken. "My mother and father couldn't have less to do with my choices. I've not seen them, not even corresponded in—"

"Did you think your little trip to Matlock was of your own making?"

I search her face, hairline wrinkles around her eyes made deeper in the low light. "They knew nothing of my plans to leave."

She chuckles. "Darling, they designed your plans to leave."

I shake my head, flashes of finding the ticket stashed within George's gambling winnings rolling through my memory.

"It is a mother's duty to ensure her offspring land where they ought to. She was disappointed, as was I, at your reaction when you learnt of the betrothal to Maxwell. And was concerned, as was I, that you might do something rash. The Hughes and Harrington families are deeply rooted, well positioned on their own. But together, well—" The thought of power twists the curve of her lips upward. "We could not allow you to throw that away."

"I don't understand …" Dread nips at the corners of my mind, the pieces of some elaborate evil, but the full picture still obscured.

"I will lay it out plainly. Your mother wrote to me, told me of her concerns. She mentioned the rumors about your preferences, and I knew just the thing—just the person to keep you occupied until such time you might come to see the wisdom of this marriage. I encouraged her to buy a ticket, to leave it somewhere you would find it. Assured her Lorelei would find you at the port, bed you. Keep you busy without the threat of some other marriage or worse, finding yourself with child and bound to some lowly man beneath your circumstance."

Saliva fills my mouth as my stomach turns. "So Lorelei has been pretending? All this time?"

"Oh, heavens no!"

A slight relief, enough to keep the bile from rising further in my throat.

"But she has always had a *type*. Sheepish." She rolls her eyes. "It was easy enough. Just had to put you in front of her."

Shock numbs the pain enough for me to ask after more. "And Viola?"

Lady Harrington's face reflects some fond memory. "My son likes to think himself skilled in this, but it has always been Viola with the true talent for reigning in wild mares."

I shudder with disgust and disbelief.

"You're not the only one with a gift. Or had you not noticed the extent of *control* she exercises over you? How your gift became wild, the need to *cure* it urgent, at the very moments you veered from our plan? Did you think it natural?"

I flash back to every instance I willed my limbs to move, but they did not. Lorelei's inability to resist my binding her in the ship. I recall the times my flesh gave way unprompted, always in the company of Lorelei, always when I tried to right my course … I knew it strange, but to hear it confirmed—

"You had your years of fantasy. Freedom, warming the bed of another woman. You've seen the realities of poverty, become disillusioned. You're of a ripe, childbearing age. Your mother and I thought it was time and, for a handsome sum, Viola was willing to ensure you made the journey home, arrive pliable enough to receive the offer you once spurned."

The revelation is nearly too much. I grip the armrests of the chair for purchase, as if the news itself might knock me to the floor. "You mean for me to marry Lord Harrington," I repeat back.

"And to take your proper place in society once and for all."

Tears begin rising, but I push them down. "But my parents—"

"Await our arrival in Lily Dale. All has been planned. You need not stress yourself with wedding arrangements. It has all been taken care of." She reaches for my hand to settle hers atop it, but I withdraw, clutching my palm to my chest.

No. "And Viola? It was some spell, the reason for her—the reason I …"

"Surely you cannot think it so unimaginable? After what your own body, well. I needn't say more."

She knows? "I don't know what you—"

She waves off my denial. "Adele, please. Spare me."

I consider whether to play naive when there's a scream in the hall and a thud at the door that makes me start. Lady Harrington's face screws up and she moves to the door, cracking it open before throwing it wide.

"Viola!" She gasps.

Though Lady Harrington does her best to block the scene with her body, I catch glimpses of Viola's nude form as she stumbles inside, hands bound behind her back, robe dangling over her shoulder.

"What happened?"

I remain pinned to my chair, overtaken by a strange mix of concern and schadenfreude.

"That bitch," Viola spits.

Lady Harrington fumbles with her binding, still trying to cover Viola's nakedness as she unties the knots. A litany of apologies and mumbled concerns spew from her, Viola responding to none, her jaw clenched, irises black with rage.

Once her hands are free, Viola locks herself in the washroom, leaving Lady Harrington and I in an uneasy silence. Lorelei must have done this. But why? What does she know about this arrangement? My questions are so many they stop up my throat, and when Viola comes out of the washroom, clothed in a robe and favoring one side over the other, I can only stare.

"She is feral, that one. Attacked me, entirely unprovoked. Lorelei might have killed me had I not escaped!"

It is unlike the Lorelei I know to become violent without cause. However, I have seen her temper, and perhaps there is some measure of jealousy …

"Well? Are you just going to sit there and gape? Or are you going to help the woman who has shown you such generosity?"

I jump to my feet, years of conditioning taking over. I pour a glass of water and fluff the pillows on Viola's side.

"Perhaps I should take my leave," Lady Harrington says.

"Not yet." Viola eases herself onto the bed with a wince, hand hovering over her ribcage. My own throbs. Did Lorelei … "Fill me in on your little chat."

Lady Harrington folds her hands in her lap. "Adele knows all, from her mother's planting of the ticket to England to the impending nuptials. Even the bit about your *talent* for persuasion."

"Good," Viola says, easing her eyes shut. "I suppose you have some questions, little dove. Fire away, we need not set ourselves up for an outburst in mixed company."

"You bewitched me," is all I can muster.

"You let me fuck you of your own accord."

I feel the blood drain from my face, my sins laid bare before Lady Harrington.

Viola takes notice of my discomfort and scoffs. "As if she didn't know!"

I shift in my chair.

"You wanted it." Viola rolls her eyes. "I only gave you the fortitude not to run from what you secretly desired."

"How?" I whisper to the floor.

Viola stretches her neck from side to side. "A few words, an offering." She looks bored.

"So you never meant to cure me." The totality of this betrayal sinks in. "There is no Aleister Crowley."

"Oh, of course there is!" Lady Harrington seems eager to join the fray. "But he's living in England and mostly concerned with"—she and Viola exchange amused looks—"male fornication."

I shake my head, as if it might wake me from this nightmare.

"It's a lot, dear, to be sure." Lady Harrington's palm settles on my thigh, a motherly gesture. "If it's any consolation, Maxwell is aware of your tendencies. I'm sure you'll find him most amenable to some kind of arrangement, supposing you keep it quiet, of course."

The women remain for hours, until the blackest part of night gives way to the pale grey beginnings of dawn. They answer round after round of questions, until I cannot deny the facts laid bare before me.

I was manipulated into finding Lorelei, into loving her.

My gift, or curse, is no secret, and I shan't be rid of it.

I will marry Lord Harrington when I arrive in Lily Dale or face disownment and destitution.

And while Viola had some magical aid, the shame of my pleasures remain firmly on my own conscience.

When Lady Harrington finally retires to her room, I fear Viola may lash out, in need of an outlet for her anger. She summons me into bed beside her, and I abide. For what else am I to do? Run barefoot from the inn? Take up residence in the woods? I could venture to get Lorelei alone and tell her of the elaborate web we find ourselves ensnared within. Viola's injuries might have been some attempt at retribution, or they might have been a lover's quarrel. Lorelei was Viola's lover too, after all. And to learn that she was a cog in this machine, a puppet of those who think themselves her betters, just might be enough to convince her our relationship was damned from the start. No, I will not plead my case with Lorelei.

So, I curl up beneath the sheets, Viola and I both lying on our left sides. I because of my broken rib, and perhaps Viola for the same reason. To my good fortune, she must be exhausted. It's mere minutes before her breathing steadies, and I know she is asleep. But I find no rest. My thoughts drift to Lorelei's room down the hall. I concoct various versions of what might have happened between her and Viola, one worse than the next.

Is Lorelei broken? Is she bleeding, just a few walls away? When Rose returned, was she greeted with a kiss? Do they snuggle up beside each other now, as I lay sleepless?

I envision my parents greeting old friends as they arrive for my arranged wedding, my mother hanging decor, my father trying on his finest suit.

I wince at the thought of Lord Harrington quietly watching me in the coach, knowing I am soon to be his. I feel the cold metal of the bit against my teeth, already smell him all over me, the taste of tack oil shoved down my throat on our wedding night. But perhaps I should be grateful anyone should have me at all, when knowledge of my proclivities have been confirmed. And the Harringtons are a powerful family. Viola was right. There is nothing left of me to love. Worse fates exist than a match above my station and the approval of my family. And yet …

I would run, if I had some place to run to.

I would sob, if it would not send fiery pain through my ribcage.

I would take it all back.

Forgive Lorelei that night. Listen to her. Not run to Matlock Bath.

I would begin again.

I would.

I would.

Chapter 31: Promise You Won't Be Mad?

Lorelei

Breakfast was a non-event this morning. Nobody seemed to have much of an appetite, so my first sighting of Adele is as we alight into the carriage for the day's journey westward. I study her for signs of Viola's temper: she still favors her left side, though maybe a little less than the night before, but there seem to be no new injuries. Viola delights in the pain I caused her, making a show of struggling to climb the steps and sit down. I imagine she told Rose and Adele that the events of last night were down to my uncouthness and temper rather than the consequence of her own actions. Adele looks at me strangely, a mixture of fear and apprehension; Viola has indeed been dripping poison down her ear.
I decide to immerse myself in my stolen book, flipping to a page which calls my attention from a crack in the spine.

Up until such point of this writing, I have conveyed myriad charms and the workings of many illusions, but what I detail now is something different entirely; something born which cannot be conjured or brought forth where it was naught. This entry shall detail the Flayed One, whom you shall know by their uncanny ability to heal, but whose gifts reach further and deeper than even this.

The Flayed One shall, through singularity of focus, learn to assume the form of another. By way of pain, they shall be cleansed of fear. Through their breaking, set free. And when such time comes as the power is learnt and mastered, their gift may be passed to future generations, through the breeding of gifted lineage. It is only through violence …

It seems so fantastical, the ravings of a loon. Is this how Adele felt all those times I scoffed at the prospect of forces beyond our natural world?
I carry on reading, each page denser and more cryptic than the last, and after a few hours I'm forced to set the book aside. There's a nagging pain at my temple from looking at the near incomprehensible writings and

symbols. Viola's book is like a reading primer in comparison, such was its simplicity. But this—this? I may lack the benefit of a formal education but I dare say even Adele would have trouble with this. A phrase I keep seeing repeated is *blood rites* and how lines should be kept pure. I know well the importance of bloodlines. I am surrounded by people who, due to nothing more than luck of having been born to the right people, have had every advantage offered to them regardless of merit. Except, perhaps, Viola. Her place in this world continues to elude me. She moves with an air of entitlement I'd normally only seen in those of higher birth, yet there's something more, a fight not unlike my own that comes from never having had enough. Something Rose and Adele claim to comprehend but are incapable of. I tried once, to let Adele in, to make her understand that hunger. She either didn't hear or chose not to.

***

Days and nights blur together. We ride, we go to our beds at night, we ride. Rose continues to be insatiable in bed, choosing a new game to play each night from her repertoire. I can't enjoy it, my mind too full of images of Adele and what she is allowing Viola to do to her, or worse, what Viola is making her do. I continue to swap out the inners of Rose's books, continue to study to try and understand what's going on. But much like Viola there's one last piece that continues to elude me.

***

Both fear and relief fill me when we finally arrive in Lily Dale. Relief that I no longer have to spend my days in captivity, caged like an animal in that coach. Fear because whatever the reason for our being manipulated into making this journey is about to become clear, and I don't know what I can do to prevent it.

Adele's parents are there to greet us. Well, they are there to greet those of importance, and that doesn't include me. Rose and Maxwell are welcomed as old friends. Viola as though she is a business acquaintance, one to be tolerated. Adele …

Adele is enveloped within their arms but remains stiff and impassive. They don't care about her reaction; they are only concerned with the fact she has returned to them, it matters not that she wishes to be anywhere else but here.

I walk off, unnoticed by the entire party, to hide my shaking hands and trembling lip. I never held any illusions that, should I have ever met

Adele's family, I would have been made to feel welcome as a husband might have been. I was never going to be their daughter-in-law, but I always thought I would have at least been Adele's friend.

"Lore?" That small familiar voice, that voice which crossed an ocean, that voice which has always followed me since the day I chased him for two miles to retrieve the gold chain he had stolen from Adele not long after I brought her home to Matlock.

"Chester?"

He slams full force into me, the impact on my stomach knocking the wind from me and almost toppling me over.

"How? What are you doing here?"

He looks down at his shoes, new shoes black and shining. He looks the smartest he ever has dressed in a gentleman's suit perfectly tailored to his small frame, hair combed. He must notice me taking in his new appearance as he says, simply, "For the wedding."

I bite down a curse. "Excuse me?"

"For the wedding, tomorrow. Lady Rose said I had to look presentable."

My head spins, but I try to keep my voice calm and measured, to do otherwise would only cause Chester to take flight. "How do you know Lady Harrington?"

"She …" He trails off, his gaze fixing on some spot behind me.

"I promise whatever it is, I shan't be mad. Just tell me the truth."

"She …"

"Chester, I always thought you and I were friends."

"We are, Lore, we are."

"Then tell me how you know her."

"She pays the rent on our house, she gives us money. Even if Mum just spends it all on—"

"Why does she pay?" *What do you have to do in return, Chester?*

"I … Remember, you promised you wouldn't be mad. I'd tell her what you and Adele were doing. I didn't have to tell her much, just that you still lived in town, that you were still together. It's only these past couple of months that I—that the other …"

It's only these last couple of months that Viola has been involved. She always knew precisely where we'd be, where we were likely to flee when upset. That night on the bridge when I'd first confronted Viola, I'd come home to find him on the doorstep, never a wild occurrence in and of itself, but the timing of it. How he had thought to tell me about her following him and Adele to the pawnshop, sowing the seeds of doubt between us.

I look over to see Rose has also broken away from the group.

"I'll talk to you later."

Chester fidgets with his cuffs, his mouth downturned.

"I promise I'm not mad at you."

A smile tugs at the corners of his lips.

"Yeah?" he asks, shyly.

"Yeah." I go to ruffle his hair, but he bats me away with a *get off*. "I've got to go now."

I have to jog to catch up with Rose. She's standing on the precipice of the center garden, seemingly taking in the view, but her eyes have a faraway look in them.

"Lorelei." Her shoulders shudder ever so slightly as I step behind her, close enough to see the fine hairs on the back of her neck stand on end. "I thought you—"

"We need to talk." I lean forward so my lips brush her ear. "Now."

***

Rose sits on the bed whilst I stand, back against the door. I can't be close to her right now.

"What is it you want to know?" she says in a resigned motherly tone, as though I've inquired about why the sky is blue or the grass green, and now she must satisfy my curiosity rather than be allowed to go about her day in peace.

"Everything."

"I put a lot of time, a lot of training into you. I thought it was all wasted until … until I discovered a way for you to repay your debt to me. Even if you were unaware of your doing so."

"I don't understand. Was it jealousy that made you employ Chester as your little spy? That you couldn't stand I was happy without you?"

"Heavens no, Lorelei. I've always been perfectly content to share you."

"Generous to a fault," I mutter.

"Pardon?"

"Then why keep tabs on me?"

"Bless! Look at you, so sure you're the heroine in this little story. You've been reading far too much of late, it doesn't suit you. No, you were a groundskeeper, Lorelei. Meant to tend and care for Adele whilst keeping her safe within the boundaries of that town until the time came for her to be returned to her rightful place." Rose laughs. "It only took the mere possibility of bedding my maid; it was me who arranged that particular tryst and I don't blame you for falling so easily for it, she was rather exquisite, to get you to run off on a fool's errand to Liverpool for … what was it? A bit of lace? So predictable."

"To be married to Maxwell? To preserve the 'bloodline'?"

"Yes. If it's any consolation, you did a fine job taking care of her. So tender. Too tender, in fact. If you hadn't been so ashamed of that rougher side of yourself, shown it to her in the bedroom, she wouldn't have been half as easy to lead. So, thank you for that."

She rises from the bed and walks over. I want to withdraw from her but I feel weighed down. "If you think you could go to her now and show her what you were capable of giving her all along, you're wrong. Viola has taken her places you would never dare tread and"—she taps her finger on my chest—"you would simply not be enough for her."

I cast my gaze downwards, the tears that had threatened to spill earlier now obscuring my vision.

She lifts my chin up, forcing me to look into her cold gray eyes. "But don't worry, darling. I love you just as you are."

***

I couldn't face dinner; the thought of sitting around the table chilled me to my core. Instead, I stay in the room and rifle through Rose's trunk. I've exhausted the books, and all I can garner from them is that this is a marriage of convenience, a way for Adele's … power? Gift? … to continue untainted. Wrapped in a pair of silk stockings is a glass bottle filled with pills. I recognise them immediately as barbiturates. Rose would give them to me sometimes to relax me before passing me around. As she attested, I enjoyed it most of the time; I felt as though I had all the power, even if it was just an illusion.

I think of taking one now, just to dull the pain a bit.

As I turn the pill over between my fingers, I remember Rose's joking about how her husband discovering them was the best day of her life, that they left him unable to *perform* and thus she was finally free from his advances.

"Not like you," she'd say, biting a pill in half and slipping it under my tongue with a kiss. "A little relaxed, a little sleepy, but still able to go on."

"Of course she'll agree." Viola's voice cuts through the door, I slip a few of the pills into my palm. "The mangy little thing won't be able to resist."

Mangy little thing.

The door opens.

"Here she is." Rose places a kiss upon my cheek. "Sit beside me, darling. We have a proposition."

"No need to look so horrified." Viola laughs. "It's nothing like that. Although I wouldn't discount the possibility in the future. We could have a lot of fun together." She pauses long enough to let the idea fester. "No, what I offer is a chance for you to have everything you've ever wanted."

"What I want is Adele."

"Is it?" Rose pushes back my hair. "Status and the respect that comes with it, that's what you crave."

"That's not …" I let my protest die on my lips, thinking of every time I lowered myself, abiding the whims of my *betters* to make ends meet. Poverty, not lethal in and of itself, has loomed like a specter over my life, forcing my hand at every turn, holding me hostage.

"See, you had Adele and you lost her," Rose goes on. "Thanks in no small part to your station. Do you wish to spend your life clawing at the veil of happiness, only to have it swept away? A foundation, Lorelei. A foundation is what you need. Without it, you've nothing to build upon."

Firm ground to build on. It is what I want. What I've always wanted. To the point that I let Rose use me in the hope she'd give me it and now here she is. Her and Viola both, offering me a place in their … I don't know what you'd call it.

Society?

Cult?

"I told you once that I'd make you believe in magic." Viola bends slightly to meet my eyes. "Lorelei, there are such wonders in this world. Wonders you'd be made privy to. Powers such as Adele's are only the surface. There are ships that sail outside of time, people who cheat death by acquiring new bodies. Wouldn't you like to know more?"

"Okay." I take a deep breath. "Tell me more."

Chapter 32: A Permanent Impression

Adele

Lily Dale is a dreadful place. The homes push in on one another, all facing the same garden circle, barely enough room between them to stretch my arms. At the helm of the neighborhood circle stands a church, taller than the surrounding buildings, looming down with a judgmental gaze from its stained-glass windows. The whole hamlet feels cramped, intentionally claustrophobic.

The reunion with my mother and father was equally unsettling, their greeting me as if I'd simply returned from a trip into town, their veneer of joy at my coming nuptials, as if we'd planned them together, as if I enter them willingly.

It's a familiar comfort when Viola leads me into the darkness of her quarters, away from my family—now strangers—and away from Lorelei's disapproving gaze. While the room has lamps and sconces, she's chosen instead to light it with a flurry of candles. They glow from every surface, perched at varying heights. She cuts the dress from my body, an act of opulence, carelessness, squandering, and leads me by the wrist to her bed, a great antique thing with four posts of carved mahogany. As she binds me, her hair flows over the headboard, and my thought from so long ago—was it only weeks?—is ratified. It is the same color.

The rope is rough. I can only suppose it is meant for some outdoor use, for fishermen maybe. Its bristles dig into my skin, chafing when I move, so I try my best to lie still. Secured to each post, my limbs are stretched, barely remaining in their sockets. But I don't bother to whine.

Not even when she retrieves a long blade from her drawer. It dwarfs the one I'm used to, double edged and the length of her forearm. My undergarments are no match for it. Their hems give up quickly, and Viola leaves them to rest beneath me.

I don't make a sound when she traces the tip from the hollow of my neck to my belly button.

"Is there anything you wouldn't do for me?" she asks, dragging it in a lazy line up my thigh.

"No, ma'am." I swallow, hoping her cuts will be quick.

"And if I fucked you with this?" She holds the blade aloft, letting it catch the glimmer of the candlelight. "Would you beg me to stop?"

Fear breaks a sweat at the nape of my neck. I've made a mistake. She means to maim me.

"Please," I say, wriggling hopelessly. "Don't."

"Close your eyes, little dove. Try to enjoy it, if you can."

I wrench my neck forward, rope digging into my wrists with the strain. I cannot—she cannot. She wouldn't.

Would she?

Even with the contortion of my body, I can barely see the blade dip between my legs. I try to twist away, but the ropes are too tight, and the only effect is a satisfied laugh from Viola.

A knock at the door.

I should be relieved. Perhaps this visitor will distract her, cause her to change her mind. But instead I feel myself flush scarlet with shame. The idea of anyone seeing me like this …

"Come in!" Viola watches horror spread across my face as she says it. She remains crouched between my thighs, making no move to cover me.

From my position on the bed, the door is blocked by a partially drawn curtain. Footsteps on the stone tell me someone draws close. I writhe again, barely feeling the burns form on my ankles.

A figure steps into view. Her long, dark hair seems to absorb the candlelight, but as she stops at the foot of the bed, drinking me in, her silver streak glistens.

"Rose." Viola leans over, letting the blade scratch my leg as it falls to the mattress, and captures her in a kiss. "So glad you could join us."

"What's happening?" I tug again at the binds, but they remain merciless.

Rose gathers her skirt and straddles my leg, Viola the other.

"Adele, allow me to reintroduce Lady Rose Harrington: Lorelei's lover, soon to be your mother-in-law, and my long-time paramour." They share a knowing look, as if meticulous planning has led up to this moment. "Is it a comfort or further pain? Knowing Rose's *reunion* with Lorelei was at my direction?"

"Either would suit her, you know." Rose tucks a strand of Viola's hair behind her ear, then catches sight of the blade. "Are we playing with her gift tonight?" Rose's eyes alight with the possibility. "I've heard much about you," she says to me, though her eyes are on my breasts, my belly, between my legs. "I would so love to see it for myself."

She grabs the knife and I clamp my eyes shut, anticipating its sting.

Viola tuts. "In time, love."

I relax and crack my eyes back open, knowing I've been spared for at least this moment.

"Just before you came in, I made mention of fucking Adele with this." Viola holds up the knife. "She didn't seem to care for the idea."

"And why not?" Rose contorts her face in mock surprise, then reaches between my legs, using two fingers to spread my folds.

"Please!" I jump at her touch, but with nowhere to go, her fingers quickly find their place once more.

"She looks ready, despite her protests." Rose dips a finger into my opening and holds it up for Viola to inspect. She runs the finger over Viola's lips, leaving a sheen of my wetness on them, then kisses her, licking every spot she swiped.

I feel hysterics pull my chest into a knot and whimper.

But Viola simply says, "I'd have to agree."

"Shall we show Adele what we did to her lover all those years back?" Rose wears a smirk that matches Viola's.

Panic courses through me. "What?" I twist. A searing pain tells me I've dislocated my shoulder from the socket. "Please, whatever you plan to—"

"No need for speculation, little dove," Viola chimes in. She flicks the knife so it spits reflected candlelight into my eyes. My stomach roils.

"You cannot mean …" I think I might be sick. It's–it's Satanic. Before I can contemplate the double-edged blade carving me from the inside, Rose continues.

"I suppose we're somewhat constrained …" She lets out a deep sigh.

"With the wedding night approaching." Viola finishes her thought, as if they are of one mind. "Yes, we'll have to show some restraint. Handkerchief."

At Viola's urging, Rose pulls one from her dress.

So they do mean to cut me. I tense once more, but am relieved when Viola wraps the handkerchief around the blade, covering its biting edges.

"I'll start," Viola says, crawling over the length of my body and crouching over my torso. I wince at the pressure on my broken rib, but she pays me no mind. Taking my bottom lip between her thumb and forefinger, she yanks until I open my mouth. The handkerchief acts as a makeshift handle, and Viola grips it firmly, lowering the true handle onto my tongue, then further still. When it touches the back of my throat, I gag.

"Shhhh," she says.

The first tears fill my eyes.

"You can do better than that." The handle is cold on the back of my tongue, and I watch it sink into my mouth, stilling my breathing to open my throat. Once again, Viola triggers a gag, this one filling my mouth with thick saliva and forcing me to turn my head and erupt in a coughing fit. She holds up the blade to show Rose.

It drips with moisture from my throat. "This should do, don't you think?"

Rose nods and Viola returns to her former position, crouched over my right leg. She presses the handle of the blade against me, and though I strain away, it pushes inside, chilling me from within. I shudder at the cold, hard fullness.

"There you go," Rose says, her eyes locked on my impaled sex.

Viola rocks her hand, pushing the handle further inside me, then drawing it back out.

As I begin to sob, Viola offers cold assurance. "Don't worry," she says. "You'll warm it up."

Rose reaches for me, running her thumb in a light circle over my clit.

My traitorous body radiates pleasure to my core. I must be wicked, truly wicked, and the thought sends more tears streaming down my cheeks.

"When were you last at church, little dove?"

The strange question pulls me out of the moment, and the climax building inside me pauses.

"What?"

Rose delivers a slap to my breast. I jolt, yanking at the binds so hard a bit of warm blood trails to my elbow. "You heard her," she hisses.

"Years!" I cry through hitched sobs. "I haven't been to church in—"

"As I suspected," Viola says, still steadily thrusting inside me. "Long overdue for a confession."

I don't understand. My transgressions have all been at Viola's urging. It's Lorelei I owe my confession to, not—

"How long did you wait?" Viola plunges the blade's handle to its hilt, and I gasp as it hits the tenderest spot inside me.

"Wait for what?" I've all but screamed it, and I know not whether to hope someone might hear me or recoil at the thought.

Rose reaches for me once more, resuming circles on my clit with her thumb while Viola presses the knife handle as far as it will go.

"After I put you on your knees in the park. How long did you wait before Lorelei's hands were filling the empty space I left?"

The sensation is blinding. Words pour from my mouth without thought. "A day!" I yelp. "Maybe less."

"Disgusting," Rose says, increasing the pressure with her thumb.

"Indeed." Viola continues her line of questioning, resumes thrusting into me. "You pretend you don't want this. But tell the truth, Addie. Have you dreamt of me fucking you?" The plunge is swift and as painful as the first time.

"I have!"

"And why didn't Lorelei want those beautiful lips on her?"

My stomach flips over. "I don't know." My voice is soft, the words floating out on an uneven breath.

"Because she found you lacking," Rose says. She pinches me and I buck, which seems to please her. "Didn't want those pretty little fingers either, did she?"

If I could sink into the mattress and disappear forever, I would. Lorelei has told her of my inadequacies. They've laughed about it together, most likely. I am the smallest thing on the Earth. The most vile. A virus upon a flea upon a sewer rat.

"She takes mine most eagerly, you know." Rose smirks.

"Of course she does, baby." Viola presses the thumb of her free hand to the curve of Rose's smile and kisses her. "She's quite obsessed with you."

Viola turns to address me. "You're doing so well, little dove, though not as well as Lorelei once did. She took the whole blade. I was quite insulted when she didn't remember me—a side effect of the laudanum, I'm afraid. Just thought I would've left more of an impression."

"Oh, but you left a permanent impression," Rose says, seemingly consoling her. "Can still feel the ropes of scar tissue inside."

It's as if they've gutted me as well. The image of Lorelei carved to pieces in this most intimate way overwhelms in every sense of the word. How could she have survived it? How could she have gone on living after—

And then I …

Refusing to let her be, I just—

The torment is too much. My agony hardens. I leave my body to drift elsewhere, my mind free from this binding. But my body is left to their mercy, as it reminds me when Rose continues her ministrations on my clit.

My captors have synchronized their efforts, moving in time as if one.

"Tell me about your family, Addie," Viola says it as ordinarily as she might anything else.

My muscles pull into a knot at my center. Not now. I cannot think of them now.

"Agh!" I scream when she forces the length of the handle into me again. "There's Mother, Father, my brother, George."

Rose quickens her pace. Viola matches it.

"And George is …"

I squeeze my eyes shut, trying desperately not to give into the pleasure forced upon me. "A gambler. A fool. Cruel to me."

Rose and Viola's breaths come in time with my heartbeat, in time with the rhythm that pulses through me. I won't last. I won't last much longer.

"Perhaps he should join us. Cruelty riles you, does it not?"

I shatter. The force of this unwelcome climax wrangles my body, fibers of the ropes snapping with my convulsions. I shiver, tears dampening the pillow, and my nose begins to run as I sob, hysterical in the face of what I've done.

"There, there." Rose moves up the bed, clearing the hair away from my face, and wipes my nose with the sheet. One by one, she unties my bindings. She retrieves a blue glass bottle from the nightstand, its contents murky in the low light, raising it to my lips. I drink, too broken, too exhausted to resist.

Viola rolls me onto my side. I don't bother to look over at them when they lay beside me and begin to make love. Here and there a hand grasps my breast or my leg, but I pay it no mind. My cries quiet as their moans grow louder. Warmth starts at my core and spreads throughout my limbs, an easy euphoria that numbs my body and mind. And by the time each woman has reached her peak, I am halfway submerged in a restless sleep.

Chapter 33: So, You're the One

Lorelei

I've avoided churches my whole life, had never felt welcome within their cold stone walls. The spiritualist church in Lily Dale, with its bright white exterior and sun flooded inside, is no exception.

I am now, as I have always been, an outsider.

I stand next to Viola, a couple of pews back from Rose and Adele's family, as though we are the couple. "I can't trust you, not just yet," she whispers as Adele enters the chapel, her fingers digging into my arm. "So, just remember what you stand to gain. Plus, sharing is a Harrington family trait. I've no doubt that I'll still be able to borrow her from time to time. Maybe you and I can finally show Adele—" My look is enough to stop her dead. "Or maybe now is not the time to explore that."

Adele is an automaton, walking down the aisle with slow mechanical steps; she stalls halfway as though the clockwork has run down. Her father unlocks his arm from hers, placing his hand on her lower back and nudging her forward until she stands beside Maxwell.

She is stunning in the fetters of her wedding gown.

Wide sleeves tapering to manacles.

The lace neckband collaring her.

She drags death behind her in the form of a white satin train embroidered with funereal lilies.

Would death be preferable to life chained to him?

Or will she come to embrace the life he can give her that I can't? Wealth, security, children. And to think, I'll have it—not the ability to give her children, of course, but the rest of it—just a moment too late.

Adele sleepwalks through the ceremony, repeating her lines like an obedient school child. Powder cakes beneath her eyes, purple darkness showing where it's cracked.

And her eyes …

They seem impossibly blue, tracing the floor as the officiant mumbles on.

Bluer and paler than I've ever seen them before, a violet haze on a distant horizon.

"You may now …"

I bow my head and stare at my clenched hands when he goes in for a kiss.

"What's the matter, Lorelei?" Viola asks, her voice dripping with honey. "I thought everyone loved a wedding?"

We trail behind the wedding party as they gather on the chapel steps, waiting for the newlyweds.

"I did as you asked, bore witness to this sham."

"And you shall get your reward for doing so." Viola clasps my wrist, forcing a handful of millet and seed into my open palm. "Provided, of course, you rise to the occasion tonight as well."

The grain digs painfully into my palm as I ball my fist so tight, I fear the tendons may snap.

"What do you mean?"

"Be sure to get that on Adele."

"What do you mean, Viola?"

My question is lost amongst the cheers and flurry of grain as Adele and Maxwell exit the chapel. I don't throw my handful, don't bestow upon them well wishes and blessings of fertility. I let it drop to the floor, a cascade of pellets through my fingers like sand through an hourglass. My time is up.

***

Adele sits at the head table, Maxwell to one side, her father to the other. I think of the pills in my pocket. It would be so easy to crush one up and slip it in a glass of champagne. The peculiar taste put down to the bottle having corked, perhaps.

Maybe we could run, Adele and I. Maybe it's not too late.

America is unfathomably large; the journey from New York to Lily Dale spanned nearly the breadth of England, and we didn't even leave the state. It should be easy to disappear.

Would she run with me? Would we get very far if we did?

Maybe not, but it would be thrilling to try.

I stand in a corner, desperate for a drink, but Viola tells me I must keep a clear head for what comes tonight.

"Lore?" Chester puts his small hand on my wrist. "It won't be so bad, you know." He shrinks away from my glare, staying quiet a moment before gaining the courage to speak again. "What I mean is, Adele will be alreyt and you and me will be too. We—we can be a family, just you and me. We don't need anyone else."

My eyes drift to Adele, to the smile that doesn't reach her eyes.

She's not going to be alright.

"I need to get some air, Chester."

I walk on trembling legs into the cool evening, the scent of smoldering firewood in the air.

"So," a male voice slurs. "You're the one Adele ran off with?" Adele's brother, George, stands beside me, two flutes of champagne in hand. "My sister has good taste, I'll give her that."

He extends a hand offering me the drink. I consider him a moment before accepting. "Yes, she does."

"Confident! I like that in a woman." He takes a deep gulp. "Say, how about you and I head off for a while? You've had one of us. Why don't you let me show you what a real Hughes can do?"

"Oh George." I lean in to whisper in his ear. "You could never make me scream like your sister does. In fact, I doubt you could satisfy any woman."

It's a small thing, but seeing his jaw tighten and his eyes harden pleases me immensely. Perhaps he'll try and strike me. I hope he does. A fight would be a fine thing tonight.

Instead, his jaw slackens, and he casts his eyes downwards.

"Suit yourself," he mumbles. "Viola told me I needed to save it anyway." He downs the rest of his glass before looking around, seemingly for another.

"Here." I thrust my flute towards him. "I don't care for bubbles."

He takes it, tipping it down his neck in one quick motion, before spluttering.

"Are you quite alright?"

"Yes." He thumps at his chest. "It just went down the wrong way." He makes his way back inside, still coughing.

I watch the sky darken to bruise purple then black before Rose places a hand on my shoulder and tells me, "It's time."

Chapter 34: The Consummation

Viola

So, it has all led up to this, a dark celebration just below the church where we held the light one. A wedding and the wedding night. A church and its mirror beneath. My little dove is sprawled upon the altar where I left her. Snapping her wings was easier than I'd thought, but somehow, she had gusto enough left in her to require a little help from my trusty liquid friends. Laudanum is a nasty thing. When mixed with barbiturates, even nastier.

I extend a hand to Mrs. Hughes, dipping as her lips swipe my knuckles. The resemblance to her protege is striking, her hair only a shade paler from sparkling bits of silver shot through the blonde. Mr. Hughes is solemn as ever as he draws the envelope from his chest pocket.

"You'll find it all there," he says, eyes bouncing about the floor.

Men never have the stomach for it.

But Mrs. Hughes cannot keep her eyes from dancing across the litany of candles, the heavy velvet curtains draped over the stone altar where her daughter's legs dangle. When she looks away, it's a show. A lie. This is her favorite part. As it is mine.

"I trust she did not give you too much trouble," says Mrs. Hughes.

"Not nearly enough."

Mr. Hughes suppresses a cough.

"You could step outside, Mr. Hughes, if the realities are too … distasteful to you. You wouldn't be the first—"

"No, no," he says, a touch of fear in the twist of his wrinkles. "I just wonder whether tonight is the best … With the wedding and all, perhaps another evening would make for—"

Mrs. Hughes throws a stiff elbow into his side. "Do you not enjoy the privilege of our position?"

He shifts his weight from foot to foot.

"You know as well as I do," I say, stepping between them. "This is the price of our position. If it's any consolation …" I slide my fingers down his chin and draw his gaze up to mine. "She will hardly remember."

He nods, retreating to a chair in the corner as if abdicating responsibility by his lengthened proximity.

"Mrs. Hughes." I curtsey and she reluctantly follows him, taking a seat beside her husband.

I cross the room to join my fellows. Rose and Lorelei stand close enough to smell the fear seeping from Adele's worn body. She could look right up at them, if the blindfold was not so securely tied. The silk sheet I'd draped over her is starting the slip with her agitated movements. The blush of her nipple peeks above the fabric's hem.

She must hear my footsteps on the stone floor, for she says, "Viola? Is that you?" There's a slight slur to her words, the drugs still pressing their kiss hard to her mouth.

"Yes, little dove." I draw the sheet up, covering her. She needn't be exposed just yet, and it will quiet her.

I glance up to find Lorelei's stare cutting daggers. Closing the space between us, and lowering my voice so Adele will not hear, I direct my question to Rose.

"Are we confident our Lorelei is ready for this?"

Rose glances at her little street rat. "I think so."

Lorelei's teeth dig into cheeks. "You could address me directly," she says.

I tut. "Ever my saucy one." It is rare we draw someone new into our circle, but I cannot deny that Lorelei has a certain fire. The prospect of having her accessible on something of a regular basis intrigues me. And she reminds me much of myself, who I once was. Destitute. Grasping for the slightest control. At the mercy of the whims of my betters. I should like to see her ascend, as I have. But I do not trust Rose's assertion that the bond between her and Adele is severed enough to allow for what must happen.

And yet, she is here.

So I press her. "What is it, Lorelei? Title? Reputation? Wealth? Which of our offerings weighed enough that you would abandon Adele to her fate?"

She swallows, a knot moving down her throat. "None."

My eyes flick up to Rose, who tenses.

"It is what comes with them," Lorelei says. "Security. Safety."

I smile. She is right, of course. "It's ugly business but well worth it, in the end. You shall have what you seek, what you have always sought. And Adele will too, in her own way."

Lorelei's gaze passes over her former lover, who still adjusts and readjusts herself on the stone, the occasional whimper escaping her lips.

"She was always going to lie upon that altar."

Rose echoes me. "It is her station. You would not deny her the opportunity for greatness, just as you would not deny yourself."

Lorelei draws a sharp breath through her nose and turns away from Adele. "You know—you have always known me better than I know myself."

Rose places a steadying hand on her shoulder. "He is coming."

Footsteps approach, heavy boots taking careless steps. In the shadows at the end of the hall is the arrogant swagger of a man.

"You don't have to watch," Rose whispers to Lorelei.

The man moves closer, candlelight illuminating the brass buttons on his black suit jacket.

"While Maxwell is not thrilled about this part, he understands—as well as any man can—the necessity of sacrifice."

Closer the man draws, his ginger hair warmer in the dim light.

A flash of alarm crosses Lorelei's expression.

Rose tightens her grip on Lorelei's shoulder. "The gift may only be passed through familial lineage. So there's no need for Maxwell to join us at the consummation."

I shudder with pleasure at the horror that distorts Lorelei's visage. She must think me monstrous. She does not yet understand: I break only what must be rebuilt, transformed into something new. But she will.

"George is a bumbling fool," I say, digging in the knife. "But he carries her blood." Tears collect in the corners of Lorelei's eyes. "So it must be him. Must be his seed."

Rose continues, "The gift is the most important thing, passing it on. We women must snatch our power where we can find it."

George's lip quivers as he stands before his splayed sister. The witless nitwit. A sheen of sweat glistens on his brow, and I think he might run, but fall at ease when I remember the spineless legacy of the male Hughes line. George may be unable to embrace his calling, just as his father shrinks from it, but there's not enough gall between them to buck tradition. They will play their parts, whining like pups or not.

"Lord Harrington?" Adele's voice carries less of a slur, but she remains sedated enough not to move from where I've placed her.

Thrill raises the hairs on the nape of my neck.

"George Hughes." His paleness blanches further when I speak his name. Adele freezes in place. "Are you prepared to receive your birthright?"

The eagerness of his nod is incongruent with the rest of him, the way he avoids meeting my eyes, his stare fixed on the stone altar beneath his sister.

"Very well then." I nod to Rose and she takes Lorelei by the hand, leading her to Adele's side. As Rose grabs Adele's wrist, Adele shrieks.

"Lorelei," Rose says, her tone stern. She indicates for Lorelei to grab Adele's other arm to stop her squirming.

As Lorelei reaches for her, Adele pleads. "Lorelei, please." Tears seep through the blindfold, darkening the black silk. "Please help me."

"Lorelei." It's my warning.

Adele thrashes, Lorelei's hand shaking as it hovers beside her. Rose tightens her grip, nails digging into the flesh of Adele's forearm.

"If you ever loved me—" Adele's voice cracks, but she steadies a bit, yielding to Rose's strength. "Don't let them do this."

"Let's get it over with," George says, unbuckling his belt.

I step beside Lorelei, ready to hold Adele should she fail. "Time to choose. Reach for all you desire, or throw it away for this wretch." I place my hand on hers, guiding her closer to Adele's arm. "Either way, it will be consummated. Tonight and every night until a child is conceived."

Lorelei extends her fingers, but stops just short of grabbing Adele's arm.

My patience has worn thin. "You martyr yourself for nothing." With a firm push, Lorelei tumbles down the steps surrounding the altar, and there's a crack as her skull makes contact with stone.

Clutching Adele's arm, I beckon George forward. I could charm her in the same way I have prior, but there's something visceral about subduing her with my own hands, feeling her muscles made weak by the cocktail I've dosed her with.

He stands between her spread legs just as she snaps them shut, her knee connecting with his groin and doubling him over.

"Fuck!" he cries.

I motion for assistance, a servant girl and the house boy stepping forth, each grabbing one of Adele's thighs. She screams.

In the shadows, Mr. Hughes covers his ears, tucking his face into his armpit. Mrs. Hughes shows a trace of dissatisfaction, but does not turn from the scene.

George continues his moaning.

"That's enough now," I say. "Get on with it."

Eyes glazed, he straightens, taking cautious steps between his sister's flailing limbs. My staff, though young enough to be struck through with fear, grip tight enough to turn the surrounding flesh white.

Still, Adele screams.

The sound seems to rouse Lorelei from her unconscious state. She rolls to her side, grasping at her head where a spot of blood mats her hair.

George fiddles with his waistband, reaching into his trousers with a look of consternation.

"Well?" I ask when he dawdles a bit too long.

Lorelei barks a laugh, spitting a mist of blood onto the floor. She wipes traces from her lips, teeth still filmy with rusty stains when she asks, "Problem with your manhood?"

Fuck. So much time spent pleasuring the fairer sex, I'd nearly forgotten the delicacies of men's ability to perform.

"George, this is not the time for stage fright. Step forward, do as your—"

"I'm trying, ma'am!" His hand bounces inside his trousers, a little pulse beating against the fabric.

"You think you're the only one capable of drugging?" Lorelei sneers from her place on the floor. "Barbiturates might have helped in making Adele compliant, but you'll find they have the opposite effect on a man's member." She attempts to rise, but stumbles onto her knees, no doubt concussed.

Rose's glance questions me as George lets out an exasperated huff and rips his hand from his pants. The groom and the servant girl look to one another. Mr. Hughes has exited through the rear door, trailed by Mrs. Hughes, taking loud, frustrated steps. I drop Adele's arm. "Go." I don't hide my anger, and George is all too quick to flee from the hall, followed shortly after by my quaking staff.

Rose lingers a moment. "Shall I help you get her into bed?" She indicates Adele, whose screams have quieted into gentle sobs.

"Just leave her. I would like to deal with Lorelei on my own."

Knowing better than to disobey, Rose departs. The stone hall is filled with the echo of Adele's whining and the shuffling of Lorelei's attempts to get to her feet.

"It's down to us," I say, descending the altar steps to peer down at her pathetic form. "I had so hoped you would choose better." I grab her by the tangled mess of red hair, wrench her neck back so she must face me. "I saw such potential in you." My spit lands in a wad on her cheek. "Disappointing."

"Fuck you, you cunt."

My fist connects with her jaw, and the crack of her teeth butting together rings out. I hear Adele fussing behind me, but I'm fixed on my target. Face down, Lorelei crawls away, but it takes less than a second to position my foot above her and bring it crashing down on the center of her spine. I know from her sucking sounds I've taken the wind out of her.

I crouch, eager to get a look at her ruined face, but she spins, sweeping my legs from under me with a swift kick. Before I can get my bearings, she's on top of me. Punches drive hard and fast into my face and neck. I've no time to return them, only to throw up my hands and try to block. She must have landed twenty blows by the time she stops. I feel my eyes swelling shut.

"Let us go. Let us go and swear you'll never come after us, never so much as think our names again."

I stagger to my feet, Lorelei already on hers, fist balled and prepared to launch another attack.

"Alright then." I throw my hands up and dip my chin in submission.

She is distracted, already moving toward the altar behind me when I grab the amulet on my chain. I go to pull my blade from its sheath, but find the casing empty.

Fear slackens my jaw. I recall the tug at my collar whilst George was fiddling.

A pinch at my neck.

I spin on my heel to find Adele, hunched and panting as a dark red liquid shoots across her bewildered face. My hands paw around the twinge of pain, fingers finding that familiar braided pattern: my blade. It's buried in my neck up to its small hilt, slippery with my own hot blood.

Adele takes one step back, then two. My vision tips and buckles.

A smack of flesh on stone and I find myself on my knees, a crimson puddle spreading out beneath me.

Another smack.

Laid flat, I stare up at her, dark edges forming around my line of vision. Ashen hair drapes her face as she looks down on me, emotionless. I press around the wound, yank the dagger from its spot. A mistake, I realize at once, as my own lifeforce sprays from the hole.

Still, Adele looks on.

Pressure from my palms slows the flow, but not enough. I know it is not enough. Lorelei joins Adele, eyes gaping in horror as she watches me take sucking breaths. I thought it would be her, if it was anyone, to make a move on me. But Adele—cold as marble, she watches, her breath even. My eyes flutter, soon to close.

"Good girl," I sputter, though it's more gurgle than words.

Before I let the pull of the other side take me, I take one last look. Spatter speckles her fair cheek, her dress marred with violence, irises pinpricks from the lingering effects of my drugs; her blue eyes behold her own power for the first time.

It is sour but fair to have been bested by one I assumed weak. And a pleasure to know, before my end, I had the power to turn a dove to a lioness.

Chapter 35: Never Like That

Lorelei

"Adele?" She stands, her gaze unwavering, over Viola's body. "Darling?" Adele turns her head towards me but doesn't see me. "Adele, we have to go. It won't be long before Rose comes back."

"Viola, she's—I—"

"Did what you had to do."

Adele nods. "I had to."

"Everything is going to be okay." I consider if it would be worth hiding Viola's body, to clean up the blood. No, that would take hours, time better spent getting a head start.

"Stay here, just for a moment."

Adele reaches for me.

"I promise I'll be back."

I rush to Viola's room and rifle through her luggage.

It doesn't take long to find what I'm looking for. The cash within the leather satchel is more than enough to get us far from here.

I grab a few items of Adele's clothing and make my way back.

Adele sits on the stone altar, draped in that silk shroud, shivering slightly. Wetting the fabric of the sheet as best I can with my own spit, I wipe the blood from Adele's face. She is unmoving, sights fixed on the tangle of dark hair, the cooling mass of flesh that was Viola.

"This is what we're going to do. You're going to get dressed and go to the stable whilst I fetch Chester and the groom."

Adele opens her mouth to protest.

"There's enough money in this bag to give him a year's wages, maybe two. His loyalty to these people will falter in the face of it."

I help Adele dress, all the while repeating what it is she must do. As I slip her shoes on, I ask her one final time where she must go.

"The stable."

"Good girl." I resist the urge to kiss her; she's in a state of shock and I'm not sure if my touch will be welcome. "I'll see you soon."

With Chester safely in tow, I wake the groom, who is more than prepared to abscond from his duties in Lily Dale in exchange for more coin than he's even seen before in one place. It isn't long until we're all safely in the carriage and on our way out of town. Adele succumbs to sleep swiftly, followed almost immediately by Chester. I hang on for a few hours more. Every noise causes my whole body to tremble, to think that they have given chase and there's nothing I can do. Eventually though, as every pop and crack proves not to be Rose and Maxwell closing in, but rather the snap of twigs under the carriage wheels, I too drift away.

***

"Miss?" The strange male voice startles me out of my restless sleep. "Miss, we need to change the horses."

"Um, yes, of course."

We climb bleary eyed from the coach, Chester running off to relieve himself, leaving Adele and I alone. I lead her into the inn where she stands behind me without a word as I make arrangements for a room for us and explain that a young lad will be along momentarily who shall need his own. When I turn, key in hand, she avoids my eyeline but follows me down the hallway and into our quarters. Something prickles in the air between us, not the thick tension of our arguments in Matlock, but something charged. It's only after I've hidden the bag of cash in the bottom drawer of the dresser, wrapped up in a blanket, that she finally speaks.

"I suppose you're feeling smug right now?" The bitterness of her words chokes me.

"What—why—no!"

"You love that you were right about Viola."

Do I? Do I love the vindication?

"I—"

"You never tried to stop it. Not really. You froze me out, replaced me in your bed. Let Rose touch you in ways you would never let me."

"I never let her fuck me. Not like you, so eager to spread your legs like a common—" The sting of her hand silences me even as her voice raises in pitch.

"You're a liar! Admit it, Lorelei, I was nothing but a placeholder. If you knew what she'd done to you, her and Viola both, you wouldn't have been so desperate to have her f-fingers in you."

"What …" I swallow down the bile and continue to ask the question that I already know the answer to. "What did they do?"

She drops her head, mumbles. I can't make out all she says but I catch the words *blade* and *whole*.

"Oh."

It's the suspicion I've held somewhere deep and buried, something too twisted to confront while accepting comfort from Rose, while allowing Adele one moment with Viola alone. And yet … had I known? Was it ignorance or convenience that drove me to continue the farce with Rose, to not drag Adele from Viola's company, if that's what it would've taken to part them? My head reels. Blood-stained sheets. Pain sharp and deep. Hot stickiness between my legs. The curl of a sneer. Several moments pass before I face Adele again. Sympathy lurks beneath a veneer of resentment. Now I know. I thought knowing for certain would bring a modicum of comfort, of closure.

It does not.

"Do you still love her?"

"What?" I should have recognised the look of quiet desperation in Rose's eyes that night. I'd seen it so many times in the early days of our relationship, when she'd been so unsure of herself, of us. It's the look she holds in her eyes now. But still the confirmation of yet another betrayal causes the bile to resurge.

"It was you that night! What were you hoping to achieve? Were you expecting to see me crying over you? You fucking betrayed me, lied to me. Not just once, but time and again. And you let that woman—"

"And I fucking enjoyed it!"

Adele closes her eyes as though readying herself for a strike.

"Go on, hit me. Hit me! That's how you derive your pleasure, isn't it? You and Viola both." She grits her teeth together and offers the side of her face. "Go ahead," she growls. "You don't know a tenth of what I've seen, what I've done. I can take it. I can take so much."

Her words land harder than any punch I've ever received, and her cornflower eyes harbor a deep and quiet pain, unlike any I've seen before.

"No, not like that. Never like that." I uncurl fists I hadn't even realized I'd clenched.

"Parsing hairs, isn't it? A strike is a strike. Pleasure is pleasure."

I reach for her, and she allows me to rest my palm on her shoulder. I feel a tremble as her eyes dart, sorting through the difference: between Viola and me, between real fear and the game of it. "It should never come from anger. It's an understanding, a trust."

"It's an abomination; I'm an abomination for allowing it, for want—"

"No, you're not. Nothing about you is."

Idly, her hand traces the edges of her ribcage.

"I love you."

"You love her," she whispers.

"I don't! I said that because Rose—you forced my hand."

Her hand rises and folds over my own. "Truly?"

"Yes. I never thought I was capable of the kind of love I have for you. And yes, maybe I haven't always been the best at expressing it, but I do. With all my soul." I clasp both her hands with mine.

"But why?" She asks it with all earnestness, as if she sincerely believes herself unlovable.

"I love all your silly Americanisms. I love how you can't make a decent cup of tea to save your life, but how you'd always bring me one in bed each Sunday morning."

"You always drank it." The ghost of a smile tugs at her lips as she gives my hands the gentlest of squeezes.

"I did! Even though it was truly, bloody awful. Because I loved the gesture, just as I love you." I get down on my knees, as is fitting any proposal. "Adele, we don't have to go back to England. We can forge a new life, make it anything we want it to be. Anywhere. Fuck it! Let everything we were before burn, raze it to the ground, and we'll build something stronger, better."

"But I–I hurt you. Betrayed you. I let you believe I was victim to some predator when it was my own vile shortcomings, my inability to speak! To just tell you what it was I desired. I let you guess at it, let you fail, then punished you for it. How … how could you ever forgive me? Why would you want to?"

"I failed because I didn't trust you enough to know your own needs and wants. I looked at you at times as if you were some innocent little girl who I had to protect, not the vibrant intelligent woman that you are. I underestimated you, and I'm so sorry."

"You saw the best in me." Adele sinks to her knees so we are eye to eye. "And you have protected me, took me in, cared for me when I could not care for myself. You've provided me with a life of warmth and comfort, even when I looked down my nose at it. I would be nowhere without you. You are the most generous, most kind woman I've ever known. And I ruined it. My regret has haunted me since that night. What I wouldn't give to go back, to actually listen to you, to hear you when you said—"

"You are listening now," I whisper.

"I am." Tears skate down her cheeks. "I am listening. I will do anything to bring your happiness back to you, whether it includes me or not. Just tell me now, and I will listen. I will hear you this time."

I grip her by the shoulders. "I want to go away with you. Start over somewhere new. We can begin again. I don't care where."

"I hear France is quite lovely. Or Italy." Her voice is still small, still shaking with emotion.

"Either one, as long as we're together. You and I. And Chester, of course. Please say yes."

Adele chews at her bottom lip, considering the possibility. "Yes, on one condition." She bats away the tears licking her chin.

"Anything."

A smile twists her lips. "Admit that it's eggplant, not aubergine."

Relief sweeps through me. My shoulders drop and I slide onto my rear. "Anything but that, perhaps I could walk across hot coals for you?"

"No," she says through a chuckle.

"Fine." I get up from the floor and draw her up with me. "The cushions are eggplant. They always were."

"Now, that wasn't so dif—" I silence her lips with my own. She kisses me back, tentatively at first, then takes a step backward, eyes wide and jaw cracked open.

Have I made an error in judgment?

But she lunges, launching into me with a force that makes me brace myself with a foot behind me. She returns my kiss with an intensity I haven't known since those early years, burying her fingers in my hair. I wrap my arms around her. There is no imagining, not anymore. This is no substitute. Adele is before me, her tongue gliding against my lip, the curve of hips in my palms. Finally, she relinquishes me. Clearing her throat and cracking a smile she says, "As I was saying, that wasn't so difficult, was it?"

"I suppose not, but no need to gloat about it," I murmur against her neck.

"I'll never let you forget it."

"I feared that would be the case." I recapture her in a kiss, determined never to let her go ever again.

Chapter 36: A Fantasy Without Fear

Adele

I am not who I once was. My drugging, it seems, turned out to be a blessing. For while I remember the day of the wedding and the night that followed in bits and pieces, the sharper details are obscured by foggy darkness. Still, I am changed. The Adele who sheepishly boarded a transatlantic crossing in hopes of escaping a marriage would have recoiled at what I plan to do. But I feel nary a twinge of guilt as I lift a man's trunk from the Astoria luggage trolley and spirit it away to the restroom.

Viola's amulet has become a macabre memento of sorts. I roll it over in my hand, warm light reflecting off the silver. There's a comfort to rubbing at the braided embellishment, a reminder that these ropes are frozen in time, impotent and unable to snare me. No, I suspect nothing could snare me now. The tiny blade slides out happily, and I strip my dress, gazing upon my reflection in the floor length mirror of the stall. A yellow bruise wraps its way around my torso, climbing onto my breast, but I shall be rid of it momentarily.

Popping open the trunk, I select a tweed suit, the finest of the mess of clothes inside. Its owner must be of a slightly lower station than my target, but no matter. Just as Viola taught me, I pierce myself at one shoulder, following the line of my collarbone. My visage melts off and slides to the floor in one, gooey chunk, and I think of Lord Harrington, of the scent of tack oil, his steely gray eyes. When I gaze into the mirror once more, I wear his face.

Before I dress, I honor the passing thought that I will never have to touch this body, to allow its weight to press down upon me, to suffer its clumsy movements, and smile. My dress stowed in the trunk, I step into the Waldorf Astoria lobby in the skin of a powerful man. For the first time in my life, I cross busy city streets without a shred of fear. Envious looks from other men at the bank tell me I've thoroughly fooled them, so when I request the teller empty my accounts, it is with all the confidence of a rich man with nothing to offer.

"Right away, Lord Harrington."

"But of course, Lord Harrington."

"Will large bills suit you, Lord Harrington?"

The money is packaged neatly and arranged in a briefcase. The teller nervously counts it out under my eye in a back room within a locked door. He even calls on his manager to ensure the bank has not displeased him in any way.

"Not in the slightest," I promise.

"Excellent, sir."

"Very good, sir."

The more I mirror Harrington's look of subtle contempt, the more they fall over themselves to please me, not knowing—for how could they?—they waste their flattery on a mere woman. There is something circular about returning to the Waldorf Astoria, suitcase of cash in hand, possibilities endless, and when I shed Lord Harrington's skin and return to my look and dress, it is with a quiet promise to myself that this will be the last time I think of him.

Chester has never been so thrilled; seeing such a large sum in one place nearly causes him to swoon. The Amalfi Coast, Lorelei and I decide, is as good a place to start over as any. Chester agrees to travel with us and, after initially balking at the idea, he promises to enroll in school and try, at least, to become a *proper boy*. In truth, I harbor a secret hope Lorelei and I might outrun the talk of all that transpired, that the journey might be long enough to heal the wounds and hide the scars, that the money might chase away enough trouble to not only project the image of a happy family, but to feel like one.

It's foolishness, though. For even in our brightly colored bungalow, mountaintops disappearing into wispy cloud cover, the gentle caress of the tide lapping the shore, and exotic tongues shouting indiscernible phrases all around, the pain has journeyed with us. Unspoken words hang heavy in the air, corroding the space around us like saltwater on iron.

I sit at my bedside, Lorelei at hers, separated by the conversation we need to have, the one so many years overdue, that's gained inertia with the passage of time and the many mistakes we've made. The sheet rustles. I should turn to face her. I should make this easier. But I cannot. It is the one thing that fear still holds me from: speaking plainly of my wants. Shame crouches over my shoulder and holds me in place. It whispers in my ear as I stare out the window, *How dare you ask her? After all you've done. You've no right.*

"Adele?"

What will you tell her? That the violence thrilled you? That you wished it was her in some hidden place, but that when Viola bent you to her will you felt …

"Look at me."

She will find you repulsive, desperate. Will always think of Viola all over you. A hand warms my shoulder. I press my cheek to it.

"We have to talk about this. I know it's difficult."

"I was bewitched. You must know Vi–that woman cast some …"

"It is more than just that though. Is it not?"

It was more. "You would never"—I crane my neck and catch the pleading look in her eyes—"understand."

"But I do!" She turns me with a gentle nudge. "I already understand. We have to talk about it."

Lorelei is so gentle, so forgiving. *You don't deserve her.*

"What is it you want to know?"

For all her insistence, this seems to throw her. Her eyes search the room. "What was it … about her?"

Here is the chance. She's asked so directly, and yet I cannot lie, much less tell the truth, so I remain silent.

"I have my suspicions," she says at last.

"It was not for lack of loving you." It's all I can muster.

"Do you mind if I—" Lorelei rises from the bed and circles it, crouching to meet my eyes. "Can we try something?"

I nod, relieved at the prospect that I may not have to explain myself, at least not in words.

She stands as she tells me, "Unfasten your dress." Her tone is stoic. It steadies the rhythm of my pulse, and I find myself less frozen, enough to do as she's asked. I let my bodice fall to my hips, exposing the undergarment beneath.

"Get up."

Once on my feet, she spins me, pushing me so I have to catch myself on the mattress.

"Do you like this?" she whispers.

"Yes."

"I figured as much." Her cold tone has returned. "And if I said it's because you're a filthy whore, would you like that too?"

My muscles tense. I long to feel her hands on me. "Yes," I whisper.

"For all you've done, the despicable behavior you've demonstrated at every turn, wouldn't you like to pay?" She hikes up my skirt and tosses it over my back. The exposure sends a bead of slickness between my thighs.

"It's what I deserve."

"So, we're in agreement." Lorelei's hand slides up the back of my thigh. "I'm willing to punish you." At the word, my heart leaps in my chest. "But only if you ask nicely."

My eyes flick up, questioning. She raises her palm, but holds it in the air.

"Please?"

The crack of her hand against my flesh tells me I've answered correctly, and the stinging pain travels from where I was struck to my center, morphing into desire, desire for more.

"Tell me, is that all you can take?"

I shake my head.

"Say it. Say, 'a bit harder, please.'"

I want her to strike me. To lash out with abandon. But the words are stuck in my throat, wedged down by years of propriety.

"Say it, Adele. Or you get nothing."

I focus on the stitching of the bed linen. I must do this. "Please." The word is strangled, but the next, more clear. "A bit harder."

Lorelei is quick to appease me, lashing the same spot with more force. "Surely you deserve a bit harder. Don't you think?"

I'm overcome with need for it. "Yes," I say. And thrice more she slaps me, alternating legs. The last crack comes down with such force that my knees buckle. "That's it!" I cry. "No harder."

I feel Lorelei's hand on the tender spot once again, but not to strike me. She grazes her fingers over the raw flesh as if to soothe it. "Good."

I crane my neck to divine her meaning, but she pushes my face back into the bed.

"Do you like this game?"

My confirmation is muffled by the linen.

"Is this how'd you like to teach me? How you'd like to show me the secret things you're afraid to put to words?

God, yes! I nod, the explosion of gratitude evident in my eagerness. How fortunate I am that she would—

She strips the thin undergarment covering my sex with a practiced tug. Fresh air mingles cool against my wetness.

"I know you like when I touch you here." Her finger slides against my opening. I'm hungry for her, a bottomless pit of need. "But what if I touched you …" It continues upward, hesitating at a place I've never …

I arch my back, hoping she'll understand.

"Say it. Can I touch you there?"

Wriggling against her is my last attempt to make clear my wish without uttering the words, but rather than abiding me, she withdraws. The cold of her absence makes me shiver, but when she delivers a slap across my rear, I am once again filled with warmth.

"It's rude to ignore your betters, Adele."

I whimper when another blow lands expertly in the same spot.

"When I ask you to do something, you'll do it. Understand?"

A flash in my periphery tells me she's raised her hand once more. Reflexively, I curl my hips to avoid it. "Yes!"

Lorelei gathers my hair, pressing her body against mine to place the length of it neatly beside me. "But I'll never ask you to do something you don't truly want. So you have to tell me."

"Okay." Feelings bloom so deep and wide I can't attribute them to just one thing or another. Could this be real? Have my fantasy without the fear?

A finger runs over my crumpled skirt, down to the very base of my spine. "So I'll ask you again." It threatens to go lower, but once again pauses, a breath away. "Would a whore like you want to be touched here?"

It feels so wrong. And the wrongness makes me want it, crave it. "I would."

Lorelei presents her finger beside my mouth. I take it onto my tongue, lightly sucking the length of it before she pulls it away. She slides one finger into my sex while the other traces a steady, up and down motion. I gasp when presses it against me, firm but gentle, and she penetrates, granting the most deliciously full feeling, fingers rocking in time in their separate places inside me.

"Good," she says.

I shudder.

"You'll have no more secrets from me. I will claim every place inside of you."

With me bucking against her, she quickens her pace, thrusting harder into me. Pleasure collects at my center and begins to build. I moan, her name curling over my tongue in breathy gasps. Lorelei knows this telltale sign, and I'm shocked when she pulls away rather than finish me.

"Not yet."

I collapse onto the bed, and when I flip over and look up at her, I don't hide my frustration.

"Cross with me?" She smirks.

I puff my lips into a pout. "I was close."

At this, she climbs on top of me, letting the weight of her hand provide the slightest pressure around my throat. "A spoilt brat is what you are, expecting everything your way. You need to learn your place."

"My place?" Emboldened by the ease with which I pull in breaths and the intoxicating knowledge that Lorelei could simply tense her wrist, stop my airflow entirely, a devious voice inside tells me to test her. "I should remind you of yours."

Her palm travels from my neck to my jaw, cracking it open. "I ought to wash your mouth out." Her lips purse as if she means to spit. I can scarcely believe she'd think of such a thing! "Would you like that?"

It is my turn to smirk, to call her on her bluff. "Yes." I open my mouth wide, confident that she would never demean me so. And I'm right, or so I think at first.

She spits onto her own fingers, then glances down at my open maw. "Wider."

I tip my head back and stretch my jaw as wide as it will go. Lorelei plunges her spit-soaked fingers inside, rubbing them briskly across my tongue. My head shakes with the force of it. "You will address me with due respect." Her eyes narrow, then flick upward, beckoning me to speak, but still her hand is wedged between my teeth. "Go on then."

Cheeks flushed with humiliation, I try to form the words, *Yes, Lady*, but the resulting sound is more gurgle than discernible language.

"What's that?" Lorelei taunts, easing her hand even further into my throat.

I gag. My eyes water, but the tears collecting in my lashes are nothing compared to the wetness between my legs. My grunts and whines are meant to say, *Yes, Lady Keyes.*

Her fist drips with saliva when she pulls it from my mouth. "One more time." Her dry thumb wipes my eyes.

"Yes, Lady Keyes."

Hearing the clear words sets her eyes aflame. She captures me in a kiss that sends me reeling. I don't realize I've dug my fingers into her back until she yelps and jolts away from me.

"How dare you?" Grabbing both my wrists, she pushes my arms above my head. Her free hand hovers above my nipple, fingers poised to pinch. "A fitting punishment, no?"

I grin. "If it pleases you."

The first tweak is uncomfortable but nothing more. She studies my face before clamping down again, harder this time. I nod. The third pinch makes me wince, and I wrap my legs around her, desperate for satisfaction.

Lorelei clicks her tongue and wags a chastising finger. "Patience, Adele."

I release my grip on her waist, letting my legs fall.

"Excellent listening." Thoughtlessly, she lets her hand glide between my legs. A second more and I would collapse around her. "Good girl." Once more she offers me her fingers and I take them into my mouth, greedily lapping up the taste of my arousal, salt and musk. "You've missed a spot." She turns her palm and spreads her fingers so my tongue can reach the crevices. "Better. Don't move." Sliding one leg over me, she removes herself from the bed, peering down on my naked body from its edge. "Who would've thought our little talk would get you so worked up?" Lorelei takes a few steps away. "Open your legs for me."

Gazing up at her, fully clothed, I'm starkly aware of my nakedness. I want to abide her, but with the light of day streaming through the sheer curtains, I find I can only part my knees a foot or so before bashfulness gets the best of me.

She leans down, eyes level with my exposed center. "You can do better than that. Show me."

I part my legs another foot, her eyes upon me like teasing fingers.

"What are you hiding, Adele? All the way. I won't ask you again."

Lorelei's stern tone makes me want to reach down myself and finish what she's started, but instead I inhale deeply, pulling my legs wide until I feel the burn of the stretching muscles. I hold them there, watching her drink in the sight of me.

"Well done. Exceptionally well done."

My need has grown such I think I might explode. As if sensing this, Lorelei advances, one slow step at a time, her gaze fixed on my exposure. She pushes on my knees, and I rock back enough for her to see the newest place she's claimed.

"It's yours." My words shock Lorelei as much as myself. Like a drain unstuck, the proclamation flows freely from my lips, without shame. I tug harder on my legs, wrench myself into a painful stretch. "It's all yours."

Her breath hitches as she grabs me, hand enveloping both holes. "It always has been."

I writhe against her, the slight pressure nearly enough to send me over the edge. But she grabs my shoulders and pulls me to my feet instead.

"Get on your knees."

I drop to the floor with a smack, knowing I'll have bruises the next day, but the thought of it is sweet. Lorelei hikes up her skirt and brings my mouth to her center, stepping closer to the bed until my head is pressed against it. There, she goes to work on me. Much as she had in the dingy cabin at sea, she thrusts herself against my tongue. I am happy to allow her to use me, clutching at her thighs and pulling her closer.

Hand woven into my hair, she steps back and wrenches my head to look up at her. "Do you like that?"

"Yes." I feel her dripping down my chin.

"Of course you do."

While I've always known Lorelei to be strong, I never thought she could toss me as she does. I land on the bed, and she strips her clothing before straddling me. Starting at my hips, she makes her way up, taking position over my mouth.

"Fuck me with your tongue."

I hesitate. When last I tried this, she rebuffed me. "Are you sure?"

"You will do as I instruct you." She lowers herself and I caress my tongue over the folds of her flesh. It passes over her clit, making her moan with pleasure. So, I continue there, tracing wide, gentle circles.

Smack! I jump when her slap lands on my thigh.

"You're not listening."

I swallow, as if I might ingest my trepidation, and press my tongue against her entrance. Her taste is strong here. I salivate, greedy for her. Fingernails dig into my scalp, and with this encouragement, I push into her, my tongue breaching her entrance, squeezed by the tightness of her.

"Fuck!" She groans, rolling her hips over my face.

Slowly, I glide my tongue in and out, letting her set the pace with the movement of her body. Her bittersweetness slides down my throat, and I find myself lost in her. Lorelei's breath becomes heavy and even, and I press my legs together, eager for relief from the ache between them. She must see this, for she lifts her body and turns, straddling me once more but leaning down to kiss between my thighs.

I spread my legs, lifting my hips. Her hot mouth sends a shock of pleasure through my core. My tongue dances inside her as hers rolls circles over me. I know I won't last. Grabbing her thighs, I thrust deep into her. She cries out, coming in powerful waves, her tongue meeting me with the perfect rhythm. I moan, face still pressed against her as I come. It's enough to send her into a second climax, her body twitching with the force of it.

When the last spurt of pleasure has diminished, she collapses onto me. We pant in time. I trail a gentle caress over her back. Lorelei turns to face me, smoothing errant hairs away from my eyes.

"I love you, Lorelei." Tears well at the corners of my eyes. "Completely. And I'm so sorry."

Her lip trembles and she gathers me into her arms. "I love you, Adele. And it was never all your fault. I'm truly sorry, and I hope you can forgive me as I forgive you."

Tears roll silently down my cheeks. I release a burden so heavy it seems impossible I didn't know I was holding it. I relax into her arms, and she wipes away my sadness, planting salty kisses in their place.

Epilogue: Good Girl

Lorelei

The cuffs are of the softest leather, but I've tightened them just enough that they dig into her wrists, her arms above her head chained to the wrought iron bed frame.

Her body, mine for tonight, stretched out before me. Waiting.

She cannot touch me. She cannot push me away or fight against me. She can only trust me.

Not a mark or a blemish upon her, save the ones I've left behind. The impression of my teeth on her left breast and right thigh. I run my hands over her lightly. She tries to arch her back to meet my hand.

"Who said you could do that?"

"No one!" she whines.

"And?"

"I'm sorry."

"I'm sorry, what?"

"I'm sorry, Lady Keyes."

"Good girl."

I get off the bed, Adele's eyes following me, kick off my boots and remove my shirt. I leave on the trousers I'm wearing but take off the belt. Without it, they drop lower, skimming my hips and showing my pelvic bone. Adele licks her lips. I know she is desperate to taste me. I might let her ... if she pleases me.

I wrap the belt tight around my right hand as I kneel on the bed, placing myself between Adele's legs. I push on her knees, spreading her wider. She's so wet already.

"Look at the state you're in." I reach between her legs, coating my fingers in her arousal. "So desperate, so needy."

"Am I wicked?"

I reach forward, putting my fingers in her mouth. She moans as she moves her tongue over them, tasting herself.

"You are."

She gasps at the words, arching her hips again, thrusting against some imagined hand or instrument.

"Are you going to punish me?"

I push her legs up and back so that she is on full display for me. There are marks, already fading, upon her arse and the back of her thighs. They are too faded. She needs some fresh ones.

"I really ought to," I say, pushing on her ankles with one hand whilst my other grips the belt tighter. "But a whore like you might enjoy that a little too much. And that wouldn't be much of a punishment at all, would it?"

"No."

"So, you promise you won't enjoy it?"

"Yes."

I turn my head so she can't see the smile upon my lips. "Very well then."

I bring the belt down on her. The crack fills the room and redness blooms instantly on her skin. I bring it down thrice more, her cries and moans louder with each one. Her promise, always made to be broken, in ruin.

I discard the belt so I may gently rub my palm across her stinging skin.

"That wasn't too bad, was it?"

"No, Lady Keyes."

I let one of her legs drop to the bed, placing the other around my shoulder so she is fully exposed to me once again.

"Do you need to come?"

She nods.

"Words, Adele." I rub my thumb over her clit.

"I need to come. Please let me come."

"And why should I do that?" I ask, two fingers already at her entrance.

"Because I'm filthy. I need it. Need you."

"And what is it you need from me?"

She opens her mouth before quickly snapping it shut. We've been working toward this moment, she and I. Her reluctance to speak profanely remains one of her last prudish strongholds. But I am determined to push her. For us.

"If you won't tell me …" I withdraw my hand from her, "I can find a better use of my time." She takes a deep breath.

"For you to f—" The letter lingers on her lips just long enough for me to raise her leg and strike the reddened skin where my belt had landed. Her body twists involuntarily away from the blow, eyes clamped shut. But then she settles, the words rolling easily from her trembling lips.

"To fuck me."

With that, I plunge swiftly into her. I give her two strokes before stilling.

"More?" I lock eyes with her, making sure she understands my question.

"More."

"Say it again."

"Please, fuck me."

I add a third, letting her get used to the stretch, to this feeling of fullness before gently moving inside her. Satisfied, I add my last finger. She winces in pain but does not tell me to stop.

"I'm sure a whore like you could take even more."

Her lashes flutter as she considers it. "Would that please you?"

"Immensely."

Biting her lower lip, she moves against me. "I so want to please you."

My heart races as I add my thumb and slowly push. She's so tight around me and it takes all my effort to move my fingers to brush against her inner walls. The sensation makes her quiet. Eyes clamped shut, face twisted in discomfort, I give her time. With only the slightest, rocking movement of my hand, she begins to relax. Hard lines on her face soften. Her breathing steadies.

I don't know how much time passes with me basking in the feel of her before she bucks her hips. She needs more, and I will always oblige my love.

I thrust into her, slowly and gently at first, before her moans spur me into going harder, faster, deeper.

It's curious that by having Adele wrapped around me like this, I hold her in the palm of my hand. I could so easily hurt her, damage her in a way that brings true suffering rather than the sweet mixture of pleasure and pain that she entrusts me to provide her with. The trust she places in me, the way she allows me to control her … There's no more powerful feeling in the world than this.

She clenches her legs together as she comes, crushing my hand and arm between her, but I do not relent. I keep flexing my fingers as she rides the wave into her second climax.

I stay still in her a moment before gently withdrawing.

"Good girl." I smooth her hair back as I place a kiss on her brow. Skin so hot it burns my lips. "I knew you could take it."

I undo the cuffs and draw her towards me, running my hands up and down her back as I whisper words of love and affirmation, until her breathing slows and she drifts into sleep

About the Authors

Rae Knowles (she/her) is a queer woman and author of dark fiction including *The Stradivarius* (May 2023) and *Merciless Waters* (November 2023). Her short fiction has been featured in *Dark Matter Ink, Ghoulish Tales, Seize the Press, Taco Bell Quarterly,* and *Nosetouch Press*, among others. Rae is an active member of the HWA and is represented by Laura Williams at Greene & Heaton.

April Yates (she/her) is a writer of dark and queer fiction, living in Derbyshire, England. Her longer work includes the novellas, *Ashthorne, City of Snares* and the novel *Lies That Bind* (co-authored with Rae Knowles).

About the Illustrator

Daniella Batsheva is a self-proclaimed "Illustrator with a design habit" whose aesthetic straddles the line between underground and mainstream. Her art boasts the beautiful intricate linework of traditional Victorian illustration mixed with imagery inspired by horror films, 90's toy packaging, and macabre history.

Batsheva's art has been published internationally. Her work can be seen everywhere from "Whole Foods" to London's biggest punk venues. She has worked with brands such as Kerrang!, Pizza Girl, and multiple musicians from Paris Jackson and Ben Christo (Sisters of Mercy). Her work has recently been featured at ArtExpo, New York, and The Crypt Gallery, London.

While her work can comfortably fit in multiple contexts, Batsheva's work is always recognizable. Her main motivation is fostering local alternative communities and contributing to the future of illustration in Goth/Metal scenes. Batsheva is also passionate about researching obscure folklore from across different cultures in an effort to preserve legends that are at risk of being lost.

Content Warnings

Intimate partner violence
Emotional abuse
Self-harm
Drugging
References to incest
References to sexual assault
Explicit sexual content including:
Light breath play
- Knife play
- Bondage
- Degradation
- Dubious consent
- Nonconsent

More From Brigids Gate Press

Dangerous Waters: Deadly Women of the Sea

Malevolent mermaids.

Sinister sirens.

Scary selkies.

And other dangerous women of the deep blue sea.

Dangerous waters takes us deep beneath the ocean waves and shows us once more why we need to be cautious about venturing out into the water.

Featuring stories, drabbles and poems by Sandra Ljubjanović, John Higgins, Patrick Rutigliano, Candace Robinson, Emmanuel Williams, Desirée M. Niccoli, L. Marie Wood, Samantha Lokai, Christina Henneman, Gully Novaro, Christine Lukas, Alice Austin, Dawn Vogel, Victoria Nations, Mark Towse, Kristin Cleaveland, Ben Monroe, Kurt Newton, E.M. Linden, Eva Papasoulioti, Ann Wuehler, Rachel Dib, A.R. Fredericksen, Daniel Pyle, Megan Hart, Ef Deal, Katherine Traylor, Juliegh Howard-Hobson, Simon Kewin, Elana Gomel, Lauren E. Reynolds, Grace R. Reynolds, René Galván, Marshall J. Moore, Ngo Binh Anh Khoa, Roxie Vorhees, April Yates, Kaitlin Tremblay, T.K. Howell, Kayla Whittle, Emily Y. Teng, Briana McGuckin, Tom Farr, Cassandra Taylor, Steven-Elliot Altman, Paul M. Feeney, Lucy Collins, Marianne Halbert, Rosie Arcane, Antonia Rachel Ward, Steven Lord, and Jessica Peter.

City of Snares

Hazel crosses an ocean, moving to the City of Dreams, not for stardom or the limelight that comes from rubbing elbows with celebrities, but for the chance to be her true self. So she's stunned when fading star of the silver screen, Diana Blake, wanders into the diner where she works and declares her intention of turning Hazel into the next, hot ingénue.

While the idea of following in Diana's footsteps is not the path Hazel would've chosen, the prospect of being close to Diana, of realising the impossible dream of winning the affection of her lifelong obsession, is too seductive to pass up.

Hazel agrees to let Diana mould her into her protege and is thrown headlong into the Hollywood star machine. Glimmers of sexual interest from Diana keep Hazel on the hook as she offers herself up, piece by piece to showbusiness. But Diana's behaviour grows increasingly controlling, suspicious accidents on set begin to pile up, and Hazel will have to fight to maintain any shred of herself, lest Hollywood eat her alive.

MARIONETTE

On the run from a life of prostitution and poverty, exotic dancer Cece Dulac agrees to become the main attraction at an erotic séance hosted by an enigmatic mesmerist, Monsieur Rossignol. As the séance descends into depravity, Cece falls prey to Rossignol's hypnotic power and becomes possessed by a malevolent spirit.

George Dashwood, an aspiring artist, witnesses the séance and fears for Cece. He seeks her out and she seduces him, but she is no longer herself. The spirit controlling her forces her to commit increasingly depraved acts. When the spirit's desire for revenge escalates to murder, George and Cece must find a way to break Rossignol's spell before Cece's soul is condemned forever.

Marionette is an erotic horror novella inspired by traditional folk tales and set in fin de siècle Paris.

Scissor Sisters

21 tales of sapphic villains, curated by April Yates and Rae Knowles.

Featuring the work of:

Hatteras Mange, Anastasia Dziekan, Ariel Marken Jack, Maerwynn Blackwood, Avra Margariti, Grace R. Reynolds, Evelyn Freeling, Hailey Piper, T.O. King, M.S. Dean, Chloe Spencer, Mae Murray, L.R. Stuart,, Alex Luceli Jiménez, Cheyanne Brabo, Luc Diamant, Alyssa Lennander, Anya Leigh Josephs, Lindz McLeod, Caitlin Marceau, Shelly Lavigne.

And a bonus tale from Eric Raglin!

Visit our website at: www.brigidsgatepress.com

Made in the USA
Columbia, SC
26 November 2024